ALSO BY ISABELLA THORNE

THE LADIES OF BATH

The Duke's Daughter ~ Lady Amelia Atherton

The Baron in Bath ~ Miss Julia Bellevue

The Deceptive Earl ~ Lady Charity Abernathy

THE HAWTHORNE SISTERS

The Forbidden Valentine ~ Lady Eleanor

THE BAGGINGTON SISTERS

The Countess and the Baron ~ Prudence

Almost Promised ~ Temperance

The Healing Heart ~ Mercy

The Lady to Match a Rogue ~ Faith

NETTLEFOLD CHRONICLES

Not Quite a Lady; Not Quite a Knight

Stitched in Love

OTHER NOVELS BY ISABELLA THORNE

The Mad Heiress and the Duke ~ Miss Georgette Quinby

The Duke's Wicked Wager ~ Lady Evelyn Evering

Short Stories by Isabella Thorne

Love Springs Anew

The Mad Heiress' Cousin and the Hunt

Mischief, Mayhem and Murder: A Marquess of Evermont

Mistletoe and Masquerade ~ 2-in-1 Short Story Collection

Colonial Cressida and the Secret Duke ~ A Short Story

CONTENTS

THE BARON IN BATH

PART I
THE BARON'S BETROTHAL

Chapter 1	5
Chapter 2	13
Chapter 3	21
Chapter 4	37
Chapter 5	51

PART II
THE BARON'S BROTHER

Chapter 6	71
Chapter 7	87
Chapter 8	105
Chapter 9	117
Chapter 10	129

PART III
THE BARON AT THE BALL

Chapter 11	147
Chapter 12	159
Chapter 13	173
Chapter 14	185
Chapter 15	201
Chapter 16	215
Chapter 17	225

PART IV
THE BARON'S BRIDE

Chapter 18	239
Chapter 19	251

Chapter 20   267
Chapter 21   277
Chapter 22   287
Chapter 23   301
Chapter 24   315
25. Epilogue   319

Sneak Peek of The Deceptive Earl   327
Chapter 1   329

Sign up for my VIP Reader List!   335

The Baron
in Bath

Miss Julia Bellevue

Ladies of Bath

Isabella Thorne

A Regency Romance Novel

The Baron in Bath ~ Miss Julia Bellevue
Ladies of Bath
A Regency Romance Novel

2018 Mikita Associates Publishing

Published in the United States of America.

www.isabellathorne.com

Part 1

The Baron's Betrothal

1

---

*M*iss Julia Bellevue and her older sister Jane traveled from London to Bath with a large party; all of whom were her sister's friends and not Julia's own. Although the seats were plush and the steeds were swift, such accoutrements could not make the travel pleasant. Julia knew that she should not complain. Her sister's connections, through her husband the Earl of Keegain, meant that Julia was traveling with the Beresfords' party in all manner of comfort, but the three days travel from London felt interminable. She could not wait to be freed from the carriage even if it meant meeting the gentleman who was the main cause of her worry: her intended.

Since most of the *Ton* retired to Bath to get out of the heat and smell of Town, it was easy for two young women of quality to find a party with whom they could travel.

When Julia had asked Jane to hire a private coach for them, her sister had been perplexed. Jane only reiterated that they would be in good company and dismissed Julia's misgivings about traveling with the large group; saying they would be safer from highway men with the earl's coach and several members of the Royal Navy along with their sisters and ladies.

It seemed to Julia that most of the Royal Navy fleet was outside the window of the coach. The men were rather loud, laughing and joking with one another, excited for their summer holiday in Bath. Several had chosen to ride astride and others rode up front with the drivers.

The men made Julia nervous. Their presence only reminded her of the gentleman she was traveling to Bath to meet. Men in general made her tense, and gentlemen in particular, tended to cause her to lose what little poise she had. Perhaps it was her mother's blood which too often seemed to come to the surface and with it, a most unladylike interest in indelicate thoughts.

Although Julia was not much of a horsewoman, she thought the gentlemen looked much happier outside of the coach. She admired the masculine cut of their jackets as they rode. She let her mind wander from one to the other, and although she was already warm in the close confines of the coach, she felt a familiar heat fill her face as she admired the form of one of the men who had loosened his jacket and stood in the stirrups to stretch. Ladies were not supposed to have such thoughts, she admonished herself especially not betrothed ladies.

She tore her eyes away and turned back to the interior of the carriage where her sister was conversing with the other ladies of the *Ton*. Julia brought up her fan to hide her blush, but she also needed it to move the otherwise stifling air in the carriage.

Even her sister Jane's normally perfectly coifed dark hair was clinging to her brow in damp ringlets, albeit neat ringlets. Julia looked like a wilted mess. Both Julia and Jane were brunettes, but that was where the similarity between the sisters ended.

Jane looked like a princess; Julia was more likely to be mistaken for a knight. Jane was regal, whereas, Julia was large and awkward both in form and speech. Jane was ever the countess. She shined at parties. Her words were kind and men sought to please her; women to emulate her. Julia was blunt to the point of rudeness, and often managed to unintentionally insult someone important. Men found her uncouth and she found them overly filled with pomposity.

Unlike Julia, Jane had looked forward to this trip and time sharing a carriage with the other ladies. Julia knew the traveling party would be rather boisterous and she had dreaded the trip before it actually happened. The reality did not disappoint.

Now, Julia sat quietly in the corner of the coach, picking at a string on the plush upholstery while her sister's friends talked around her. Julia would have liked to remain invisible, but it was hard to be inconspicuous when one's breeding and stature were so obvious.

Some said she was an unnatural Amazon. Julia towered above the other women, including her sister. It made her uncomfortable and self-conscious. In an attempt to alleviate this fault she shifted downward in the corner. At least she was sitting in the coach, so her monstrous difference in height was not so apparent.

Before they departed Julia had admonished her sister that under no circumstances was she to try to draw her into conversation with the other ladies, and Jane had reluctantly agreed. In polite company, Julia tended to make one gaffe after the other, so she tried to be silent. Jane was quite the realist and knew trying to converse with her sister in the coach would be a disaster. Julia would have nowhere to flee if she made some *faux pas*. Sometimes however, her tongue seemed to have a mind of its own.

Julia had only a sparse handful of friends herself due to the rumors of her birth, and was really only comfortable speaking with them. None of these friends were with her now, but at least she could look forward to seeing them in Bath – that is if this odious journey ever ended.

She turned her body towards the window and looked out of it again. They were now on the last day of travel, and Julia could no longer ignore that there was a reason for their trip to Bath, other than the summer holiday. The thought made her stomach tie up in painful knots.

When the conversation in the coach turned into a heated discussion over which man was more of a rake: Neville Collington, the Earl of Wentwell or Godwin Gruger, the Baron Fawkland. Julia wanted to sink into the floorboards of the coach. Lord Fawkland, was the very man to which her father had so thoughtlessly betrothed her: the gentleman who caused her trip to Bath to be fraught with such anxiety. Though it seemed, according to the ladies' gossip, that the baron was less than a gentleman. Julia simply bit her tongue and blushed.

She could only hope the other women forgot about her entirely. She slid further down in her seat and wished she could disappear, but she was far too large a girl to even become inconspicuous, never mind invisible.

"I have heard that Lord Fawkland escorted a lady home in his carriage," a blonde friend of Jane's said. She paused for effect, fanning herself. "Without a chaperone."

"It has come to my notice that this was not the first time," the other lady, a pert red-head added.

Julia must have made some noise that drew their attention, for the first woman turned to her. "Is it true then," The blonde asked. "Did your father truly betroth you to the Lord Fawkland?"

The lady's startling blue eyes were fixed on Julia and she found all she could do was murmur.

"Yes."

"Well, he is very good looking," the blonde replied. "In a rather large and over-bearing sort of way. You must admit that."

The second lady tsked. "Oh, dear, you know looks are not everything. The poor girl, how perfectly horrid." She looked sympathetically at Julia. "Is there not some way around it?" she asked.

Jane shook her head at her friends, answering for her younger sister. "My husband, has his solicitors looking into the matter, but he suggested we go ahead as if it cannot be broken."

Julia noted that mercifully, Jane did not go into great detail here amongst near strangers. "But perhaps it can be changed," Julia murmured to herself. At least Jane had asked her husband to check into the matter, even if he offered little hope. Julia reached across and gripped her sister's hand in thanks. Jane smiled at her briefly, but offered no other encouragement.

Julia supposed that her father had planned with her best interests at heart when he made the arrangements for her after his death. Yes, he had left her with a last request, which as it was a last request, it was not a request at all. It was a command. He had betrothed her to Godwin Gruger, the Baron Fawkland, all unbeknownst to Julia, thinking he was a childhood friend. Without a doubt, this was prior to the soiling of Lord Fawkland's reputation. Her sister Jane was initially quite elated that Julia would become a baroness, but Julia did not share her sister's love for titulature.

Julia was not a social person. She could not possibly be a baroness. No. She did not want to marry the Baron Fawkland. Julia and Godwin Gruger had never been friends, even as children. Their age difference had been too great, and Godwin thought himself already a baron. When his father died and Godwin had actually inherited the barony, he came home from the Navy even more cool and distant.

The one time she had spoken with him since Julia felt entirely out of her depth. She had never gotten on well with Godwin, and now if rumor was to be believed, he was a terrible rake. He had not changed from the wicked boy who had broken her dolls; for it seemed he was now just as careless with women's hearts. Everything was wrong with her father's decree. It was Lord Fawkland's younger brother Cedric she remembered. Cedric was much more lighthearted, ever involved in some trick.

Oh why had her father not chosen Cedric instead of Godwin? Julia was nearly of an age with the younger brother, though she must have been about ten when she had last spoken to him. Still she *had* played with the younger brother as a child when Cedric had invited her on his mischievous jaunts. He had even played tricks on the ladies who teased Julia on her behalf. Some of those, she now thought, were quite cruel, but his older brother was over six years her senior and a stranger to her.

If only the words had not also been immortalized in her father's will, an irrefutable document that sealed her fate. Still she clung to the hope that the earl's solicitors may yet find some way to twist the will to her favor, a loophole to slip through.

Julia had given the matter considerable thought. It was not as though she did not wish to honor her father's dying wish, but the terms of the arrangement were entirely unfair, and she knew that if she had had but a moment to confer with him, her father would have changed the conditions. If her prayer could be answered, she would have asked for just five more minutes with her father, but if that prayer would be so granted Julia was sure she would not have used those precious moments to speak of her marriage.

She loved her father, and missed him terribly. Melancholy filled her. She sighed, uncertain how to proceed. Her father had always taken care of such things for her, and although she had her sister to help her, Julia still felt bereft without their father. It was not her sister's responsibility. Nor was it the responsibility of her sister's husband, the earl. She needed someone of her own. Julia wanted a husband, just not Godwin Gruger.

She could only hope that the road to Bath would soon be at an end. God be good. She would be so awfully glad to make an end of it. She didn't think she could endure much more of this carriage ride. The worry and the confined space, as well as Jane endeavoring to explain Julia's distress to her friends, who were nearly strangers to Julia, was all starting to be quite wearing. At last the little group had let off discussing her life in detail, and Julia was left once again to her troubled thoughts as she sat and gazed unseeing out of the window at the passing scenery.

2

---

*W*hen the party finally arrived in Bath, Julia fled the carriage and left her sister to deal with supervising the unpacking. The only good thing to be said about a trip was that eventually, one did arrive at the intended destination.

The Bellevue townhouse in Bath was modest in comparison to the manors and estates in the country. Fewer rooms, less space, but the clean white stone exteriors and classical lines were without compare. Julia loved the weather in Bath, mostly warm and mild, but she even loved the breathtaking storms that rolled in, cooling the cobblestone streets in the evenings. Julia's future home, if she married was her favorite place in all the world.

If her father had just deeded the house to her, she would not be in this pickle, but Father was old-fashioned and Jane had exclaimed in horror when Julia had suggested as much. It just was not done! A woman of her station did not own property. But there were highborn ladies who owned property. Surely it was not the norm, but neither was it the horror Jane said it was.

Julia loved the townhouse in Bath. It was not so different than the other townhouses on the block, but it was quaint rather than spacious. It had been redecorated not long before her father's death and Julia had overseen the choices of colors herself. She had chosen a vivid rainbow of hues matching the mood of many cheerful summers spent here.

The parlor was a comfortable smoky blue. The dining room a rich russet which enhanced the shine of the candelabra, softened flaws in skin tone and deepened the red mahogany of the table. There were paintings throughout the house that she herself had done and others by old masters which made her feel as though she were one of their esteemed company.

Indeed Julia would rather have a paint brush and palate than a whole room full of dancers at the finest ball. The most beloved room in the house was her attic study, the room she used to paint. She climbed to it now, the heat increasing as she ascended the staircase.

The room was done in golds and yellows and greens which were some of her favorite colors. The room made Julia feel cheery when the world made her sad. She hurried up the stair to look out the window at the view. She could see much of Bath from that window.

She loved the even cobbled streets and the stark white buildings set in neat rows. She loved the order of it. She could even see the Grand Pump Room where people came from all over to take the healing waters.

A servant had already brought up her box of paints and brushes. The easel was set where she preferred in the far corner, and the window was open allowing a breeze into the room. She stretched out across the pouf. She was home.

"Miss?" One of Jane's servants had followed her up the flights of stairs and was a bit out of breath. The maid placed her hand over her heart and continued. "Oh goodness," she breathed. "I am sorry, Miss." She apologized as she curtseyed. "Lady Charity Abernathy called earlier this morning and said I was to give this to you the very moment you arrived."

The maid held out a note and continued. "She heard you would reach Bath today and wanted to call, but only if you arrived before tea. She has a to-do this evening. Would you like me to send word, Miss?"

Julia glanced at the letter which said much the same thing as Charity herself had apparently told the maid. "Yes, please," Julia said, pulling a sheet of parchment from her desk and wrote a quick note to her friend asking her to come for tea.

WHEN LADY CHARITY ABERNATHY ARRIVED LATER THAT afternoon, the house was still in a state. Jane was a little put out by the fact that Julia invited company when they had barely settled in, but Julia protested saying that Jane had spent time with her friends for the whole ride to Bath. So Jane relented but declined making an appearance.

"I have too much to do," she said. "Presently, I am soiled from travel and am entirely unfit for company."

Julia thought that if Jane was unfit for company she must be truly dreadful. She was still in her traveling clothes, when Mrs. Manchester set tea in the garden. Although the roses were a bit overgrown and not blooming yet, the airy setting was just what Julia needed after the close confines of the coach, and Lady Charity would not mind her appearance.

Lady Charity Abernathy and Miss Lavinia Grant were Julia's friends, and she had few enough ladies to call friends. If Charity wanted to visit on short notice, Julia would not refuse her. Both Charity and Lavinia were blonde and smaller than Julia. Lady Charity was soft and feminine, with curves that attracted masculine attention like honey. Lavinia had the appearance of a china doll and a droll wit. Julia could see no reason why either should befriend her, but they had.

In fact Lady Charity was the reason Julia was not allowed to stand ignored at parties, because Charity herself would not be ignored. She had taken Julia under her wing and regaled her with stories. Now, when Julia complained over tea of the staunch attitudes of her last days traveling companions, Charity lifted her spirits with tales of Lady Amelia Atherton's time in London last season. Julia laughed when Charity told her of Lady Amelia's antics, but still, Julia begged off the evening party her friend suggested, complaining of fatigue from travel.

"I cannot possibly be ready. Most of my clothes are

still packed. Nothing is pressed. I would not do such a disservice to our staff, and I am truly weary."

"No," Charity said. "Fatigue does not keep a young lady from a party. It is a dowager's excuse. Now tell me true."

Julia paused as a servant brought the teacakes before she finally capitulated and revealed to her friend the cause for her melancholy.

"Father has left instructions for my marriage," Julia said at last.

"In his will?"

"The exact same. He states that I am to marry the Baron Fawkland."

"Oh, Julia!" Charity exclaimed. "You cannot. He is a terrible rake. Everyone says so. He has ruined more than one young lady."

"So I have heard," Julia said glumly. "But what am I to do? The will is set. If I do not marry him by the end of the summer, I shall lose the house here in Bath."

"Oh, but you love this townhouse!" Charity exclaimed.

Julia nodded "Believe me, it breaks my heart that I must choose between a house I love and a man I do not."

Julia told Charity how, her sister's husband had been trying to find a way around the terms of Father's will for months now, because Julia had been so distraught, but to no avail. The earl's solicitor had said the only gap in the agreement were if she were willing to give up the house to her grasping Cousin Rupert.

The thought gave her a turn. Father had never planned that. No, he had planned that she be married to

Lord Fawkland! Still, the thought of a lifetime with a man she could not abide, made her quake in her shoes.

"You should go to the soiree tonight," Lady Charity urged. "It will do your heart good to forget your worries for a while. I'm sure one of your sister's fancy maids can get something ready for you to wear."

"I cannot," Julia said as she poured the tea. "I am still sore from bumping about in that awful coach for three days. The trip was ghastly."

"You made good time," Charity offered.

"I wish we could have made it in two."

"Traveling in what? A mail coach?" Charity teased.

Julia scowled at her and continued to demolish her tea cake with her fork. Some did indeed travel with the mail coach, but not ladies of quality.

"At any rate, your problem has a simple solution," Charity said, lifting her teacup daintily.

"Pray tell. What is that?"

"Fall in love with a man who can buy the house with pocket change," Charity said airily. "It is after all, not a very big house. Any gentleman above a baronet should be able to afford it. Request it for a wedding present."

"I do not want to marry a baron or a baronet," Julia protested. "I just want this house."

Charity hummed her sympathies, "Do not fret, my dear Julia. We shall think of something I am sure. Now I must go and prepare for this evening's festivities. If I am late my mother will never forgive me, and I want a bit of time to visit with Father before he retires." Charity stood as she spoke and Julia stood with her, but they did not leave the garden. "You may not attend the soiree tonight, but I will expect to see you tomorrow. My mother is hosting a musicale and she has engaged the renowned Mr. Andrew Lodder. You cannot miss it." Charity shook a finger under her friend's nose. "I shall be very vexed with you if you should do so."

"Oh, very well," Julia agreed. "I shall endeavor to be there."

"Mr. James Poppy is escorting me. You know the Poppy family, do you not? James has a brother...Michael." Charity's eyes seemed to brighten as she considered. "Perhaps Michael could..."

"I do know the Poppy's," Julia said. "But sadly, I do not think they could afford my house in Bath along with their other expenses and their many sisters' dowries."

"So you would accept Michael then?"

"No. Oh, I don't know," Julia said miserably. "He's handsome enough in a broody sort of way."

"*You* are the one who is broody," Charity accused with a laugh.

"I am not," Julia said pouting.

"Why not let Lord Fawkland woo you?" Charity said. "He is a baron. For all that he is a rake; he is so terribly good looking. Or there is always the Earl of Wentwell. If you must choose a rake," Charity said plainly, "and are to be caught out, you should choose the man with the higher title."

"Charity you are awful," Julia said with a laugh. She knew her friend was only teasing in an attempt to cheer her. "I would never do such a thing. Besides, if I wanted to marry a rake, why not choose the one I am already engaged to?" she said. "Trapping a man cannot be a good way to start a life together."

"You would not be the first woman to catch a man so."

"Not a gentleman," said Julia.

"No. Not a gentleman," Charity agreed.

"Oh, what was Father thinking!" Julia cried.

"He was thinking to save you from gossip when he could no longer protect you," Charity said wisely.

"Jane said much the same thing," Julia confided as the women moved towards the door together. "But I cannot think the baron can protect my reputation when his own is so sullied. Oh Father..." she sighed and looked at her friend for a moment.

"I miss him," she said softly, and Charity who had a special relationship with her own father, put a hand on her friend's in camaraderie. "Do not think of anything sad," Charity counseled as she hugged her.

If only Julia could do that. "I wish I could."

"I shall endeavor to help you on the morrow," Lady Charity promised. "I believe the Gruger brothers are invited to the musicale. I do not know if they have replied, but I will check with my mother."

Julia nodded and went inside to help Jane with setting up the household for the summer. She would worry about husbands tomorrow.

3

When Julia awoke early the next morning she was still plagued with disquiet. She decided to paint. It would settle her. She could forget everything while she painted. She went up to her attic studio and laid a canvas on the easel.

Julia bit her lip and studied the scene outside of her window. She loved this view. She could not lose it. No matter what Charity said, she was not broody. She was usually an optimistic person; only the fact that she could see no way out of her circumstance was depressing her.

As she chose the colors and immersed herself in the art she imagined the scene was her life: calm and beautiful and still, just like the picture she was creating. She clung to that thought. If not prevented, she would have endeavored to jump into the picture and sit quietly in anonymity, feeling the sun on her face and smelling the sweet air of Bath; the air of home.

The door stood open to allow the breeze to circulate,

and soon the sounds of the house awakening carried up the stair, as well as the smell of baking cakes and brewing tea. She heard the shuffling and laughing of the servants and considered going down to breakfast, but she wanted to come to a convenient stopping place in her painting.

Perhaps a lighter blue and a bit of yellow for sun, she thought. She knew the sky would turn lighter as the day progressed and the light would change. She mixed the paint with a bit of white on the palate. She paused; brush in hand thinking her canvas looked more cheerful than she felt.

The sky was a pure azure with no clouds at all, but she debated whether she should put them in anyway. The blue today didn't have the nuances she loved so much. It could be painted a single hue with just a bit of yellow and white for the sun.

Well, perhaps even the stark blue had some hint of gradation. One only had to look for it more diligently. She knew that later today, the sun would shine strongly, delineating the clean lines of the town. The pure white marble would shine like a gem under the bright summer sun. It would look different than it did now. Did that make it necessarily less beautiful, she wondered?

As she painted, Julia remembered poking about the history of Bath with Charity and Lavinia. Lavinia could always make her laugh. Together they imagined they could see the Roman commanders rolling down the cobbled streets in their chariots. She and Charity often made up stories about those proud Romans, and laughed at their fantasies.

She had even once painted the chariot scene from her

very vivid imagination and Lavinia teased her about the strong arms and set jaws she painted on the Romans. They fell into giggling as they compared the picture with real-life men, and could barely breathe with the merriment as they lay across Julia's bed and laughed, their stays reminding them that rolling about and laughing was not a ladylike activity.

Julia had managed to roll off the bed to her feet, but Charity lay stuck on her back like an upturned turtle, snorting with mirth, and flailing her arms as her bosom shook with hilarity. Julia stood choking with laughter and could not even manage to pull her friend upright. Instead she just stood there laughing until her stomach hurt.

"Fie!" Charity exclaimed. "You are unkind. Help me up." She waved a hand at her friends.

Julia and Lavinia continued laughing so hard they couldn't breathe. But at last together they had managed to pull their friend up and then, Charity had accosted them both with her fan saying, "You are horrible friends, both of you; leaving me to lie there stuck like a round backed tortoise!"

Lavinia giggled telling Charity, "But you are rounder than I am; you should have rolled right off of the bed!"

"Rounder! Am I?" Charity exclaimed. "Do you think I am accustomed to rolling in and out of bed?"

Julia gave her a look, and Charity reddened as she realized her words, "Oh! Don't you say a word. You are too cruel."

That was how Jane found them, wrinkled and flushed in the summer heat and still giggling with mirth. Julia had a bit of paint on her nose and the maid had to crawl under the bed to retrieve the paintbrush Julia had lost.

Jane chided them for their appearance. "Pray, what is so funny?" she demanded.

"Romans," Charity had said.

"Men," Lavinia replied at the exact same time.

The girls could not share the cause of their mirth with Julia's upright sister, Jane, but every time they looked at one another they burst into renewed giggles. Why were the men of today not like those stout Romans? Lavinia lamented.

"Men no longer have that sort of masculinity," Julia said, "and if they do, then they are unkind."

"I do not think the Romans were kind," Charity proposed and Julia agreed that was probably true, but the gentlemen she knew who were kind, were somehow less charismatic than those Romans.

"I do not think those two traits come in the same man," Julia said. The three friends sighed and continued imagining the perfect men who were obviously born too early in time for them to appreciate.

No matter how vivid her imagination, Julia could not imagine a life without the Bath home. Almost as unsettling was the thought of the brash, overbearing Fawkland calling the house *his home*. He was charismatic. That was certainly true. Dare she think he had any kindness within his character? He may surely have passion, but how could she have peace if kindness was not in his temperament?

She sat and stared out of the window, her paint brush still loaded with paint in her hand. How would it feel to have her home invaded? Perhaps it was better to let it fall to Cousin Rupert, but she did not want to live on her sister's charity, although Jane would never complain. The problem was, Julia wanted to be married, but did not think there was a worthy man alive. Her sister told her she was too particular.

"May I come in, Julia?" Jane stuck her head into the room and Julia startled. She was so wrapped up in her thoughts and her painting she did not see nor hear her sister until she was at the door.

"Are you coming down for breakfast?" Jane asked. "I feel as though I have not seen you since we arrived yesterday. Miss Grant has come to call."

"Oh!" Julia said excited to see her friend; Lavinia would cheer her.

"I will be down in a moment," Julia said looking back at the painting with longing. She wanted to at least finish the sky.

Lavinia with typical curiosity had followed Jane upstairs to the attic retreat. One could not really leave Lavinia behind. Julia heard her light foot on the stairs.

"Why that is beautiful," Lavinia said. "My paintings always look like they were done by a clumsy child. You really have such a talent, Julia."

Lavinia was not being entirely truthful. Her paintings were not as detailed but she could draw passably well, and she was much better at needlepoint. More than that, Lavinia was a graceful dancer, beautiful and personable, with curls that were never out of place and a smile that never wavered.

Her hair could be damp with perspiration or even wet

and it would still curl. It did not fall straight or puff up into a head of fuzzy dandelion fluff as Julia's did. Lavinia never groped for conversation or did anything out of place. Even when she did, everyone found it quaint or droll; a talent Julia lacked. Julia envied that poise more than Lavinia's beauty, but she also loved her friend, so she did not fret. Lavinia was only Lavinia.

"I know your future husband will find your painting most endearing," Lavinia added.

"Please, Lavinia, can we not talk about husbands." Julia set her paintbrush down on the palette, beside the splotch of summer's day blue. It was clear that her sister and her friend would not let her finish.

"Julia, we must speak of husbands," Jane said gently.

"Yes," Lavinia commented. "Lady Charity spoke to me at the soiree last night and told me of your ... engagement, and your melancholy. Oh Julia, you must not leap to the conclusion that all is lost. You are not married yet."

"And you must not stay in your attic studio with no company but your own bitter thoughts," Jane said.

Julia sighed.

To her sister finding a husband had been a breeze. Jane was a beautiful woman with all of the necessary qualities, a fine dancer, a skilled hostess, and soft speaker

"Julia, you must at least meet him," Jane coaxed.

"Hmm?" Julia said distractedly. The sky was still off. Perhaps she would have to wait until it dried a bit and try to soften it with clouds.

"Julia, please finish," Jane said urgently. "Put the paint brush aside and listen to me."

Julia applied herself more diligently to her painting. "I have met him," She replied bluntly

"When Lord Fawkland was a child. He is a man now. There is a difference between the boy and the man," Jane said. She put her hand on Julia's arm. "I'm sorry. I didn't mean to be cross with you, but this is why we came to Bath. You must meet with him."

Julia began to clean her brushes while Jane spoke. There was no hope to finish her painting. Jane would continue to pester her until she had her way. Jane did not know the meaning of defeat. She was talking in her matter of fact way, and Julia had to listen, but her eyes kept straying back to her painting. When she painted she forgot all about the issues in her life. She forgot about the house and husbands and balls, but Jane did not.

"Julia do you hear me?" Jane said in exasperation.

"I hear you," Julia said lifting a shoulder in a shrug and looking back at her sister. "I just believe that I have not changed so much. I am sure he will not have changed. I did not like him as a boy. I will not like him as a man."

"Julia, you cannot know that," Lavinia urged. "I was just telling Charity last night." Lavinia paused and Julia got the impression that she was the subject of much discussion between Charity and Lavinia. "You should meet him," Lavinia continued. "If he is not to your liking, find another. Many gentlemen in His Majesty's Service are currently in town. Some are quite handsome."

"None could afford the townhouse," Julia said.

"If Cousin Rupert would even sell it," Jane added. "If you fail to marry Lord Fawkland by summer's end, the house reverts to Cousin Rupert, and his grasping wife has been trying to find her way into Society for years. If she gets her hands on this house, she will not give it up."

Julia wrinkled her nose with the thought. "Oh, why did Father not leave the house to me directly instead of tying it to my marriage with Fawkland?" Julia said.

"I'm sure Father thought to have you well settled, before he passed." Jane said softly. "He did not plan on dying."

"I know," Julia said chastised. "It is just that this house is everything I could ever need."

"I know you love the city, Julia and want to keep the townhouse," Jane added. "So will you not try to find out if the man interests you at least a little? Give Lord Fawkland a chance. Perhaps he will be better than you remember."

"Better than the gossips say?" Julia asked.

"Gossips have been known to be wrong," Jane pointed out. "If not, then Lady Charity and Miss Grant have the right of it. We can make a pitch for another match for you. If Cousin Rupert will not release this house, perhaps the gentleman will have one of his own and you can decorate it to your liking. You can do none of those things in this attic room."

Julia paused in her brush cleaning as a breeze blew in ruffling the curtains. The windows were thrown open and Julia had tied the curtains back into a knot of bright yellow. The air came through the high window in a soft breeze, just enough to comfort the painter. It was a perfect room. She did not want to lose it, but she could decorate another house. She didn't want to, but she could. That was not the only problem though.

"No one wants to marry me, Janey. The rumors are that I am not even truly a Bellevue and everyone knows it. The *Ton* has been more than vocal for my whole life. Perhaps that is why Father gave me to Lord Fawkland." Julia's voice dropped to a whisper. "He knew no other would want me."

Julia saw Jane's back stiffen. Her sister hated when Julia brought up the rumor. Both Jane and Father had been insisting for ages that it was meaningless talk, but of course, it wasn't. Meaningless talk eventually burnt itself out. These rumors did not.

"I have heard the gossips call me an Amazon and an unnatural giant. The gentlemen need only to glance at me, and they see my father's brawny appearance, Jane. Look at me." Tears filled her eyes.

"Oh, my dear sister," Jane began, reaching out to hug her. "You are my sister. Father completely denied the rumor that mother was unfaithful. It angered him that the fudge would not die." Jane held on to Julia's hand and declared, "You should ignore it Julia. It is of no consequence."

"How can I find a man to marry when I can barely find a man to dance with who I am not head and shoulders taller than…?"

"When a man is in love," Lavinia interrupted taking Julia's other hand. "It does not matter."

Julia sighed. Lavinia was ever the optimist, ever the romantic. Julia supposed Lavinia could afford to be with her bright blue eyes and golden hair, but *her* life was not like that. Men were not like that. Not for Julia. Surely what happened to her mother taught her that.

Julia had few memories of her mother, but she had heard much, perhaps too much. First that her mother had tried to run away with a rake of a man; and then that he had not even been part of the *Ton*, just a brawny good-looking fellow with a silver tongue. Some said he was a bastard as well.

Julia was supposedly the child of that union. So Jane and Julia were not true sisters, but only half-sisters. Some said that the day, the man had booked passage to America Julia's mother had been on her way to join him, to run away with him, but she had been killed when her carriage overturned.

Father had called the stories preposterous, and as Julia got older he still repudiated the rumor. Still if her mother was going to run away, wouldn't she have taken Julia with her? Would she leave her child, with a man not her father? For that Julia had no answer, but secretly thought perhaps even her mother did not want her.

Her father had been good to her, and never reminded her of her questionable parentage. In fact he laughed at the rumors and simply claimed people needed something to talk about. *If it is not your mother it will be someone else.*

Jane had always believed Father, but Jane was not the one with the Amazonian build. Jane was not the one tormented. One only had to look at Julia beside Jane to see it was so. If the rumors were true, then she did not know her real father and had no desire to know him.

Any man who would abandon the mother of his child was not a man worth knowing. He was a bastard who sired a bastard. As much as she hated it, Julia could not look in the mirror without thinking the rumors were accurate. She and Jane had nothing in common except for their brown hair.

"I can see in the glass, Jane."

"I wish you would not say such a thing, Julia. Father would be furiously upset to hear you speak those awful rumors aloud. He must be turning in his grave. He always believed in mother's fidelity. Always. Why can you not do so too?"

Julia just shook her head. She sat down upon the edge of the pouf now that her brushes were laid out to dry. The pouf and the window seat were the only chairs available in the attic retreat.

"You are his daughter. Don't you see?" Jane continued. "Even after his death Father is trying to do the best thing he can for you, and see you safely married, to a titled lord so that no one will be able to say you are not his daughter."

"But even if there is no truth to any of the talk, Lord Fawkland's rumors, added to my own make everything worse."

Jane made it sound so simple. She just had to accept Godwin, as her husband, a rake and a libertine, and a man who would have full control over her life. The thought terrified her. No man Julia had ever met, excepting perhaps Father, had been even the slightest bit honest. In fact few women were.

Society demanded a certain type of behavior. If everyone was wearing that mask, the mask of polite social behavior, how was she ever to get to know anyone? More than that, he would know of her birth. How much respect could he give her? The Godwin she remembered didn't even respect her dolls.

Perhaps her sister could weather rumors better than she could. As a child the taunts had hurt Julia, and when the ladies' children didn't want to play with her, it left her to her own devices until Cedric Gruger, the baron's younger brother, dragged her along on his schemes. At last she had a friend, even if he was a boy and often rougher than she preferred, in childhood he had been her only friend. Oh why hadn't her father betrothed her to Cedric instead of Godwin?

"You do not know for sure what sort of man Lord Fawkland had grown into," Lavinia urged. "My Mr. Hart says he is upright and good."

Julia stared heavenward. "Are you still in correspondence with that captain's clerk?" Julia asked.

She had expected Lavinia's infatuation to burn out long ago, but Julia latched onto the distraction to draw the attention away from her own problems.

"Oh yes," Lavinia said producing several letters from her reticule which were written by the aforementioned naval clerk. She hugged them to her breast.

"Lavinia!" Jane said appalled. "You must turn him away. What does your chaperone say?"

Lavinia only held the letters closer and beamed. "She says I must forget him, but I cannot. I will have no other."

A captain's clerk would be near penniless, Julia thought. Anyone of quality would at least start as a midshipman.

"Isn't it romantic?" Lavinia said.

"Are you quite mad?" Jane asked. "He is completely unsuitable. Not even a gentleman."

"Perhaps we shall run away together." Lavinia's eyes were alight.

"Do not even say it," Julia added.

She hoped Lavinia was teasing, but she was not certain. Lavinia was ever with a jest. Sometimes Lavinia's simple understanding of life seemed better than her own, but at least she herself was in no danger of falling for a rogue and running off to have an illegitimate child. The same could not be said for Lavinia.

"At least I shall not end up as my mother did," Julia said somewhat sadly. "No man would want to carry me off. Even if they wanted to, they would have to be a behemoth to carry off this great weight."

Lavinia chuckled. "I am sure love will find a way. Trust me, Julia. When you find a man you love, this house will cease to matter."

"I very much doubt that," Jane added dryly.

"I would give myself only for love, not money," Lavinia repeated stubbornly. "I could never marry for power or position, and I think less of one who would. It is ghastly." She shuddered.

"Gads," Jane said tartly. "You are naught but a child. You would rather live in the streets like a beggar?"

Julia could see that her sister was beginning to get angry.

"I think at the first sign of rain and cold you would like to have the house, Lavinia. You are mistaken."

"And what of love," Lavinia retorted. "She cannot marry Lord Fawkland if she does not love him."

"She will come to love him if she marries him," Jane said stoically.

"I would never give up love for the sake of a house," Lavinia said. "It is only a house!"

"Stop it!" Julia snapped. Both her sister and her friend reddened when they realized how they had been carrying on.

Julia sighed. She knew they were only arguing because they loved her. They each saw a different way to help her. Jane was ever practical, but Lavinia was a social flower who would wilt without the praise of the men of the *Ton*. Still, perhaps she was right. Lavinia could not survive without love. She had a softness and vulnerability about her that men seemed to fawn over. Perhaps some of that grace would rub off on Julia. She could only hope.

Would Julia trade her Amazonian looks for such naivety? She thought not, and yet she loved Lavinia like a sister. Julia put her hand on her friend's. "Never change, Lavinia. For you, love is like sunshine and water, but I think love is not in the stars for all of us."

Lavinia smiled. "I do believe that you too will find love, my dear friend."

"And I think you will be happier married," Jane said. "With Lord Fawkland you will have this house which I know you have always loved. But you are my sister and I will always see that you are cared for no matter what happens."

It warmed Julia's heart to know that Jane would provide for her, if need be, but she could never allow herself to be a burden. Jane had her allowance from her husband, the earl, but she had her own home, her own life. Jane had taken this summer in Bath, leaving her own husband behind, to spend time with Julia and to help her. Julia wanted this to be the last time she inconvenienced her sister, but she did not know if that was within her ability.

"Shall we have breakfast?" Jane urged. "It will make you feel better, Julia."

They left the attic study but Jane did not descend the stairs as Julia thought she would.

"I shall send for the tea and cakes to be brought up to my room. We can have a quiet morning to ourselves, without any of the fuss. I can see you are distraught and hanging on to maudlin thoughts," Jane said.

"No," Julia said. "We shall go down. What will Lavinia think of us?" She smiled at her friend.

"I am your friend, Julia," Lavinia said. "I think nothing at all."

Julia blinked at her, and Lavinia stared back nonplused. Sometimes Julia thought Lavinia said these silly comments just to make her smile. It worked.

"No. I am quite alright. Thank you," said Julia softly catching their hands as they turned to go down to breakfast. "Thank you both."

4

I t was late for breakfast and the dining room was bright with the morning sun shining on the mahogany furniture. The table was set with tea and biscuits. Julia was buttering a scone, when breakfast was interrupted.

Jane looked up from cracking her egg as the butler entered with a letter. "Yes, Harrington?" Jane said.

"A messenger just arrived," he replied, offering the letter to Jane. Julia recognized it as being from the Lady Shalace, Charity's mother. Jane opened it and smiled at Julia.

"We are invited to a musicale soiree this evening at Lakewood Place," she said. "I presume you already told Lady Charity we would attend?"

"I have," Julia said. She could not disappoint her friend.

"Oh how wonderful," Lavinia said clasping her hands.

"It should be great fun. I am so looking forward to Mr. Lodder. I was privileged to hear him perform last year."

"And you listened to the performance?" Julia teased.

"A lady has two ears," Lavinia stated, "So that she can listen to the gentleman at her side as well as the gentleman singing."

Julia laughed feeling in much better spirits.

"Please inform the messenger to send our acceptance," Jane said formally, and Harrington left them to their breakfast. Jane turned back to the conversation. "We also heard Mr. Lodder perform at Vauxhall, before he moved to Bath, oh several years ago. His voice is quite exquisite."

The women continued with their breakfast and conversation. Jane looked at her sister covertly, her attention seeming to be on her breakfast as she said, "The Gruger brothers have both sent their acceptance to Lady Shalace. They will be at the musicale, Julia, so you will be able to meet them again at last, and see if the elder brother will suit."

Julia had the scone to her mouth when Jane spoke. The mood of melancholy returned post haste.

"Very well," Julia said. She sipped her tea while Lavinia and Jane chatted; their earlier argument forgotten as they spoke of men and music. Julia wanted to sulk. She really did, but she could not. She did need to make an appearance at the musicale. She had promised Charity. And like it or not, she did need to speak to Lord Falkland. If she was too overcome, she would just call the carriage and leave as soon as she was able.

"I will see you then at the musicale," Lavinia said as

she took her leave. She kissed Julia on the cheek and whispered. "You will find love, dear Julia. I just know it."

LATER THAT AFTERNOON, JULIA AND JANE STOOD IN JULIA'S dressing room with an abundance of clothing and accessories strewn about them as Jane tried to find Julia something suitable to wear. Julia was lounging on the chaise while Jane worked to outfit her. Julia's dressing room was spacious, but did not have the breeze of the attic room. Her suite, while bordering on austere in furniture was done in all vibrant tones.

The bold and beautiful colors spoke loudly to Julia's soul. Both her bedroom and the dressing room were small, but Julia did not care. Everything of importance; everything that made her herself, was encompassed in the attic room where she painted. Sometimes she fell asleep on the pouf, and did not return to her room at all. She cared nothing for her dresses and regularly soiled them accidentally by painting in them whenever she got a whim.

"You have nothing to wear," Jane declared.

"Surely that is not so," Julia protested thinking this whole ordeal was maddening. "What about the white one?" she asked. It was simple and cool in the summer heat.

Jane looked askance and sighed as the maid entered with another armful of clothing. There was nowhere convenient left to lay the garments.

Jane waved ineffectually at the maid.

Julia knew her rooms were nothing like the rooms Jane shared with her husband, the Earl of Keegain. Even here in Bath, Jane's room was packed to the gills with all of her things. Clothing, jewelry and accessories burst out of wardrobes and drawers that could never contain them. Jane's maid had brought in several loads of clothes for her mistress' perusal, to outfit Julia for tonight's event. Jane had found fault with everything in Julia's closet.

"None of your dresses are suitable," Jane said shaking her head. "I have already been through the lot of them." She held one of the dresses with two fingers as if touching it would soil her hands.

"It is only a musicale. You act as if we are going to court. It doesn't matter if..." Julia broke off as she rescued a tippet from her sister and clutched it to herself as her sister tossed out several of her favorite pieces. Jane had already decided that none of Julia's shoes were pointy-toed enough to be worn. They were in a pile to be given away, but Julia had secretly retrieved her favorite slippers and tucked them under the edge of the blanket.

"You are meeting your betrothed for the first time since you were a child," Jane protested. "You must look your best. When is the last time you replaced any of your dresses, Julia? They are nearly three seasons past being in fashion. They all look like something a dowager would wear," Jane said with a scowl. "You should have given some of them off to a seamstress to be remade."

Jane held a flowing dress aloft as she exclaimed. "What is this relic? There is enough fabric here for three dresses."

"It is not as bad as all that" Julia said. But Jane continued undaunted.

"This neckline? Oh, Julia. Even Grand-mamma would not wear this."

"But it's so comfortable," Julia lamented as Jane threw it aside. "I like it. Its fine for morning wear."

Jane scowled at her.

Julia snatched up the dress and sat on her bed clutching it like a lovey.

"I could paint in it," Julia said reasonably. "I have to have something to paint in shan't I? I should not want to get paint on my best dresses. Even you have to agree with that, Jane."

Jane ignored her as she tossed dresses on the bed beside Julia, and her maid sought to sort through them. "Oh! Does this one have paint on it as well?" Jane asked exasperated. "Yes, paint!"

"See," Julia said. "I need dresses to paint in."

"Why didn't you paint in that one?" Jane pointed to the dress with the draw string neckline.

"I don't know." Julia said. She hung her head shamefacedly. She snatched up the aforementioned dress and hugged it to herself as she lay on the bed. "I can use this one only when I paint," she said. "I promise." She laid it with the other one that Jane had discarded.

Jane sighed and continued looking. She finally pulled a fashionable dress from her own wardrobe and laid it beside Julia's prone form. She held another aloft. "Which do you like?"

Julia shrugged morosely. They both looked stiff and

uncomfortable. There were entirely too many bows and ruffles and doodads.

"You could be more helpful, you know," Jane said.

"Then you would think I am agreeing to this," said Julia, sitting up on her elbows.

Jane shook the chosen dress free of wrinkles and held it to herself. "Oh, Julia, look. This will look splendid with your dark hair."

Julia scowled at her. "It will be too short," Julia said.

"Perhaps," Jane said, hanging the dress back in the wardrobe. "The Beresford's will be at the musicale. They are both taller than you, and you got along quite well with them at the coaching inn."

Julia scoffed. She barely spoken to either of them for three days on the coach ride and the younger Beresford was already betrothed to Jane's own friend, Amelia Atherton. What was her sister thinking?

"The elder was quite personable I do declare, and will one day be an earl. Even if you lost the house here, he would be able to buy something lovely for you. I suppose that would be a possibility if you truly can't abide the baron. There are advantages to being a countess."

"Did you not see how he looked at Lady Patience?" Julia asked as she unobtrusively kicked another pair of her favorite shoes under the bed where Jane could not see them. Honestly, if Jane kept going she would be attending the musicale shoeless!

"Well, there are others of consequence. What about the younger Beresford's companions?" Jane frowned at another dress as Julia attempted to rescue it from her sister's zeal. "Samuel Beresford is a Commander in the

Royal Navy, and his father is an earl certainly some of the others in his company have enough coin to get on with."

Jane's lady's maid, who had come in to help, pulled another dress from the wardrobe. "How about this one, milady?" she asked, but Jane shook her head. "No. I know that one is too short," she said. "Try the violet one there. What about this one?" Jane asked Julia as she spread the skirt out for perusal.

Julia grimaced and Jane waved a hand. The maid put it away.

"In any case, Julia," Jane continued as she searched. "There is hope that some of the gentlemen in Bath will have some property from their families, and even if they don't they may be able to purchase a home in Bath. We have only to search them out. There is another naval man that Commander Beresford was meant to meet here in Bath." Jane tapped a finger on the door of the wardrobe as she thought.

A second maid came into the room to do their hair, but Jane waved her away impatiently as she tried to remember the man's name. "I heard Lady Patience speak of him. A Captain, I think although I don't know at what rate. You know, a naval man might be just the thing." Jane said, putting a finger to her chin. "He would not be home long to bother you," she said tartly. "But there would be less money, Julia. A captain makes barely more than four hundred pounds per year. He could not afford to purchase your house, nor keep a proper establishment at all unless he had family money in addition to his military stipend. Certainly a stable would be a problem. Hunters could not be kept on that amount; perhaps not much more than a cook and a carriage," Jane said thoughtfully. "But if you loved him…"

"I care nothing for horses or hunts. I am not extravagant, Jane. I only want my home, and of course my paints. But in any case, I do not think I would like a navy man," Julia said. "Most are over-bearing."

The thought of a man like the outspoken Samuel Beresford as her husband terrified her, but so did the thought of being a baroness. In all probability, a navy man would want to live nearer the sea, probably in London. She wrinkled her nose. She did not want to spend the majority of the year in London. She liked Bath, although she could probably get by with a country home; if she lost the townhouse. The thought sent a stab of pain through her.

"Don't scowl so," Jane said. "There is no help for it. There are the Poppy brothers…They always come to Bath for the summer. They haven't a title but their country house is not far from here. You used to play with the brothers as a child; do you recall?"

"I did not," Julia said. "I played with their sisters, when they would have me." Aside from the Beresfords the only boys she remembered from her childhood were the Gruger brothers, Godwin and Cedric.

She frowned at the dress Jane was holding up.

"Do you hate this one too?" Jane asked exasperated.

"No," Julia sighed.

"James and Michael Poppy are both quite handsome now," Jane continued.

"Jane," Julia said, but her sister kept right on talking.

Jane turned and tossed the chosen dress, a

diaphanous light pink, beside Julia on the bed. "Stop sulking," she said. "Now, put that on and let us hope it does not want for a seamstress. I never went back for the fitting to have the seams taken in, so it should fit you.

It was also a little long on me and it won't matter if the petticoat hangs out a bit. You have that one with the roses embroidered on the flounce. If you need the length, that should do. I will have a seamstress look at some others so you have something decent to wear later in the week. I think yellow will look positively gorgeous on you."

Julia knew there was no point in arguing. She would be going to the musicale because Jane had already given their regards, and otherwise Lady Charity would be disappointed. So would Jane. Julia did not want to disappoint Jane. In spite of their differences, she and her sister had always been close.

Still, she could not resist a small dig. "Yes, Countess," said Julia.

Jane stuck out her tongue in a most *un*-countess-like behavior and for a moment Julia remembered what it was like to be carefree children.

"It fits like a glove!" Jane exclaimed when the last tiny button was buttoned. She smoothed the skirt and straightened the lace. "You look lovely. Look how the color brings out the highlights in your hair and the blue of your eyes."

"It's too short," Julia complained pulling at the dress.

"Nonsense," Jane said. "Any longer and it would be trailing on the floor. As you reminded me, this is not a ball. When we arrive, men will be lining up for permission to marry you and you can have your pick of the lot. Then you will not have to worry about losing the house or marrying Lord Fawkland if you do not wish to do so. Your new husband will buy your own house."

"I do not want my pick of the lot, Janey, I want none of them," said Julia, stepping in front of the glass to look at her reflection. She was no breathtaking beauty, but she did look neat and prim. Her eyes were large and liquid, but of course all of her was rather large. That was the problem.

"I have heard you comment on a number of men's good looks when you, Lady Charity and Miss Grant are in a state."

Julia flushed as she thought of the way her thoughts went when she saw a handsome gentleman. She tried her best to deny the wantonness her mother had seemed to leave in her soul.

"You are not blind to men. I know you do not wish life as a spinster."

"I would get a cat," Julia retorted.

"A cat!" exclaimed Jane. "You want a cat instead of a husband?"

"Well, perhaps two," she teased.

"Why all this fuss when it comes to a husband?" Jane turned her attentions to the collection of accessories. She flung fans and combs blindly on to the bed behind her until she had quite a stack. Her maid was hard pressed to keep up.

"I do not think a cat shall ever tell me what to do and what not to do. A cat shall not betray my trust."

"We shall find a man you can love," Jane said softly. "A gentleman is much preferred over a cat, Julia."

"I like cats."

Jane scoffed. "I am sure you do, but a cat cannot own a house," Jane said in her practical voice, "and surely you do not wish to remain a spinster?"

"No," Julia said softly.

She could not tell Jane that she feared picking the wrong man, as her mother had. Her eyes were always drawn to the worst of them. Yes, brash powerful men frightened her, but they also excited her. If she let herself get swept away by a hint of fancy, she would end up in the very same scenario as her mother found herself. The sort of men she should be interested in, kindly respectable ones like her sister's earl, never caught her eye. No, like her mother, she secretly picked out the rakes.

She thought of the uniformed men she had seen from the carriage. She didn't know a single thing about them, but that was the sort of man who made her heart beat fast, a well-formed man instead of a well-connected one. Her eyes always lit on the ones that were unsuitable and her heart raced. It was a flaw in her makeup.

She was not the gentlewoman that Jane thought her to be. This sort of attraction was not the temperament of a lady. Perhaps her father was wise to this fact. Perhaps that was why her father chosen for her, but she had no liking for the Fawkland boy...no, not the boy, the man. She corrected herself.

"A husband is forever." Julia said seriously. "If I do not make the right choice, Jane, I must live with that day after day for the rest of my life."

Suddenly morose again, Julia flopped back down on the bed. The pile of accessories bounced into the air. "Oh,

Jane, I would never want to be a spinster and a burden upon you and the earl, but how can I choose? I am so frightened I will choose wrong."

Jane stopped sorting and turned to her, a string of pearls in her hand. "You would never be a burden, and even if you marry no one and lose the house by the end of the summer, you are my sister. You are family and as far as choosing, that is why I am here. To help you."

Jane laid the pearls aside and helped Julia sit up.

"Up, up," she said. "If you lounge about in that dress, you will be a mess of wrinkles come time for the musicale."

Julia groaned but sat up and straightened her dress so that it didn't wrinkle. Her curls were like a dark lion's mane around her head adhering to her neck in the midday humidity and sticking this way and that like a briar patch. Jane was glowing, a faint blush of pink on her cheeks that could have been painted there with a brush. Some women were just born to be elegant, Julia thought, but she did not think there were ever two in the same family.

"Here." Jane came over to the edge of the bed with silver comb inlaid with tiny pearls and held it up to Julia's hair. "Perfect. Now we will need a fan of course, maybe this one with the gardenias? I like the bright cheery colors, don't you?"

So that's the sort of flowers they were, Julia thought. She had painted them once, but never cared to find out the name of the flowers. "Anything you put in my hair is going to be swallowed up by it," Julia grumbled.

Jane tucked an errant curl behind Julia's ear, and then

pressed a kiss to her forehead. "You are beautiful; you are a Bellevue, and you will find a husband that makes your heart sing. This house will be all your own by the end of summer."

Solitude and quiet, that is what Julia needed. Not the distraction of a handsome man with loose morals to lead her astray. How was she going to get through this summer?

"My *own*, yes. All alone, just me and this house and not a single other soul," Julia said with a grin. "Though maybe if you ask nicely I will let you come visit on occasion. Or perhaps I shall name my cat Jane... maybe Countess."

Jane tossed the fan at her. "I shall get Jacqueline to do your hair," Jane said.

Julia supposed if anyone could do anything with her unruly hair, it would be Jane's French maid, Jacqueline.

Jane's surety infected her. Julia looked in the glass, as Jacqueline worked magic on her hair. You are a Bellevue, she told herself. You will get through this evening, and the next days to come.

5

_____

*J*ulia and Jane arrived at the musical just after the hour and the festivities were in full swing. The music had not started, but those gathered visited with one another over drinks and hors d'oeuvres. The heat of the day was already subsiding and the open windows let in a refreshing breeze.

Charity's mother, the Countess of Shalace bustled over with an effusive greeting for both of them. She turned almost immediately to Julia. "Charity tells me you are engaged," she gushed.

"Yes," Julia answered simply.

"Splendid, just splendid." Lady Shalace replied brightly.

Julia looked for Charity. She hoped to be able to spend time some with her friends before being introduced to her betrothed, but she did not see Charity or Lavinia. No doubt Lady Charity was engaged in her hostess duties, but Lavinia was also not in sight.

Charity's mother talked briefly to Jane about their travel to Bath and the availability of some eligible men at the musicale; Julia supposed Lady Shalace was thinking of her daughter, but she knew Lady Charity was in no hurry to marry. After a moment Lady Shalace excused herself to greet her friends Mrs. Thompson and Mrs. Sullivan who had just arrived together.

Jane was pleased as a fox in a henhouse, a state due entirely to the numerous attractive and available gentlemen in attendance for Julia to peruse, even though the reality was she would probably still be forced to marry Lord Fawkland. Jane dragged her around to meet what seemed like every male in attendance.

Every time one of the men looked at her across the room, Jane gave her a knowing smile. "The gentleman are entranced, Julia," said Jane. "You are the prettiest lady here. Why you could have a wealthy husband by the end of the evening and spend the rest of the summer doing naught but relaxing and painting. Does that not please you?"

It would please her, but Julia did not believe the men were craning their necks to look at her rather they couldn't help but notice her extreme height. Either that or they noticed her sister; the resplendent countess next to her. Julia refrained from comment.

Jane kept a running dialogue on who were members of the Peerage and not; who had houses in Bath and in the country. She knew titles and acreage, she even had a rough guess of servants employed. Julia wasn't sure that Jane didn't somehow know their very worth in pounds and shillings. It gave Julia a sick feeling in her stomach.

There was Percival, Lord Beresford, the eldest son of the Earl of Blackwood who was well connected and would one day be earl himself. Julia and her sister had traveled to Bath with his party, but it was clear to Julia that Lady Patience had laid claim to that one, even if her sister could not see it.

Patience barely let loose of his arm for the entire trip to Bath and he did not seem to be bothered by her clinging. There was Lady Patience's elder brother Reginald, Lord Barton who would also one day hold an earldom. As well as, Commander Samuel Beresford, Lord Beresford's younger brother, but Commander Beresford had recently announced his betrothal to Lady Amelia Atherton.

The Poppy brothers, Michael and James, were both fit and comfortable. They couldn't afford the townhouse, but they had their own country home close by. Jane reminded her neither had a title, and she reminded Jane that she did not aspire to a title.

She found Lavinia with the Poppy brothers along with Miss Flora Muirwood and several Poppy sisters. Julia would have gone to join them, but Jane spotted Godwin Gruger, the Baron Fawkland, speaking with the musicians.

It seemed whether Julia was ready or not, the time had come to be introduced to her betrothed. It was a most queer situation. They were somehow betrothed through her father's writing so he had obviously given his permission, but Lord Fawkland had not courted her nor had he asked her to marry. And she had not yet accepted, she reminded herself. Julia was not sure what to say to

Lord Fawkland with the awkwardness of Father's will between them. She wet her lips nervously as she watched the man look their way. It was as if he were somehow alerted to her speculation, and called over by her interest.

Lord Fawkland excused himself from the group of musicians and stepped languidly down from the dais where they had set up. He moved with purpose. Julia looked covertly at him trying to see some sign in his face of his feelings for her. There was no indication of agitation or appreciation, but his lips held the ghost of a smile.

He glanced once around the room, a cool inspection; and then his attention was all for her. She felt herself pinned by his gaze. She fanned herself for something to do with her hands, forcing herself to move her fan slowly as befitted a betrothed lady. If only her mind could be as easily occupied as her hands.

Lord Fawkland was, if possible, even more handsome than she remembered, and tall. He was definitely tall; at least she would not self-consciously tower over him. His long stride covered the distance between them in no time at all, and she realized she could look him in the eye, with only a slight upward tilt of her head. She quickly looked at her shoes.

They were fashionably pointy-toed and somewhat uncomfortable, but they matched the pink of her dress. Oh, she looked like a candy confection. A rather large sugar flower she thought glumly. She bit her lip; terrified she would say the wrong thing and embarrass herself.

"Lord Fawkland," Jane said with a slight curtsey. Her greeting pulled Julia from her thoughts. "You of course remember my sister, Miss Julia Bellevue" she said. "She was only a child when you last met I believe, but under the circumstances, I am sure you have much to discuss."

Julia latched on to her sister's arm. Jane was not leaving her alone with the man, betrothed or not. Of course, they were not really alone with all the people gathered to hear the musicale. Did Jane have to bring up that she had been a child when they had last seen one another? It was embarrassing. She was certainly not a child now. Couldn't Jane think of anything more flattering to say?

Julia glanced up and found Lord Fawkland's dark charcoal eyes pursuing her. She squirmed under his scrutiny, still feeling like that plump woe-begotten child. She remembered seeing him in his Royal Navy uniform and hearing his commanding voice. It was such a rich, deep voice like smooth chocolate and cream.

It had been years since she last saw him. Heard him. She had had a tizzy of calf's love at the time, but she was certain that the reason was his uniform: it was only the fine clothe of His Majesty's Navy that turned her head. She always thought gentlemen looked quite dashing when in uniform. He was only the first of many a passing fancy. He was not special.

Lord Fawkland cleared his throat. "Ladies," he said with a curt bow. "Lady Keegain. Miss Bellevue."

Julia was surprisingly pleased with his manner when she offered her hand. He did not take liberties, but only quickly brought her gloved knuckles to his lips and then released her. He did not press her, but his eyes were very intense, as they met hers. They were quite dark for someone with blond hair; the grey in them was varied like a brewing storm and she wondered if she could capture that color on canvas. It was intriguing.

"I was shocked and dismayed to hear of your father's passing," Fawkland said his voice melodious and soft. "Words cannot convey my most sincere condolences."

The words were not just said in passing He actually did seem sincere, Julia thought, or perhaps he was just better at lying than most.

"Good afternoon, Lord Fawkland" Julia said at last finding her voice. "Thank you for your condolences."

He continued smoothly as if he had planned his words. "Mr. Bellevue was of great service to me when my own father passed," he added. "I would have been lost without him."

And now she was lost without him, Julia thought. She met Lord Fawkland's eyes again briefly and then looked away confused. He did not seem rakish. How would a rake seem? He would not ravish her here with the other guests. How could she know if he was what others said of him? She shoved the unwelcome thoughts away. Julia knew that their fathers had once been friends, but she had not known that her father had helped Lord Fawkland in any way. Was that why Father had chosen him?

Lord Fawkland turned to Jane with another small nod. "And please thank Keegain for seeing to the arrangements. I am in your husband's debt. This deuced war..." He broke off, the sudden passion squelched. "Pardon," he said taking both women in with a glance. He took a breath. "I was out of the country when your father passed," Lord Fawkland explained. "Or I would have contacted you sooner. Mr. Bellevue was as kind and wise a man as I have ever known."

Wise, Julia thought? Was he in agreement with this ridiculous arrangement her father had foisted upon her?

"Thank you for your correspondence on the matter, Lord Fawkland," Jane said.

"Yes," Julia added inanely. She had returned that correspondence at Jane's insistence, but it seemed they had danced all around the facts in those brief letters. Now that they were standing face to face, conversation did not come any easier.

"Thank you," Lord Fawkland replied, "Your letter was a bright bit of sunshine, in an otherwise dull day, Miss Bellevue."

Well, there was a lie, Julia thought. That single letter, written under duress, was as business-like as his answer had been: no kind words of affection, only a brief outline that she understood she was engaged to him according to her father's will. Apparently Father thought she would be married to Lord Fawkland before he passed, so that upon his death, her father wished the house in Bath to be deeded to Lord Fawkland, her husband, rather than to Cousin Rupert. It would have been so much more palpable if Father himself had told her of his plans first, but he had not.

"It must have been quite distressing for you to find out about our engagement from the solicitors," He said sympathetically. "I would have spared you that."

"Actually," Julia said. "Jane told me. The solicitors wrote to the earl."

"Of course," he said. "I only meant I would have started our courtship on a more romantic note, if I had known our time was so precious."

Romantic? What on earth was he talking about? Was he trying to woo her?

"I never wished to set you with an ultimatum. You must know, I only recently found out about the townhouse myself."

"And that was a boon," Julia blurted.

"Of course," he said after moment. "It was, but your father was always generous. I had expected a dowry, not a house."

"You could deed it to me," Julia said.

"Julia!" Jane hissed.

Lord Fawkland opened his mouth and closed it again as if he was not sure what he should say to her. She thought it was very simple. He should give her house back to her.

He turned those intense eyes on her then, and spoke. His voice penetrated down to her toes with a soft resonance. "If we do not marry," he said at last, "as I understand it, the house goes to your cousin." He took a slow breath and asked. "Do you find our engagement distasteful?" He seemed shocked, as if he couldn't quite believe that she did not find herself delighted to be married to him.

Well, she was not delighted. "I do not know you," she said flatly.

"Our fathers were friends. We were children together."

"Many marriages start with less," Jane added trying to calm the tension.

"No. We were not children together," Julia contradicted him. "It was your brother I was acquainted with, not you."

"Cedric." His voice was like ice.

"Yes, I..." Julia began but Lord Fawkland was no longer looking at her.

She followed his gaze over her shoulder to realize that Lord Fawkland was not replying to her comment, as she originally thought. He was speaking to his younger brother. Cedric Gruger had approached and stepped up just beside her.

"Hello brother," Cedric said an impish smile on his face. "Do introduce me to your betrothed."

Something passed between the brothers but Julia could not deduce exactly what it was.

Cedric seemed lighthearted as he had been as a child. Godwin said nothing, but his jaw hardened.

"Never mind," Cedric said blithely. "As the lady said, we are already acquainted." He stepped forward and took Julia's hand, kissing it. His bold action was quite on the edge of good manners, but she *had* just said they were acquainted and she was reminded of the fun they had as children. It was ridiculous to pretend they were not introduced, although polite society would hold that they were not, after all this time.

"Charmed," Cedric said still holding her hand. His eyes were bright as if they were on the edge of a joke, his full lips curving into an infectious smile. "You are much too beautiful for my brother, Miss Julia," he teased, blatantly using her given name as he had when they were children. "He will not appreciate you."

Julia could not tear her gaze away from the younger brother. As children it had seemed Cedric Gruger was less attractive of the two boys, with a too-large nose and mess of curls to rival her own, but time had proven otherwise. His face had grown into his nose, and his curls begged to be touched.

She stilled her hands and reminded herself that she was a lady. He was the sort of man that women lost their minds over: charming and virile. And he was actually taller than his older brother by a good inch. She knew she should say something, but she was rendered speechless.

"Mr. Gruger." An elegant woman who was already bearing the signs of intoxication waved to Cedric. One of her companions held her steady with an arm around her waist as she stumbled a bit, righted herself and came on smiling and talking with animation. "You promised to escort me," she sing-songed as she approached.

Julia blinked. The musicale performance had not actually begun. How could a woman so early into her cups hold a conversation better than Julia herself? She was truly hopeless. The fact was, only half of the guests would sit and listen to the music. Most were here more to mingle than to actually hear Mr. Lodder sing, although Julia thought she would enjoy the performance more than conversation.

"I do hope to call on you on the morrow, if it is convenient, Miss Bellevue," Lord Fawkland said.

"Certainly, my lord" Jane answered.

"I thought we had planned to go to the Pratt's picnic," Julia interjected.

"I would be honored to escort you," Fawkland said. He bowed stiffly. "Please excuse us."

Julia watched Lord Fawkland practically drag his brother away, the tipsy woman clinging on Cedric's opposite arm. Lord Fawkland still treated Cedric like a child. He was unkind she told herself as she watched the brothers walk away. Still, there was something about Cedric that had unsettled her even in the brief moment she had spoken to him. Of course, she had been unsettled since she left the house this afternoon.

"Well, that was something," Jane said, when the brothers were well out of earshot. She looked after them for another moment. "He is taller than you. They both are."

"Yes," Julia said as if this was a feat. She breathed a sigh of relief. At least they were gone, but Jane seemed intent upon torturing her. "What are your thoughts?" She persisted.

"I wish Father had betrothed me to the younger," Julia blurted.

Jane nodded. "You remember him as a child. You are more comfortable with him?"

Julia wasn't sure if the unsettling feeling in her stomach was actually comfort, but she did remember his infectious smile.

The musicale was starting and Jane and Julia moved to sit. Julia hadn't yet seen Lady Charity, but she hoped she could find Lavinia to sit with her. Before they reached their seats, Mrs. Thompson and Mrs. Sullivan hurried over.

Mrs. Thompson was a brunette, where her friend Mrs. Sullivan was fair. Slight wrinkles creased the corners of Mrs. Thompson's eyes, and she had laugh lines, but she was the more beautiful of the two. They exchanged pleasantries with Jane, but wasted no time before revealing their true purpose in speaking to Julia.

"Now just between us ladies, who has caught your eye?" Mrs. Thompson asked.

"Though we are out of the game, I'm sure we can help," Mrs. Sullivan added.

"Out of the game?" Julia repeated. Whatever did she mean?

"Mrs. Sullivan and I know all of the bachelors." Mrs. Thompson clarified. "We can introduce you if you like."

Julia shuddered with the thought.

"Oh, to be young and on the hunt for a husband." Mrs. Thompson heaved a sigh.

"Do you remember?" Mrs. Sullivan began, as she elapsed into what could only be a lengthy story, but it would be terribly impolite to give the woman the cut. Julia's eyes wandered back to Cedric who was engaged in conversation with several young ladies now.

She remembered how he had played tricks on some of the girls who teased her and would not speak with her. At the time she had thought it great fun, but now? What did she think? She thought about the games they had played as children and remembered how fast they had run. There seemed to be a lot of running if she remembered correctly. At last a poke by Jane brought her back to the present.

"You will be disappointed," Jane said. "My sister is somewhat... discerning."

"And so she should be," Mrs. Sullivan replied.

"I had heard your father decided," Mrs. Thompson said. "A proper lady heeds her father's wishes."

"We shall see," said Jane, when she saw Julia fumbling for words. "She has only just met the Grugers, our old family friends again. It has been an age since we were acquainted and then only as children. This is our first excursion to Bath this year."

Mrs. Sullivan gasped. "The elder Gruger or the younger? Where the younger is concerned, a more charming and fashionable man you would be hard pressed to find. He is a perfect match for her! That they were childhood friends can only mean that it was meant to be, do you not think so, Mrs. Thompson?"

Mrs. Thompson nodded vigorously.

"Are you terribly excited," Mrs. Sullivan asked.

Uncertain what else to do, Julia nodded.

"Yes, it is fated," Mrs. Sullivan said. "I do so love when fate takes a hand."

That is hardly the conclusion Julia would have jumped to.

"Yes, indeed. Just stay far away from the elder Gruger brother. Lord Fawkland's title is not worth the trouble." Mrs. Thompson shook her head, making a tsking sound. "He is not the boy you may remember. I have heard some dreadful talk about him."

"What sort of talk?" Mrs. Sullivan's mouth formed an

'o' of feigned surprise, which she artfully hid with her fan.

"Simply dreadful," Mrs. Thompson repeated in a conspiratorial whisper, but there was a smile in her voice as she exchanged a look with Mrs. Sullivan.

The pair had missed their calling as stage actors, the way they performed their roles. Still, Julia could not help leaning in to hear what Mrs. Thompson had to say about Lord Fawkland.

"I have it on dit that he has a brood of children; all from different women. And that he keeps the women quiet with expensive allowances." Mrs. Thompson nodded. "Now, I don't think that is the sort of man a young girl of quality should aspire to."

"Of course not," Mrs. Sullivan said primly.

Mrs. Thompson pitched her voice in a stage whisper. "He threatens anyone who speaks of it. His temper is quite legendary."

Julia almost felt sorry for Lord Fawkland, knowing personally the sting of gossip. Julia wondered how much of what Mrs. Thompson had to say was even the truth. She and Mrs. Sullivan both seemed to be the worst sort of busy bodies. Though it could be the truth; he had a decidedly virile appearance. Of course, so did Cedric.

Jane's face had paled. "You should not say such things, Lady Thompson, and in front of my young sister no less. She does not need to be frightened into thinking all men are rogues, especially not on account of baseless rumors. She is an innocent."

Although Julia could claim no actual experience with

men, she also did not think of herself as completely innocent. Had she not just this day feasted her eyes upon the very man spoken of? She felt a hot blush filling her face.

"Shame on you for spreading such stories," Jane said. "Look, you have made my sister blush."

Was it entirely necessary for Jane to point out how she blushed, Julia wondered.

"Now I have known Lord Fawkland since we were children, our fathers were old friends," Jane continued. "And I will not believe rumors about him."

Of course Jane would say so. She could not give any credence to rumors attached to her sister's betrothed, Julia thought. This was a disaster.

Mrs. Thompson shrugged an elegant gesture that showed off her shapely, pale shoulder. "As I said, 'tis only a rumor." She flipped open her fan with a flick of her wrist and shared a look with Mrs. Sullivan behind it. "But as you know, most of these things have at least a kernel of truth."

"Julia!" Lady Charity's voice brought her back to the present. "There you are! I have not had a moment to myself all afternoon," she said petulantly. "Come, sit with me, and we will listen to the music." She turned to Mrs. Thompson and Mrs. Sullivan. "Ladies, my mother wished to speak with you. I do believe she is in the drawing room." In the next moment, Charity had led Julia and Jane back towards the music room leaving the other women to find their own way to Lady Shalace.

"You looked like you needed rescuing," Lady Charity whispered. "We certainly do not want them to find anything to talk of. It will be all over the *Ton* by tomorrow."

Julia hurried to keep pace with Charity. The musical performance was beginning. She looked again but could not find Cedric nor the woman who had come to fetch him.

Jane reached down and caught hold of Julia's hand, threading their fingers together as she had since they were young. "I'm sorry you had to hear that, Julia. Those women should know better than to speak so in front of you."

"I am not a child, Jane, and it did not offend me. Nor shock me. An indecent child grows into an indecent man." She was beginning to think dichotomy was a staple in siblings. "I am not so naive Jane."

"Still, if you refuse him on hearsay, Julia..." her sister began.

"No, Jane. Men who stray, stray. If he is of loose morals now, that will not change." Julia said with finality she did not feel.

The three women found Lavinia and sat to enjoy the rest of the musicale together. Julia considered her plight as she listened to the music. She could not stop thinking of the Gruger brothers. Despite what she had told Jane. How had they become so handsome, and tall? It was not at all fair.

Her heart leapt at the thought of Cedric, but her heart had also raced when Lord Fawkland had been introduced to her. She stifled a groan. It was her wanton blood given her by her mother. She saw a man and her blood raced and her tongue tied itself in knots. How could she tell which man would be the best husband when they all made her feel giddy and stupid?

How could she know what to do? The *Ton* was so confusing. How could she decipher the truth? No one was what they seemed. Everyone hid their true feelings and no one ever said what they meant.

Julia was no closer to an answer by the time she and Jane arrived home. But she was determined to make the best choice. She refused to marry a rake.

Part 2

The Baron's Brother

6

$\mathcal{T}$hough he had only met her again yesterday, the Lord Fawkland, Godwin Gruger considered Miss Julia Bellevue his betrothed. Of course, he had not really met her yesterday. He had grown up with her, or rather his six years younger brother, Cedric had. Godwin remembered Miss Bellevue as a dark-haired child, running wild with his brother, but somehow while he had been at sea, the girl had grown into a striking woman.

He knew Julia was the younger Bellevue daughter, but he wondered who she was now. What did she like and dislike? He found himself excited to get to know her. Long ago he had been struck by the strength in Miss Bellevue's face and the confident way she handled his brother's shenanigans though she was only a child. He thought then if his brother had not reduced the girl to tears, she should be of stern stuff.

She seemed a steadfast girl, his family knew hers and she was not so fragile a thing that he felt he might break her. He only remembered seeing her, and being intrigued by her when he had arrived home from The Royal Navy. He had chosen her specifically. He had been seventeen, and Miss Bellevue...considerably younger. Nonetheless, she had met his eyes fearlessly, and he wanted to take some courage from her that day, and perhaps he had...the day he had come home so unprepared after his father's death.

Julia's father, Mr. Bellevue had been invaluable to him in that trying time. The man had patiently mentored Godwin when he had first inherited the barony and indeed, became not just his late father's friend, but his own as well. It seemed completely natural then, when Godwin thought of marriage, he should speak to Mr. Bellevue, not to ask for advice, but to ask for permission to court his youngest daughter when she began her season; the young girl who had so intrigued him.

Godwin assumed that the girl's father would speak to her of the arrangement. He did not yet see the need to approach the girl directly. She was young and there was plenty of time. Then Mr. Bellevue died and there was no time at all.

A letter informed him of Mr. Bellevue's death and it was with a heavy heart that he read the particulars. According to the solicitors, her father's will indicated that the girl would now be expected to marry him or lose her house in Bath. At first he thought just to deed the building to her, but there was some complication with a cousin. Godwin realized he had to go and meet with Miss Bellevue and speak to her in person.

He could not consign such news to a letter; so he shelved his other business and planned to travel to Bath. He had sent a short correspondence to his now fiancée, the youngest Bellevue daughter informing her of his desire to see her. He wanted to speak to her personally. He called his manservant and ordered the London house closed and preparations made. The girl was his responsibility now.

When he had met with Miss Bellevue yesterday, she was as striking and stately as he remembered. A woman who could look him in the eye, and she did, sizing him up, and finding him wanting. He realized almost immediately, to his great chagrin, that she preferred his brother Cedric's company to his own. He was dismayed, but he was also never one to shrink from a challenge.

She merely did not know him. That could be remedied. He would begin by escorting her to the sunset picnic at the Pratt residence. Cedric would undoubtedly be at the picnic, but Godwin could not let that concern him. Miss Bellevue might think she knew Cedric; but he would show her he was the better man.

It had been a while since he was so excited to go to a picnic, or in fact, any kind of a party. He usually shunned such events, but this evening it seemed not such a chore. He called for the carriage and made sure that it was in perfect accord for the ride, even though the Bellevue residence was only a few blocks from the Pratt's, and the weather was warm and fine. It was truly the perfect day for a picnic. He smiled as he straightened the cuffs of his shirt beneath his coat and climbed into the carriage.

MISS JULIA BELLEVUE WAS IN A STATE OF ANXIETY. LORD Fawkland would be here any moment, and she still sat trapped at the glass with her sister's maid, Jacqueline, fussing with her hair. Although Julia could not blame the woman; her hair was a mass of dark curls that tended to turn into something akin to wool with the heat and humidity.

Julia's hair, like her tongue, often had a mind of its own. The fact that Jacqueline could do anything with it at all was a miracle, but Julia squirmed eager to be done with the primping. In fact, she wished she was done with the whole picnic. Her dress irritated and her shoes, which were actually her sister Jane's, were uncomfortable.

What made Julia most sore was the fact that she would be expected to converse with her betrothed, Lord Fawkland, and perhaps she would be required to speak with some other gentlemen of the *Ton* as well. Julia found such social events taxing. The only thing that she could look forward to was the fact that Lady Charity Abernathy and Miss Lavinia Grant, her dear friends would also be at the picnic.

Jacqueline pulled on a stubborn curl and pinned it in place and Julia winced. Surely, her hair would soon be completed! She reminded her sister Jane and her maid that the event was a picnic, not a ball.

"Lord Fawkland will be here any moment," Julia said. "Are you not yet finished, Jacqueline?"

"Un moment Mademoiselle," The maid said as she placed the comb Jane had chosen in Julia's hair.

"Gentlemen are accustomed to waiting for their ladies," Jane reminded her.

Julia scowled at her sister as the butler announced Lord Fawkland's arrival.

He was here! Julia felt her stomach turn over. "Oh, Jane," she said, turning her head so that Jacqueline had to hold onto a curl "Ouch," Julia winced.

"Pardon Mademoiselle."

"What if I say something awful?" Julia said worriedly.

"You shall not," Jane said with more confidence than Julia felt.

"Magnifique," Jacqueline exclaimed at last, proud of her own handiwork.

"You look beautiful," Jane said.

Julia had her doubts, but she took the compliment gracefully thanking both Jane and Jacqueline.

When at last she was dressed and ready Julia walked down the staircase with special care. Lord Fawkland was waiting in the drawing room and examining the paintings on the wall. The painting he stood in front of was one she herself had painted; of birds taking wing from a garden path. Next to it was another of her paintings, a simple depiction of Bath with a cat sitting contentedly on a wall.

Oh why had she let Father hang them so publicly? At least her name was not on any of them, only her initials in the lower right corner. She gripped the rail. She did not want to embarrass herself before the evening even started; by tripping and falling down the stair. She watched Lord Fawkland as she descended and wondered if this man could really be her future husband.

Lord Fawkland turned and smiled at her. The smile lit his whole face, and Julia relaxed a little. He did seem happy to see her, and not quite so stern as he had previously. He came to the bottom of the stair and took her hand as she stepped down. She was again struck with Lord Fawkland's large stature. Though she was quite tall herself, standing on the last step, she could look Fawkland in the eye.

He has rather intense grey eyes, she thought as she stood fixed in his gaze. Her breath caught as he spoke.

"Miss Bellevue," Lord Fawkland said as he bowed over Julia's hand, holding it for only a brief moment before releasing her and turning toward Jane who came down the stair just behind her.

Now that Julia's feet were firmly on the ground she realized that he was indeed a head taller than she. She had only a moment to study him covertly while he was speaking with Jane.

Lord Fawkland was quite handsome with his blond curls brushed back from his face. He had a strong jaw and a rather prominent nose.

He looked back to Julia still smiling; his voice deep and melodic, "I do not know when I have more looked forward to an outing. I am eager to get to know you, Miss Bellevue. Your father always spoke so fondly of you."

Julia was anxious too, but she did not think it had anything to do with getting to know him; and rather everything to do with what she already knew. What had Father said of her? She wondered.

Lord Fawkland helped her and Jane into the carriage before sitting on the seat opposite them. He smoothed a hand over his perfectly folded cravat and then laced his fingers together in his lap.

"It is such a short walk to the Pratt's," Julia commented. "It is hardly worth the trouble of a carriage." After she said it, she wondered if she had sounded churlish.

"Perhaps," Lord Fawkland said, "but I wished to have a moment with you before I lost you to the crowds and festivities of the picnic."

Julia did not answer. She did not know what to say. It would be rude to stare out the window, as she usually did during carriage rides, but it seemed equally rude to stare at him. She looked at her shoes, or rather Jane's shoes on her feet.

"It is a very nice carriage," Jane said trying to save the moment and Julia had to agree. The carriage was well-built, neat and fresh, as if it had just been cleaned, but she did not say so. She kept her own council.

But Lord Fawkland seemed intent on drawing her into conversation. "Do you like to take walks, Miss Bellevue?" Lord Fawkland inquired of her. "Do you have a favorite place?"

Julia startled. She was unused to being addressed directly. Everyone who knew Julia knew that she took time to warm up to a person. They left her to add to the conversation as she liked. Lord Fawkland did not know her.

"I suppose I do," she said at last answering the first question. Then she lapsed into silence again, creasing and re-creasing the folds of her dress. "Not always, of course," she added, looking at him covertly through her lashes. He was so very handsome...and a horrible rake, she reminded herself; if the rumors could be believed.

"No, not always," Lord Fawkland agreed. "I do not believe anyone enjoys a walk through some of the London streets, especially in summer...It can be... distressing," he finished somewhat hesitantly and then changed tack. "Though I often enjoy a walk in brisk weather, just to see the flora and fauna, or perhaps the birds."

"I think it can be rather indolent...just walking," Julia said. "That is if you have nowhere you mean to go." Had she just said that aloud? Did she call him slothful for walking without a destination? Oh dear. She was a horrible person. She should just be silent. She always said the wrong thing. She threw a hopeful glance at Jane. Her sister would hold this conversation together. Julia knew she would, but Lord Fawkland began yet again, addressing her, more specifically now. "I noticed you had several paintings of birds and cats. Did you buy them locally?"

The birds? She thought, and then she realized he meant the paintings themselves...her paintings. Julia looked at him wide eyed, her heart in her throat. "Yes," she said at last. "They are local."

"One depicted a scene here in Bath, but I did not recognize the painter."

Her mouth became dry as a desert.

"That's because they are Ju..." Jane began and Julia sent her a horrified look. Her sister changed mid-word. "Just a local artist," she finished.

"They are quite good. Cheery," he added, "and bold."

"Are you a collector?" Jane asked.

"No. I would not call myself an expert, but I know what I like." His eyes were back on Julia.

Julia was about ready to leap from the coach. It was only a few blocks to the picnic. Surely they should have arrived by now. She found herself sinking into the corner, and Jane poked her, albeit unobtrusively. This whole outing was a horrible idea. She was sure to disgrace herself.

"Miss Bellevue," Lord Fawkland said as the carriage stopped. "I am quite determined to get to know you and hope you will wish to get to know me as well."

THE PRATT PICNIC WAS BEGUN IN EARNEST. A CHEER WENT up from a group of ladies just as the sisters alighted from the carriage and Julia's eyes were drawn to them. The ladies were playing a game of shuttlecock. Julia watched for a moment.

It did not look like a complicated game. One just needed to hit the shuttlecock with the racquets. That was straightforward enough. There was a bit of an error as one lady got a tad tangled in her skirt and the group let out a sad sigh to see a point lost. However, Julia found it quite entertaining to see the husbands cheering the women on to victory. For most of the games, it was the women cheering their men. She smiled at their antics.

Lavinia hurried up to greet them.

Jane's friend, Lady Ebba followed Lavinia. After introductions were made all around, Lavinia turned from Julia to Jane, "We were looking for someone to play shuttlecock," she said. "We need another pair for the game. Married ladies are playing against the unmarried," Lavinia explained. She looked back at Julia, pleading. "Please play," she said.

"Where is Lady Charity?" Julia asked somewhat hesitantly.

"She was paired with one of the Poppy girls earlier," Lavinia said.

Jane had already engaged in conversation with Lady Ebba. Julia realized she could either play or stay and converse with Lord Fawkland. She did not think herself adept at shuttlecock, but conversation was even a more distressing pastime than the game.

She looked back at Lord Fawkland, uncertain. Apparently he took her uncertainty to mean that she wished to play. "Enjoy yourself," he said. "We will meet again before dinner." He bowed smartly.

"Yes, thank you," she said, feeling completely at odds. She did not want to play shuttlecock, but she also did not want to be left alone with Lord Fawkland. There seemed to be no third choice.

"I do not want you to feel coerced into ...anything," he said. He took her hand momentarily, and looked at her with such intensity it took her breath. "Your father and I were more than acquaintances, Miss Bellevue. I counted him as my good friend and mentor: perhaps even as a second father."

Well, she thought. Although she did not know Lord Fawkland, her father had trusted this man. She could at least attempt to get to know him.

"I think we will be able to find some common ground, if we but try. Do you agree?" he asked.

She nodded. She had no idea if she agreed or not, but he released her with a smile.

She hurried off with Lavinia to play the game. She hoped this was not a mistake.

Julia and Lavinia played against Jane and Lady Ebba. She did not know the other woman, but that was not unusual. She had met few of the crowd here, though it seemed Jane had known them all for ages by their enthusiastic greetings. How Jane had actually met them all, Julia had no idea. Jane always seemed to have a cluster of friends. Julia had enough trouble keeping a conversation going with only one.

It did not take long for Julia to learn that her life as a near recluse did not prepare her for an afternoon of sport. She could handle a paint brush with ease and put paint exactly where she wanted it, but the racket was not so amenable. She had a difficult time getting the racket to connect with the shuttlecock at all.

Julia swung and missed several times since the start of the game. Once she managed to bat the dratted thing back, quite by accident. Shuttlecock did not seem as if it should be a complicated game, but Julia could not master it. She held the racket at an awkward angle and after a while, it got heavy so she switched it to her non-dominant hand.

That did not help her aim, but it seemed that Lavinia was doing well enough without her aid; taking up where Julia was lacking. Laughing, she batted the shuttlecock back to Jane who missed it, and Lavinia hopped in excitement.

Julia glanced around the lawn as Lavinia held up their side. Her gaze caught Lord Fawkland looking their direction and she looked quickly away. Oh, why was he not otherwise engaged? She did not want him to see her make a fool of herself with this silly game. It was rather warm in the sun, and once exerting oneself in the game, it became quite uncomfortable even though the heat of the day was already subsiding.

Men and women played at cricket and shuttlecock on the far hill while others lounged, sipping from glasses beaded with condensation. Now that sounded like a nice pastime. She was actually quite thirsty. She looked again but did not see Lord Fawkland now. If she had stayed with him, she could have been sipping some sweet drink. She turned, searching for him, wondering if he was still watching her. She hoped not. Certainly he had nothing to cheer for.

A shuttle cock flew past her head...again.

"Julia!" Lavinia called. "You are not even trying," Her friend chastised her.

It didn't matter. Lavinia had scored all of the points for their side. Although Jane and Lady Ebba were maintaining a sizable lead while Julia stumbled about and swung wildly. She looked like a pigeon with a broken wing, fluttering about without hope of taking flight.

She knew the game was named for the feathered

implement she was supposed to hit, but it seemed it could also be named for a headless cock which ran about in its death throes. She was an apt example of said bird. She missed once again, but this time she attempted to at least do so with grace. When the shuttlecock landed just out of Julia's reach for what must have been the tenth time, she dropped her racket on to the grass and threw up her hands.

"I give up" Julia exclaimed, panting. Sweat did not mar the other women's dresses as it did hers. They all looked as cool as they did when they started the game. Julia's hair, which Jacqueline had worked so hard to achieve, was sticking to her neck in ringlets. "I am sorry, Lavinia. But we will never catch up, and sweating like a sow is not the way for me to impress my future husband. Jane, I'm going to find Lady Charity," Julia said as she turned to leave the field.

Jane caught up with her momentarily. "Oh Julia, you have stained your slipper!" Jane pointed down at the toe of Julia's shoe. The embroidery was covered with a green grass stain. Well, Julia thought, what else could one expect playing such a game as shuttlecock.

"What will your future husband think of you, with a stained shoe? You mustn't appear slovenly. Perhaps I can beg a spare pair off of Lady Pratt."

Jane turned a fretful gaze around the lawn, searching for the hostess.

"Jane, if my future husband will not have me with a single grass stain, then I do not believe we would ever manage to make a marriage work." Julia responded dryly.

"I am not a dainty woman, like you sister. He will just have to accept that."

Jane sighed and re-pinned a curl that was dangling in Julia's face.

"Is it hopeless?" Julia asked of her hair.

"Of course not," Jane said brightly adjusting a few pins. "Shall we find some refreshment?"

Julia nodded. She was parched.

Lavinia caught up to them laughing. "Do not worry, Julia" she said with a cheerful smile. "It was a fun game even if we lost." Julia was glad that Lavinia had been her partner instead of Jane. Jane would not have been so magnanimous about her sister's ineptitude.

Lavinia made to follow Julia and Jane off the field, but was waylaid by Flora Muirwood and one of the Poppy sisters who had just won their own game. She hesitated.

"Shall we meet you again before dinner?" Jane asked Lavinia.

"Yes, of course" Lavinia agreed.

Julia started to move away, following her sister, but as she turned she caught her breath and paused. Jane grinned at her. If she had tried to spy on Cedric she could not have gotten a better view. The younger Gruger brother was engaged in a game of cricket and she was to his back. He was up at bat, crouched in the ready stance; his trousers pulled tight. Julia blinked and looked again, although a lady would have turned away.

Cedric appeared at ease and prepared, and when the bowler's throw came, his hit was perfect. The ball flew up and in a wide curve. He ran to the wicket as the ball bounced across the field.

A moment before she looked away, Cedric caught her watching him and flashed her a smile, too knowing by half. Julia stiffened and turned away. At the last moment, she saw Lord Fawkland. His eyes were upon her. Did he see her observing his brother? She was utterly mortified. She wanted to run, but there was nowhere to go.

7

---

*G*odwin watched as Miss Bellevue played shuttlecock with her friends. He wanted to speak with her about their betrothal, but he did not want to stand in the way of her fun. He knew she had reservations about their marriage and he wanted her to understand a bit of his character.

He would not rule her with an iron hand. He had no wish for a silent and sullen wife. He wanted her to have her friends and her fun. He had always liked her spirit. In fact, her spirit was a large part of her appeal.

As soon as the shuttlecock game began he realized that she was truly terrible at the game. He nearly laughed aloud as she sprinted wildly after the shuttlecock only to miss again. He realized that Lady Ebba and Lady Keegain had taken the better side of the field and left the side facing the sun to Miss Grant and Miss Bellevue. The older women were already the better players and the handicap was too much for Miss Bellevue.

Her teammate struggled to hold their end; still Miss Bellevue tried valiantly even switching her racket to the other hand. Although her command of the game was awful, he found that he was quite impressed with her mettle. More than ever he was determined to convince her to accept his suit.

As Miss Bellevue was safely playing shuttlecock, Godwin looked for Cedric. He knew his brother would be here at the picnic; creating gossip no doubt. He searched the crowd for his brother's blond hair. Like himself, Cedric was tall and easily found. Godwin spotted his younger brother busy playing cricket, with a throng of women cheering for him, and decided to have a drink while watching Miss Bellevue's game, but he was waylaid en-route by Mrs. Thompson.

By the time he managed to extricate himself from her questions, the shuttlecock game was finished and the ladies were nowhere in sight. He had a moment of alarm and he looked automatically for Cedric, but he was still safely playing cricket.

Godwin looked for Miss Bellevue's dark hair above the bevy of blondes. Normally, when he was obliged to attend such events he found a way to avoid them, but somehow the parties, ridottos and gaieties were not so abhorrent when Miss Bellevue was in attendance.

He smiled at the thought of talking with her more over dinner. He wanted to know her favorite foods and desserts. He wanted to know everything about her. The more Godwin saw the girl, the more he wanted to protect her. It was uncanny. He searched for her in the crowd. Not that it was difficult. She towered above most of the women and some of the men. She had the carriage of a queen.

He grinned as he found her, not amidst the crowd, but walking off by herself, with only her sister headed towards the archery range. He finished his drink and followed her. A prideful voice inside of him urged him to show off for her. He was a crack shot with both bow and musket; a perk from his time in His Majesty's Service. He would impress her. His brother did not stand a chance.

JULIA AND HER ELDER SISTER WANDERED OVER TO THE archery field. Thankfully, it was deserted, and Julia was glad to leave the crowd behind. Five targets were set up at increasing distance down the lawn. Julia, feeling brave without an audience, pulled a bow from the rack and set up across from the closest target.

She and Jane had practiced archery with Father when she had been younger, and she knew her mother was quite a good shot, but it had been quite a while since Julia had shot a bow. She had never been an expert marksman, but it couldn't be worse than shuttlecock. She had already done embarrassingly poorly at that sport. Archery could be no less appalling. No doubt Jane would best her, but at least archery would keep Jane's mind off of the marriage mart and Julia could have some peace. The thought gave her some respite but, Jane was looking back towards the other party goers and did not pick up a bow immediately.

"I will take your reluctance to participate as a sign you are frightened I will win." Julia teased her sister.

Jane shot her a withering look. She rubbed her hands together and marched over to the bow rack. She traded her kid gloves for the more durable shooting gloves as she spoke.

"More that I did not wish to embarrass you in front of your potential suitors, but I see there is a lesson to be taught here," Jane retorted.

"What suitors?" Julia asked. She chuckled and felt more at ease with just her sister beside her. Perhaps this day would not be an entire travesty. It could not get much worse after the disastrous attempt at shuttlecock.

Jane nocked the arrow and drew with textbook form, smoothly, unerringly. A heartbeat later, Jane released and the arrow flew straight and true, burrowing into the target just a hair off the center mark. She always was Father's star pupil, but at least challenging her older sister made Julia forget about husbands for just a little while.

Julia tried to copy Jane's form. She tried to remember Father's lessons, but even though Julia was the larger of the two women and should have no trouble with the bow, her arm quivered as she drew the bowstring back. Jane had made it look effortless, but the act required more force than Julia had remembered.

"More quickly," Jane urged. "Swift and sure. Remember what Father said."

"Easy for you," Julia said as she wrestled the bow into place at last, but holding the position was hardly any easier than getting it there in the first place, and she was forced to release before she was steady. The arrow wobbled in the air and landed on the ground five feet from the target. Flat.

"Well, ladies, this hardly seems a fair match." Julia did not need to turn to know who that deep voice belonged to. Lord Fawkland had returned.

"Hello again, Lord Fawkland," said Jane. There was no sign of disapproval in Jane's voice. She did not listen to the talk of the *Ton* but Julia could not help but remember what she had heard about Lord Fawkland: that he was a rake of the most low regard. Jane was merely too polite to let on.

She reminded herself that Father had trusted Lord Fawkland. Still, rumor laid credence to what Julia knew as a child. She remembered the day she had come into the school room to find her favorite doll trussed up and hung from the ceiling with a hangman's noose; broken. She had never really discovered which brother had done the deed, but Cedric claimed that Godwin had wanted a ransom. She had always wondered what that ransom had been. It was only a doll, she reminded herself. It was years ago and did not matter.

Her nanny had only clucked and said, "Boys will be boys." Still, the sight of the ruined doll came to Julia now. She looked at Lord Fawkland a little nervously and her heart did flip flops. He was so terribly handsome. He did not look like the sort of a man who would torment a young girl. She shook her head. She would not have her head turned by his manliness. She would remember the cold arrogant child he was, and she would be just as cool. She lifted her chin and looked away.

Julia had expected Lord Fawkland to melt under Jane's smile like every other man seemed to, but when she glanced over her shoulder Julia found him looking at her instead of Jane. She felt a blush heating her cheeks and her stomach clenched. She looked away again. His cool eyes were so mocking, as if looking for some flaw.

Perhaps he was dismayed that she was so tall. She glanced at him from beneath her lashes.

"Do you shoot, Lord Fawkland?" Jane asked.

Julia thought it was a silly question. Of course he shot. He was a gentleman, but he seemed unperturbed by the inaneness of the question.

"I do," Lord Fawkland replied to Jane. "As I remember, you always had a knack for archery, Lady Keegain, but I see it is not a family trait."

How dare he expose her shortcomings? Julia peeked at him from the corner of her eye. He was looking at her again!

Did he believe the rumors said of her? Had he mentioned family on purpose, supposing that she was not truly a Bellevue? That would be just cruel. But wasn't he cruel?

She thought about her dolls. She could see no reason why would a twelve-year-old boy do such a thing. Though she had, in the intervening years, learned that people were not kind, and young boys were less so.

She would have taken him to task on his manners, but all the words she had in her head would not leave her mouth as she wished them to. She convinced herself she did not want to spend enough time on him to reprimand his impropriety. She turned away and hoped he would stop making her so nervous. Instead, he took a bow from the rack, larger than either Jane's or Julia's, and tested the weight of the draw.

Julia's felt a trickle of heat run down her spine as he moved closer.

His eyes swept over her. Immediately her hand started to shake as she realized he was looking at her. She gritted her teeth trying to still her disquiet.

"We all have our strengths," Jane replied. "My sister is a better painter than I am. She has the patience to mix oils to the perfect shade whereas I can barely make a proper scene with watercolor, though I have devoted many hours to the study."

Did Jane think she was making this better? Though her sister could never resist coming to Julia's defense, Julia glared at Jane. She hadn't wanted Lord Fawkland to know she had done the paintings back at the townhouse. Oil painting was not a common ladylike pursuit. Jane glared right back as if to say Julia was being silly.

"Julia is the proper artist." Jane said with finality.

"Your father spoke of it," Lord Fawkland replied.

He turned to look at Julia and she blushed under his gaze, or her sister's praise, she was not sure which.

"I'm sure you find the same with your brother," Jane continued. "There are things you do well and things he does well."

Julia watched the smile fade from Lord Fawkland's face. "Humph," Was all he said by way of reply.

It seemed there really was some animosity between the brothers. Julia could almost feel it crackle around Lord Fawkland even at this distance. Her natural curiosity made her want to ask about it, but she held her tongue. Asking questions like that only got her in trouble. The man was entitled to his secrets.

Julia put her concentration on righting the arrow. She struggled to aim. Lord Fawkland lifted one eyebrow and a shoulder in a half shrug before turning back to Julia. She felt heat pool in her belly and she looked away. She should be looking at the target she reminded herself. She released another poor shot.

"Cedric could never stand for being anything but first. It drives him mad that I was born first and no amount of work or money will overcome it," said Lord Fawkland. "Everything I have, my brother wants. His jealousy blinds him to what good he holds himself."

"Surely not," Julia said.

She remembered her gad abouts with the younger brother and felt the need to speak. She had all manner of berating comments running through her head, warring to be spoken, but none of them would actually come out of her mouth. Had she just called the man a liar? Oh bother. She should just pretend to be mute. Yes, a mute woman would have a better chance of making a good impression than she did. Did she want to make a good impression, she wondered? Did it matter if he was a rake? How could she marry such a man?

Fawkland didn't answer her random attempt at conversation. Perhaps that was because there was nothing to say, and partly because he probably did not want to contradict her, not if he was a gentleman. Of course rumor said that he was not.

Instead of speaking, he unbuttoned his jacket, ran his

fingers along the smooth curve of the bow, then set an arrow in place all in one smooth graceful motion. Julia's gaze was drawn to his hands as he pulled back the bowstring effortlessly. His movements were confident, assured. Was he so assured with everything he did she wondered? A shiver ran down her spine although the day was hot.

She saw at once why he had unbuttoned his coat; his muscles flexed and pulled the fabric of his shirt, bunching his jacket around his shoulders, and it may have torn without the extra space. His waistcoat strained across the muscles of his torso. The heat caused the cotton to cling damply. Julia felt a hot blush fill her face. She cleared her throat.

Only his strong fingers moved with his release. The arrow sunk solidly, penetrating the dead center of the target, exactly where he had chosen to put it, the fletching obliterating the small yellow circle from this angle.

"Bravo, Lord Fawkland." Jane applauded. "Oh, here comes Lady Montgomery, looking for me. Excuse me, just a moment."

No! Thought Julia, as Jane began moving away, but the word stuck in her throat.

Lady Montgomery had been a dear friend of Jane's since their debut. She looked harried now, crossing the lawn with her dress bunched up in her hands, and a look on her face like she had much to tell Jane. The woman could talk for hours. Julia was doomed.

"Of course," said Lord Fawkland. "As long as your sister can stand to be left on her own with me." He smiled, and his eyes were warm upon her. Julia panicked. What would they say to one another?

"Julia?" Jane asked. "You don't mind? I shall only be a moment."

Julia could not speak and Jane took her silence as assent. She did mind. She did not want to be left alone with Lord Fawkland, but even she knew it would be rude to say so and she did not want Jane to feel like a nanny, glued to her side every moment of the summer. She did not need such a close chaperone. She didn't. She only wanted one.

She threw a glance at Lord Fawkland. He was so tall, nearly a head taller than she was. Her eyes lingered on the broad expanse of his chest. Jane was already moving away. She could call her sister back. Oh, she was being silly. All of the *Ton* was just a breath away; it was still daylight and the picnic was in full swing. There was no real privacy. She didn't need a close chaperone. Still, Julia was nervous. Jane glanced over her shoulder, beamed and hurried off to meet Lady Montgomery. She thought she was doing Julia a favor!

Julia was alone with Lord Fawkland. Well, as alone as one could be in a party of some hundred people, all occupying a single lawn. But it was a very big lawn and no one was paying her any particular attention with the exception of Lord Fawkland who was watching her curiously.

They stood in silence. Julia's skin was alive with tension. All she could think of was his strong fingers holding the arrow with such precision, and then letting it fly. Her imagination brought those fingers to her skin. She shivered; her face aflame.

Her thoughts flew. She should speak. She should say something witty. Her sister would know what to say. Lavinia would know what to say. Even Francesca the littlest Poppy sister, who wasn't even out for her Season yet would know what to say.

Julia's tongue felt dry in her mouth, and she cleared her throat. Dear God. She could at least talk about the weather, couldn't she? *Beautiful day isn't it?* She could say that. Of course he could see that it was a beautiful day. It made her sound like a ninny to repeat it. And standing here mute did not make her look like an idiot? She chided herself.

Lord Fawkland had turned from her and she breathed again. He shot an arrow himself, and then another. She watched him mesmerized. Why didn't he start the conversation? He was surely no gentleman.

"You are a quiet one," he said his voice soft, like velvet. He had stopped shooting and turned towards Julia again. All of his attention was on her and she wished he would turn back to the targets...and wished he didn't.

"I'm not," she said.

"But you do not share your sister's love of parties, I see. Though you were more boisterous as a child, if I do remember correctly."

He smiled at her awaiting a response. Julia said nothing. She blushed and looked at her shoes, thinking that if she wasn't looking at him, she could get her bearings and speak. Why did he bring up her childhood? She was no longer a child. She noted the grass stained toe of her shoe. Did he notice? She tucked one foot behind the other self-consciously.

"I will never forget the day you and Cedric stole a berry pie right out from under our cook's nose and ate it all yourselves. You ran the servants in a merry chase that day."

"I didn't," she said. The words were strangled. It was strange he remembered their childhood quite differently than she did. She had nothing to do with the stealing of the pie. That was Cedric. She did have to admit to sharing it with him though. It was delicious, but Cedric had forgotten to steal spoons and she had stained her pinafore digging in with her fingers after Cedric's dare. She had been covered with blueberry stains. Her nanny was quite cross with her.

"Cedric was ill that evening, but still maintained having no regrets," Lord Fawkland said with a soft laugh. He sounded wistful. "I was home on a furlough."

Julia remembered the day. She had not gotten sick but she had been given a scolding. Only Cedric had such fun running from the cook and dodging those who tried to catch him. Later, Cedric had taken her to a secret place and regaled her with the adventure.

He told her of the chase and shared his stolen pie. He showed her his treasures: A number of baubles she remembered. It had meant nothing at the time. Now, she wondered what they all were. Those treasures? And why had he hidden them? To whom did they belong?

"I remember those lips covered with sweet blueberries." Lord Falkland reached out as if to touch her, and she thought again of those hands on her skin and shivered. For just a moment anticipation filled her, and her lips parted, but his fingers stopped a hair's breadth from her lips. She could see his gentleman's ring shining in the summer sun. She dare not look at his face. *What was she doing?*

She dodged him and the movement seemed to have unstuck her words. "I detest parties," she said. "Being thrown together with people I do not know, only to have them say awful things about me the moment my back is turned."

Julia knew it sounded mulish, but she could not stop herself from blurting out the tumble of her thoughts.

"People say all sorts of things when they believe there are no consequences for lying." Lord Fawkland said as he took up his bow and nocked another arrow, aiming sideways at the farthest target, his body completely relaxed. "People are cruel. Sometimes they need to be put in their place."

He shot the arrow and chose another one, moving with smooth precision like a dancer...or a painter, placing the paint just where he wanted it.

"Are you saying I should threaten them as you do? I have heard..." She broke off. She could have kicked herself. Why had she said that? Why hadn't she just been quiet and looked demure?

He stiffened, just for a moment, and she thought she caught a flash of heat in his eyes. Then he shot another arrow. It flew unerringly and struck dead center once again, sinking much deeper than the previous arrows. The intensity of Lord Fawkland frightened her, but she stayed nonetheless. He shot several more arrows, each one hitting the target with unerring ease and the boiling nervousness in her stomach turned to a soft simmering as if she were expecting something. She was not sure what.

"What have you heard?" His voice was almost a whisper, but she heard it still.

"I—I should not give any account to gossip," she said, feeling her face flame. "I know how it feels to be the brunt of it." What would he think of her? Did she care what he thought? She supposed she should. Her Father had tied her future with his. All she had to do was figure out how to avoid that future; that is if she still wanted to avoid it?

When Lord Fawkland turned to face her, there was no sign of anger in his face, just weariness. "Gossip is a coward's weapon," he said.

Lud, who was he speaking of? Her gossip or his own?

"Pardon?" she blurted.

"I am saying; people lie. People do things they should not, and hide under a mask of respectability."

Well, that was true, Julia thought. Hadn't she just said the same to Jane earlier today? But she didn't want to agree with him. And yet to disagree seemed churlish. "Do you do that?" she asked.

"Do what?"

"Hide. Under a mask—" she broke off before she spoke her thought aloud: a mask of respectability. Was she seriously going to ask him *that*? What was wrong with her?

Lord Fawkland did not answer immediately. Instead,

he considered his answer for a moment. "I do what I must to protect the reputation of my family."

Not himself, she thought. His family. He could not just let the talk stand. Like Jane. She could not let injustice stand either. That did not seem like a man who would take liberties. Julia studied his face a moment and he turned back to the target again, aiming and shooting with perfect precision.

Julia admired his form. She thought she could stay here all day and just watch him move with such precision and grace, but it was unseemly.

Julia, for want of a distraction, picked up her own bow and stood again across from the nearest target. "I do not think my threats would have the same effect as yours Lord Fawkland; it would only prove those people right in their assumption that I am wild and ill-mannered and prone to fits of passion because of...because of..."

She broke off uncertain where to go with this confession. Once again, she had said things that were better off unsaid. She bit her lip, angry with herself for letting her tongue take off with her. She pointed her arrow at the ground. She took a shaky breath before beginning again.

She was trembling with anger, and emotion, cursing her stupidity which did not help her form. Lord Fawkland stepped up beside her when she began to draw again. His fingers hovered just above her elbow, never touching, but close enough to feel the heat of them.

"I have never felt you were wild and ill-mannered," he said. "I know my brother sometimes led you astray, but..."

"It was not him, truly," she said. "Mr. Gruger was once my friend."

Fawkland's smile was extinguished as quickly as a snuffed candle and the sun in the sky went behind a cloud. A chill shuddered through her. What had happened between the brothers she wondered to make the animosity between them so pronounced? She pointed her arrow to the ground and released the tension from the bow, as she waited for him to enlighten her, or not; as he wished.

Godwin took a breath, and spoke. "My brother can be charming," he said. "Amusing even, there is no doubt of that. However, Cedric never much cared who might be harmed by his amusements."

"Your brother was the only one who never teased me about the circumstances of my birth," Julia said.

Lord Fawkland's jaw tightened and she bit off the flood of words that threatened to fly from her mouth. What was the animosity between him and his brother? The question was on the tip of her tongue, but she bit it back. She could not ask such a thing. Even she was not so socially inept, but there was certainly more here than she had first realized.

When at last Lord Fawkland spoke, his voice was sure. "Do not let anyone tell you it is wrong to be yourself. The *Ton's* talk of your breeding has more to do with their manners than your own," he said. "Never forget that."

Her own father had said much the same thing when she was inundated with rumors of her mother's infidelity and her own tainted birth. "That sounds like something my father would have said," she commented.

"It *is* something your father said," he replied. His voice was wistful. He really had known her father well.

She raised a hand and then stopped, uncertain. She wanted to reach up and brush her fingers against the strong line of his jaw, to ease the tension there. Surely that was a forward thing to do. A lady would not even think of it.

Lord Fawkland looked at her then, and his eyes were the cool grey of a storm cloud. She felt they held the same intensity as an oncoming storm. She could nearly feel it blowing along her skin although the sun still shone.

His jacket was still open. His white waistcoat defined his chest and the heat which had moistened his body, made the garment cling. A baron had no right to be so well built. And she had no right to look. What was wrong with her? A decent lady did not think about a man's form! She tried to tear her eyes away and failed. She felt her face heating. He was so close she could smell the faint scent of sandalwood on his skin.

A shadow was on his cheek. His beard would grow darker than his hair, she thought, and she wanted to feel that rough stubble against her own skin.

His eyes alight on her lips and the moment stilled. Was he thinking of blueberries, she wondered and her heart pounded? She realized she wanted him to kiss her. Oh she was such a hoyden. She should look away. She should make some witty remark. Say...the sun was shining today...Oh, she was horrible at this.

She realized she was holding her breath, and let it out with a shaky sigh.

He cleared his throat. "Shall we try another arrow?" he asked.

She nodded dumbly and chose another.

"Lower your elbow so that is in line with your arm. A bit more. A straight line here will make for a straight shot," he said, drawing his hand along her arm, but still not touching her.

"Do not try to hold the arrow," he said. "Nock, aim, fire all in one smooth motion. There. That's it. Now, release."

She did. The arrow flew. It did not wobble but flew through the air. It landed point first in the target and stuck; in the outermost ring, but still. Julia danced in place and Lord Fawkland cheered for her.

"Did you see that? I hit it!" Julia laughed, forgetting her manners completely and jumping up and down like a small child. She all but flung herself into his arms. Where was her decorum? Oh she was a ninny. She took a deep breath and settled herself. There she went, getting worked up and emotional.

"A marked improvement," Lord Fawkland said. "You are a quick learner."

"Thank you for teaching me," she said.

"I enjoy teaching you." There was a hint of a smile still playing on his lips, and it almost looked genuine.

8

———

"*I*magine, my brother the, taskmaster, teaching such a beautiful lady," Mr. Gruger's mocking voice came from behind Julia. "And in such disarray," Cedric tsked marking Lord Fawkland's unbuttoned coat. Julia realized how close she and Lord Fawkland had been standing and took an immediate step back.

"Speak of the devil and he shall appear," Lord Fawkland whispered under his breath, though Julia caught the words.

"Hello Cedric," Lord Fawkland said aloud as Cedric strode onto the range, pushing his blond hair back into place with one hand.

"I could not allow you to commandeer all of Miss Bellevue's time, when I have hardly had any of it myself, brother," Cedric said.

The setting sun was obscured by fine high clouds, tinged golden by the light behind them. Lord Fawkland's shadow stretched across the grass as he stepped away from his brother, and re-buttoned his jacket. His face was hidden by the low light.

Julia wished Jane would hurry back. She had been gone a long while...too long. The air between the brothers felt like the moment before a storm, crackling with threatening energy and she felt Lord Fawkland's cool grey eyes on her like a physical touch. She was not sure what to do.

"Go on and draw," Cedric told her and she obeyed. He was so close to Julia's back that she could feel his heat; his breath on her neck. Then he touched her. His fingers were as warm as Lord Fawkland's had promised as they brushed her shoulder.

"Cedric," Fawkland said, but Cedric ignored him.

"Stand straight," Cedric said, correcting her tendency to slouch by pulling her shoulders back against his body as he stood behind her. She could feel the heat of him in the summer sun and the firm line of his body behind her. She couldn't breathe. Her hand shook.

Lord Fawkland took a step toward them, but Cedric had already moved. He stepped around to her front and brought his hand up to her cheek. "Pull to here," he said his eyes on her lips. "Right there. That is the perfect spot." He touched the corner of her mouth.

"Cedric," Lord Fawkland said again. "You are too familiar with Miss Bellevue."

Julia's mind was buzzing. Her body was screaming three kinds of alarms. She couldn't even see the target. Her eyes were blinded with his closeness. When Cedric dropped his hand from her face, she sighed in relief. She lost her head so easily. Hadn't she just been so discomposed by his brother? She was indeed a hoyden. Even Lord Fawkland commented on how she allowed his brother's familiarity. She started to relax her draw to simply put the arrow down, but Cedric interrupted.

"No, no, no," Cedric coaxed her. "Draw to the corner of you lip. Yes, just so." If her proximity affected him the way his did her he did not let it show. He stepped aside. "Now shoot."

Julia shot at his word, but she was not even looking at the target. Her arrow flew past it and the next one, landing ten feet off to the side of the third target out. Cedric groaned humorously and covered his face with his hands as he chuckled; his eyes sparkling with mirth.

"Are you laughing at me, Sir?" Julia asked. There is no hope for me. I am awful, she thought. Can I do nothing right? At least if she was competent at archery she would not have to talk. They could just stand companionably together, and shoot, but that was not to be.

Cedric was still chuckling, but he dropped his hands from his face and showed his wide grin.

Julia could not help joining in. It felt good to laugh. She felt like a child again in on some rambunctious joke Cedric had played.

"My apologies, I am afraid you are hopeless, but you are so beautiful while you try that the results of the shot are not important."

Julia's laughter died on a breath. She was not beautiful, and she did not want to hear lies. She was thankful for the dusky light, that he could not see the way her cheeks reddened at his words. Then she remembered they were not alone and she turned around, embarrassed, Lord Fawkland's name, on her lips, but Lord Fawkland spoke first.

"I believe your chaperone is returning, Miss Bellevue," he said tightly to Julia. "And dinner will be served soon." He was standing just few feet away with his arms crossed over his chest and a look of censure in his eyes.

She turned to see Jane ambling across the lawn. Julia pulled off her shooting gloves and tried to put on her kid gloves again, but her hands felt damp with perspiration and getting the gloves back on was a chore.

"Perfect," Cedric said rubbing his hands together.

"The lanterns are being lit," Lord Fawkland said, ignoring his brother. "We should return, Miss Bellevue. It is after all, a sunset picnic." He turned to look at her, but Cedric had already captured Julia's hand and tucked it around his own elbow before she even had the second glove completely on. There was a bit of fabric loose at the end of each finger, and now that Cedric had captured her hand, Julia was unsure how to proceed.

"I am quite excited to see if Lady Pratt can outdo last year's stuffed peacock," Cedric said.

What was it stuffed with? Julia wondered.

"And here is the elder Bellevue daughter for you to escort to dinner, Fawkland," Cedric said with his ever present smile. "The elder sister for the elder brother."

Jane looked momentarily from Cedric to Lord Fawkland, and Julia remembered she had told Jane she preferred the younger brother. Lord Fawkland did not look happy, but he held out his arm for Jane while Cedric helped Julia to smooth the gloves, finger, by finger. The action was helpful, but certainly on the edge of propriety.

Lord Fawkland glowered at him.

With her hand already tucked into Cedric's arm, Julia was uncertain what to do as he smoothed the glove of her opposite hand. She looked to Jane for help.

"Lady Keegain," Lord Fawkland said coolly as Jane came forward and took his arm. With her very presence, Jane calmed the tension between the Gruger brothers.

"I am sure we will have a lovely dinner," Jane said. "Lady Pratt is the perfect hostess."

They walked somewhat companionably back to the main area of the picnic. Jane chatted amicably about the Pratts while the others listened.

Tables were set away from the edges of the trees in the stone courtyard. The scent of flowers hung in the air covering the faint mineral scent of the Bath waters. The food was as beautiful as the gardens. Lanterns hung all about the courtyard, and candelabra were on every table. The place was aglitter with lights and silver. Flowers and fountains added to the magic of the moment.

"It is so beautiful," Julia said as Cedric helped her to her seat. Propriety said that she should talk only to those on her left and her right, not across the table; not that she wanted to talk to anyone at all, but she was forced to speak near exclusively to Cedric and Jane. The food was plentiful and what she ate was delicious, but she found she had little appetite. Cedric commented that the Pratts had served several fish and fowl dishes, along with three different styles of venison which was a bit presumptuous.

Julia merely nodded. She supposed it was so, but she did not want to criticize their hostess. It seemed impolite.

Cedric continued undaunted. "You remember the deer park on our property, do you not?" he asked.

"Yes," she answered monosyllabically, thinking that remembering the deer park did not make the venison more appetizing to her.

"We had some great adventures there, did we not?" Cedric asked. He launched into a story of which she had no remembrance, but Julia put a bite in her mouth and nodded anyway. The one dish which was venison filet medallions in a creamy mushroom sauce smelled delicious, but she was never that fond of the dark game meat so she chose fish and fowl instead. Julia picked at her stuffed pigeon. She divested it of its decorations and pushed it around the plate, while Cedric tried each of the venison dishes and coaxed her to taste them.

Jane was chatting amicably with Lord Fawkland and Julia was left much to her own devices with Cedric. She tried to settle her nerves and smile at him.

"That's my girl," he said softly when he saw her smile.

Julia blushed. She was most certainly not a girl. Not his girl at any rate.

"I remember a young girl who had a spirit of adventure," he continued leaning close.

She did not remember that herself. She remembered wishing she was more adventuresome. Julia found herself nervous again. She supposed it was because she was forced into such a social situation. Jane attempted to aid her in the conversation, engaging Cedric from the other side of Julia, leaving Lord Fawkland to his own musings.

Finally dessert was served: a multitude of cakes and tarts as well as fresh fruit which Bath was known for in the summer. Julia nibbled on a cherry tart.

JULIA WAS RELIEVED WHEN THE GENTLEMEN AT LAST WENT apart to smoke and the women excused themselves to the retiring rooms.

"Are you quite alright?" Jane asked, when Julia had refreshed herself. "You look pale."

"I shall just be glad to be quit of this whole endeavor," Julia said as she anxiously smoothed her dress.

"I know you would rather be home," Jane said. "But did you not enjoy your conversation with Lord Fawkland this afternoon? Is he as you expected, or do you still prefer the younger?"

"No," Julia said. "Yes. Oh, I do not really know what to expect, Jane. It is just that I still feel I do not know him."

"Shall we go out into the garden?" Jane asked. "The men will be back soon, but the garden will give us a moment's peace."

The garden was quite beautiful with roses blooming on all sides, but it appeared many of the party-goers had the idea of a walk after dinner, so there was no privacy for Julia to talk to Jane. The day was moving well into evening now, but the path was swept clear of obstacles and the garden was well lit. The walk was pleasantly cool and other small groups of women walked along various paths. Lady Charity and Lavinia caught up with them, along with the Poppy sisters. Julia smiled as the women conversed, but she did not attempt to join in.

Before they had walked very far, Mr. Gruger greeted the women again. His smiling face reminded her of the gaiety he always brought with him even as a child and Julia found herself smiling back at him in spite of herself. When Cedric learned that the women were enjoying the gardens after dinner, he said he would escort them, giving a running commentary to the entire group on the different roses the Pratts cultivated in their garden.

He offered Julia his arm and she took it, feeling some of the camaraderie they had as children. They did find a bench near the main thoroughfare, where some of the dowagers were already sitting. Mr. Gruger paused to greet them and they tittered like young girls. They liked him, Julia thought. Everyone seemed to like Cedric Gruger.

They passed a beautiful place near a pool, and paused to watch the carp coming to the top of the water. Their golden scales were lovely and Julia thought this would be a wonderful place to paint. She had never painted fish before. The water would be a challenge. Perhaps she would ask Lady Pratt's permission to paint here. They walked around the pool and Julia considered how the sun would hit the water in the morning.

Julia's friends, Lady Charity and Miss Grant were still nearby along with some of Jane's friends. They had walked a bit in front of Cedric and Julia while Cedric regaled Julia with tales of their childhood and she felt as if she had gone back in time. Here was the Cedric she had known as a child. Here was the Cedric whose company she enjoyed. She laughed at his antics and his bright eyes sparkled as he reminded her of a pond on the Gruger lands.

"I remember it," Julia said.

Cedric regaled her with a tale of pushing some bully into that pool.

"Who?" she asked, and he shrugged.

"I don't remember."

"Did you get a scolding?"

"Didn't I always?" Cedric said.

"I do remember some of these escapades," she said, "although I do not remember them being such fun. I was telling Lord Fawkland…"

"Oh let us not speak of Godwin," Cedric said, placing a finger against her lips. "What else do you remember?"

"I remember a lot of scolding," she said.

"Ah, yes," Cedric said. "There was scolding. Now that must have been my brother." He laughed.

"I thought we were not speaking of him," Julia said in a flurry of relevant wit. She was quite proud of herself when Cedric smiled at her, but the moment was lost as Cedric brushed the curls from the nape of her neck and she froze in place. He stood a little behind her, and shifted her so that she was nearly leaning against him, the heat of him soaking into her skin as he held her, close. She felt the touch of his fingers on her bare neck, just beneath her hair.

She tried to say, he was too close and this was unseemly, but the words would not come. The scent of him muddled her mind, and she could not speak. Where had everyone else gone? When had she and Cedric wandered so far away?

Cedric's lips followed his fingers a moment later, pressing a feather-soft kiss behind her ear. This could not be happening. He could not kiss her. This would ruin her. She must speak. She tried to make a sound. It came out as a little squeak.

"We are alone now, and it is too dark for anyone to see," Cedric said.

When had it grown so dark? She wondered. She had spent the whole afternoon, first with Lord Fawkland, and then his brother...his brother. Whatever she thought, she was his brother's betrothed. Cedric's breath tickled her neck as he pulled the comb loose from Julia's hair and her elaborate updo collapsed. All Jacqueline's hard work destroyed in a moment; precious pins rained down, lost in the grass.

She wanted to scramble to pick them up. She wanted to pull away. She never wanted to move. Her body made the decision for her, refusing to budge as if her limbs were filled with lead. His lips felt hot on her skin and she shivered. Such kisses were reserved for married couples. She should stop him, but for the life of her, she could not think how to accomplish this. He tipped her head up; his thumb ran along her lower lip. She felt frozen. He was no longer a child and neither was she.

The thought of Lord Fawkland seeing her like this snapped her back to reality. She thought suddenly of the blueberry pie and his words earlier this afternoon, *Everything I have, my brother wants...everything I have.* No, her father had chosen the elder brother. Not the younger. Not this.

Julia stepped away and spun around.

"This is not... appropriate," she said, breathless. She was proud of herself for speaking, but he did not let her go.

Cedric caught her hand with both of his. The comb was on her palm reminding her that he had pulled it from her hair. She must look a wild thing, with her hair all streaming down. She knew her eyes were wide with surprise. "Unhand me!"

He did not release her.

"Come now, Julia, it is just us here, alone. I will not tell a soul about us. I know you can keep a secret." Cedric said as he moved in closer again, his hand on her waist, he pulled her close, his lips inches from her own.

"You have joined me in so many explorations, Julia. I know your spirit of adventure is alive and well. I only must help you find it again."

She must have made a sound. A squeak of protest.

"Shh," he warned. "I know that you are not like other girls, stuffy and cold, unwilling to share their affections," His words were whispered against her lips. He brought his other hand up to her cheek.

Was he truly hoping to romance her by reminding her that she was not truly a member of the *Ton*? By telling her she was not like the other young women?

Julia's body went from melted chocolate to iron fury in a flash. She swung her hand at Cedric, catching him off guard. Her hand connected with his cheek, though not as solidly as she would have wished, and he let loose a curse and released her. Before he could respond, she ran. She knew he could catch her if he wanted to, but he did not come. Julia did not look back to see if he followed, or if anyone had noticed their altercation. She did not stop running until she had left the party far behind.

9

___

$\mathcal{J}$ulia soon found herself back on the familiar cobblestone streets, far from the Pratt residence and the garden, but closer to her own home. Jane would be horrified. It was then she remembered she had left behind Jane's silver hair comb, and the pins all through the grass.

Would Cedric deliver the comb; tell Jane what had happened? Though she did not know how, Julia knew she must have led Cedric on in some manner. She had no idea what she had done. Or had he just assumed, knowing what he did of her mother, that she would be welcoming to those sorts of advances?

She felt her face fire with a blush and put her cool hands against her flaming cheeks. The truth was she had welcomed it. She had not moved when he first kissed her. She had not reprimanded him. She had said nothing. She had even leaned into his hand when he touched her lips with his thumb. She had leaned into his kiss. She groaned and covered her face with her hands.

Cedric was known to everyone as a good man. No, the fault was in her. Julia ran her hands through her hair and pulled out all of the remaining stray pins used to hold her updo in place. She may as well look as wild as she was. Her curls tumbled down to her waist and people passing by stared, but she ignored them, hoping the darkness was enough for anonymity.

If the *Ton* found out what happened, no one would ever marry her and then Jane would fault herself. Anger came more naturally than tears and Julia lashed out, kicking a lamppost as she passed it. The kick made her toes momentarily numb and then the pain blossomed sharp and overpowering. She grabbed her toes and held them for a moment trying not to scream.

She held the throbbing digits in her hand until the pain eased. At last she started to walk again. Her foot ached from the sudden shock but the throbbing was less than it was a moment ago. She kept walking, keeping the weight on her heels and flexing her hands into fists to keep from striking out again. She had gone from frightened to furious and back again in a moment.

She wondered if she should go back to the picnic and try to find Jane, but she couldn't be seen like this. Instead, she walked in the direction of home until she found herself in front of the Grand Pump Room. People dressed in their finest, bustled in and out of the wide doors, faces pink and damp. Coifs somewhat wilted in the heat, but none as bedraggled as she.

Although the sun had sunk behind the hills, the air

still held the warmth of summer. The noise of the orchestra followed them out as the doors opened, and cut off when they closed. None of the patrons spared her a glance. Julia could smell the minerals in the moist air, the scent of the water said to cure any ailment. Could it cure what was wrong with her? Could it cure the fire in her that flamed with an attractive man's attention? Perhaps if she asked Jane, they could go together to take the waters.

"I will *not* be a burden on Jane to deal with her entire life. I will not be the odd spinster sister she must always fret about, never free to enjoy her own life like she could if I were normal," said Julia, staring up at the building.

The women passing by glanced at her then broke into titters. She stepped aside and hastily braided the wild thatch of hair that hung down her back. Although most had their hair done up, some of the younger girls wore plaits. If she were smaller, she may have been able to pass herself off as a child. As it was, no one was fooled. Anyone who saw her; saw a wanton.

Had her father known? Did he understand? Is that why he arranged her marriage? Had he known she could not choose for herself? Did he know she would choose wrong? Tomorrow she would come back. She would take the waters. Once her wantonness was healed she would marry. She would find a husband who was not a Gruger, and she would marry him before she could do any more damage to the Bellevue reputation.

She didn't care about the house. She would find another place. The thought of giving up her attic study shot a pain through her heart, but there was no help for it. She would paint outside if she must. She had a plan, and now that Julia had a plan she did not feel so hopeless. Her anger faded, but she could not return to the picnic with her hair in such a state.

She would send a servant back to search for Jane and tell her sister that she had returned home. Yes, that was a plan.

Julia's foot throbbed each time she stepped on it. Her walking became a hobble. Eventually she stopped and pulled off her slipper, for the foot had swollen past the point of being comfortable trapped in the shoe. There was blood on her stocking. She rubbed the toe gingerly, and then gasped as she hit the nail and pain sparked through her.

"Done with the picnic already?" Lord Fawkland appeared in the shadows of the townhouses and easily caught up with her. "Are you all right?"

He straightened, taking in her shoeless foot and the state of hair. Another Gruger thinking she was unhinged; just what she needed.

"I am fine, thank you. My home is just up there," Julia said, limping past him. She could not bear to put the shoe back on. Instead she carried it and walked in her stocking feet, and holding her dress out of the dirt.

"No, you are not fine, Miss Bellevue. You are hurt, let me help you," he said.

His face said that refusal was not an option, but she was done with overbearing men tonight. She stared him down. He ran a hand over his rather crumpled cravat and looked at her. She felt him taking in every bit of her own rumpled appearance. He could as easily force himself on her as his brother had done, but he did nothing. He waited and finally said again, very softly, "Let me help you."

He simply waited until at last she gave a reluctant nod. He stepped up next to her. He offered her an arm to steady her, and she took it. They began walking slowly at her pace.

She could smell the pungent pipe smoke on Lord Fawkland's clothes and could even catch the faint scent of spicy sandalwood soap on his skin beneath cherry pipe tobacco. His arm was so warm under hers and she shifted nervously, feeling a flutter that began in her chest, settled deep in her heart. She should move away from him; she thought and leaned suddenly on his arm as she stumbled at bit.

He stopped, one hand tightening on hers to steady her. "I should carry you," he said.

"No," she said horrified.

"It would be the most expedient way to get you home," he said reasonably, but she did not feel reasonable. His suggestion made her feel giddy. Her heart beat faster. Carried in his arms...she couldn't speak for a moment with the thought of it. He could do it, she thought. He was large enough to pick her up and carry her.

For just a moment she imagined herself nestled against his chest. A wave of delight washed through her. She was a large woman. She never thought to be carried again since she had outgrown the practice as a child and perhaps she wanted someone to comfort her tonight. When she at last gained her voice she spoke much more confidently than she felt.

"You would not dare," she said. She believed his brother would do so no matter how she protested, but Lord Fawkland was not his brother.

"I'm worried for you," he said in a gentle voice. "You are going to damage your foot more than it already is with walking on it. Let me carry you."

She pulled away from him. "You needn't worry for me," she said. "I can take care of myself."

"I see," he replied.

She took a hobbling step away, and he offered his arm again. She took it.

After a moment, Godwin said. "This betrothal. This... business I contracted with your father...We find ourselves in an untenable position, betrothed and yet virtually strangers. I did not plan it that way." He paused "We should speak of it," he said softly, but then he said no more.

She supposed he expected her opinion, but she did not know her own mind. If she spoke, she would only make things worse. She always did. She only knew his arm felt good under her hand. She only knew she had inherited her mother's hoyden blood and if he knew, he would not want her any longer. She thought about the rumors about him and the thought of her husband with another woman...she gritted her teeth with sudden anger. She shook her head. These thoughts had to stop.

He stopped walking.

Why had he stopped? She looked up at him.

"This is your house is it not?" he asked and she realized they were in front of her home.

Her home, for she thought of it as hers, did not look

much different from the other townhouses in the row although the curtains in the windows were yellow like sunshine, and her neighbors all had white. The stairs were going to be much more difficult than the street.

"May I carry you?" he asked again, gesturing to the front steps, but when she shook her head stubbornly, he did not insist.

He helped her up the steps one at a time, with him holding her arm and letting her lean heavily on him. The task was a laborious, and meant she had to put weight on her big toe with each step. After two steps she would have asked him to carry her up the next set, but she could see no way to ask without seeming forward as well as indecisive. Well, she supposed she was both. She blinked away her tears and continued; she refused to cry.

"This is fine," she said as they reached the top step.

She really didn't want anyone to know he had accompanied her home unchaperoned, especially since the day was moving quickly into twilight. The gossip would never stop. She could only hope no one had seen them; or no one recognized them. It was a vain hope, but she held onto it.

"As you wish," he said and gave her a little bow in front of her door.

"Thank you," said Julia. The moment hung, and she had the feeling he wanted to say something more. Was he as tongue-tied as she was? Were they so much the same? It was too strange a thought to think. Would he ask to call upon her? It did not seem such a burden as it had been earlier today. "Good evening, Lord Fawkland" she said.

"Good evening, Miss Bellevue" he repeated. He

turned, and then turned back. "Kick a bush next time," he said. "It will break before your foot does...a small bush," he amended.

He opened the door for her and then trotted down the front steps. She turned to watch him, and realized that if he saw her kick the lamppost, he must have been watching her with his brother. The thought could have been uncomfortable, but right now, she was glad he had been watching. She felt protected, and then she realized how it must have looked to him; her betrothed. She had let his brother kiss her! Oh, he must think she was awful.

"There you are," said Jane as Julia hobbled into the sitting room. She wrapped Julia in a hug. "Are you alright? I was worried sick when I couldn't find you at the picnic. Why did you leave without saying anything? If you were tired of it we could have taken the carriage back together."

Cedric had not told anyone yet, then. Julia breathed a sigh of relief. Perhaps he wouldn't. Perhaps he would be a gentleman.

"I am sorry, Jane, I just could not stand to be there a moment longer." It was not a lie, at least.

"Did someone upset you? What happened to your hair?"

"You know my hair never stays in its pins," Julia said avoiding the question.

Jane's eyes narrowed. "Did you walk home? Alone?"

She blushed. "No. Lord Fawkland accompanied me."

Jane raised an eyebrow. "Oh Julia! I wish he had not done that. It would not do for you to be seen with him, not with his reputation."

"I am his betrothed," Julia said as she bent and pulled off her other slipper and limped from the entryway. "Or have you forgotten?"

Jane appeared not to hear her. "Good heavens! Your foot looks as though a horse stepped on it," said Jane kneeling down to get a better look. She touched the toe and Julia winced. Jane gave her the most pointed of looks. "Julia, what on earth happened?" she asked.

"I stubbed it on a stone; that is all," Julia lied.

"A stone," Jane repeated.

It would not do for Jane to know Julia had so little control over her temper. She wasn't sure how to begin to explain this evening. She limped off to the sitting room sofa and put her foot up. Jane followed her into the room and turned to the windows. She began shutting the draperies.

Once they were all drawn and the house was quiet, Jane came back to Julia. She laid a hand on her sister's. "Julia?" she said.

Julia said nothing. She just squeezed her eyes closed.

"I can send for the doctor tomorrow," Jane said.

"Please do not." Julia touched her toe again. It was tender and bruised beneath her now ripped and ruined stockings.

"Then, shall we get you upstairs?" Jane asked. "You should soak that foot," Jane decreed calling for help to take Julia up to her room and a maid to bring hot water and salts.

In no time, Julia was sitting in her own room soaking her wounded foot in a basin.

Jane worried over her sister, but that upset Julia more,

so Jane worried over her slippers instead; now stained with both grass and blood. Once the maid had left, Julia knew that her sister expected an explanation, but Julia changed the subject.

"Might we go to the Grand Pump Room tomorrow?" Julia asked. "I wish to take the waters."

"If you would like. We could get dressed up and invite Lady Charity and Miss Grant along." Jane saw Julia's face at the thought of a crowd, even her close friends, and amended, "Or go alone, if you would rather. Though we must go early. No lying abed, for there is a ball to attend at the Assembly tomorrow evening. Oh how on earth you are going to dance with that foot? Is that why you want to visit the Pump Room? To heal your foot?"

Julia nodded, forcing herself to stillness. She would not cry. She was not a weepy woman, but at last in the comfort of home, she still could not relax. Not just yet. She took a deep breath and gathered her strength. "Thank you, Jane," she said.

It did not sit right, lying to her sister, but she did not think Jane would be so eager to go if she knew the real reason behind Julia's request. She wanted the waters, not to heal her foot, but to heal the malady that came with her birth.

Julia lay awake in bed tossing and turning well into the night. Had Cedric told his brother what had happened between them? Had Lord Fawkland really seen them? What must he have thought? The thoughts churned her mind.

She wondered what she had done to give Cedric the expectation that his advances were welcome. And now

Lord Fawkland knew. He had seen Cedric kiss her and yet he had walked her home. Oh, what must he think of her! And he mentioned the betrothal. Did he want to rescind it? Was that what he was trying to say? How could he want to marry her when he saw her with his brother?

Of course Cedric would not want to marry her, not after she slapped him. But she could not be sorry. She could not help but think he deserved it even if she somehow gave him the impression that she would accept such advances. When had she done that? Julia groaned into her pillow. The thoughts would not cease and sleep was long in coming.

10
----

*G*odwin was furious with his brother, Cedric. He wanted to throttle him, but first he had needed to see Miss Bellevue safely home. Now, however, he felt almost light-hearted as he walked back from Miss Bellevue's townhouse. When he had first seen her with Cedric, his heart had sunk. After all, she hadn't seemed pleased by their betrothal when he first met her, and then, she had all but told him she preferred his brother.

He hadn't exactly followed Miss Bellevue when she left the picnic. Well, perhaps he had, but only to keep a watchful eye on her. He knew Cedric fancied her and the fact that Godwin had offered for her meant that she would be in his brother's sights. But, he had her father's word that she was his. He only had to convince Miss Bellevue of his sincerity, though it seemed he was doing a poor job of it.

He tried to warn Miss Bellevue about Cedric but he

couldn't blame her for being deceived. Cedric was a born charmer. He could bring the most resolute to his side. Miss Bellevue only knew Cedric as a boy; she could not know what he was like now.

Godwin knew this evening had nothing to do with any remaining feelings Cedric might have had for the girl and everything to do with his feelings for his brother. Cedric may have liked the Bellevue girl at one time, but this hateful behavior was solely because Godwin was now betrothed to her. Cedric never could stand to lose.

He smiled as he thought of Miss Bellevue slapping his brother's face. Why, he had seen grown men quelled by his brother's size, and now this little slip of a girl... Alright. So the lady was not small, but she was still a lady. His lady. He wanted her to be his lady. She was so fierce. Godwin had been interested in the girl when she was young, but now, he saw her in an even more favorable light. She was quite the spitfire, proud and regal. He sighed.

Godwin visited Cedric's usual haunts searching for his brother until he could think of nowhere else to look, except the upstairs of a bawdy house. At least there, the women would be receptive to his advances. Godwin still wanted to strangle his brother for toying with Miss Bellevue's feelings just to spite him, but as the night wore on his anger cooled somewhat and he realized it may be better to avoid having words in public...again.

Neither his reputation nor Miss Bellevue's could take much more maligning by the *Ton*. Anyway, he could not think of where else Cedric may have gone to, and searching public rooms was different than searching private ones. It was not yet dawn. Cedric had not returned to his rented lodgings. That much Godwin knew. No, Cedric was probably out accosting some other girl, he thought morosely. Godwin could only hope Cedric paid her.

Godwin decided to visit one more club. Cedric may be there, and if not, it was likely some of the naval men were. He could enjoy a drink with friends before heading back to his own lodgings and sleep.

"Fawkland. Come. Sit," Lord Percival Beresford called as Godwin entered the club.

Commander Samuel Beresford waved Godwin to their table. Godwin gave a quick look around as he moved to join the Beresfords, but did not see his own brother drinking or at cards.

"Percy. Samuel. Jack." He greeted his friends, and nodded to the fourth man at their table.

Samuel Beresford, his brother Lord Percival Beresford, Captain Jack Hartfield and another Navy man were playing whist.

"I am done," said Samuel Beresford, as he gave up his seat to Godwin. "If I lose any more I shall not be able to afford my own wedding." He ran a hand through his already thoroughly mussed hair.

"Surely it is not as bad as that," Godwin said.

Samuel stood and picked up his drink.

"No, Stay Samuel," Percival Beresford said to his brother. "What shall I do without my partner?"

"Take Fawkland," Samuel suggested.

"I'll stake you, but then you must share your winnings," Percival said. "We can switch to *Vingt-et-un,*" He suggested noting there were five players now instead of four so partnering was not possible. "I shall deal, unless you wish to, Samuel?"

"Ha!" Samuel commented, but he sat back down smiling at his brother. The men shifted over to make room for Godwin and Jack Hartfield pulled up another chair and shoved it towards him.

As he sat, Godwin envied the easy camaraderie of the Beresford brothers. He and Cedric had fought since they had come from the womb.

"There are quite a number of navy men here in Bath this summer," commented Godwin as he sat. "It looks like the fleet landed."

"Aye," agreed Captain Jack Hartfield. "Too many ships sunk by the damned French," he said as he sipped his drink. "It leaves good men without a ship. At least we have a bit of a holiday. I pity the poor blighters on half pay at port."

The lieutenant agreed with Captain Jack. "Time we take a few of those ships off of Boney," commented the lieutenant as he threw in his cards for the new deal.

"Yes," Samuel added.

Godwin knew that Captain Jack, like himself, was the son of a baron as well as a captain and Commander Samuel Beresford was the second son of the Earl of Blackburn. The lieutenant was the son of a viscount, all doing their duty for King and country.

Godwin had not continued in the navy because his

father had died young, and he had taken up the barony, but the men in the service of the Crown were his friends nonetheless. He was closer with the Beresford brothers, Percival and Samuel, than with his own brother. He had met Samuel first when they served on the same ship. Captain Jack was only a midshipman then.

Godwin had become friends with Lord Percival Beresford afterwards, when he returned home and tried to do his best to become the baron his father had meant him to be. He supposed he managed that well enough. He was always able to manage everything. Everything but his younger brother.

Percy shuffled and dealt the cards for twenty-one. Play continued for a while with money changing hands from one to another as they bet and the conversation picked up again. The drinking picked up as well, as playing twenty-one did not take a great deal of concentration and no partner depended upon each other's wits. None were so in their cups that they could not count.

Conversation was centered on politics and the war with Napoleon. "Why pursue this talk," Percy Beresford said. "We are whole, and dry and well fed. Soon enough we will all be back at the work of war. Let us linger over our good fortune for the moment."

"Good fortune," Captain Jack exclaimed. "My ship run aground is not good fortune."

"At least you are not at the bottom of the sea with her," the Lieutenant said.

"Fie, a good captain goes down with the ship." Captain Jack said.

"Not when you can climb out and walk to land,"

Samuel said with a snigger. "You would have had to lie down in the drink to drown, Jack." All of the men laughed at the circumstances that put the ship aground, but that was only due to the liquor for it was no laughing matter as it happened.

"Only Captain Hartfield's good sense managed to get most of his crew ashore safely. The ship however was so badly damaged even the French didn't want it," the lieutenant offered.

"Bah, the worst of an English ship is better than the best French one any day," Captain Jack said.

"Spoken like a true patriot," Lord Percival Beresford added.

"Perhaps you will find a better lady to sail with, Jack," Samuel said with a wink to the captain, and the conversation turned to the Beresford brothers and their impending weddings. Congratulations and toasts were passed around the table as the night wore on towards morning.

"What of your lady, Hartfield," asked Percival as he passed on the last toast.

"Yes," Samuel added. "Has her chaperone let her loose? Or is she still jailed?"

Captain Jack shook his head. "I am as unlucky in love as I am at sea. She has said I played her false, and it is not so...well tis not I who played her false, but Mr. Hart, and now since I, in the guise of a captain's clerk am barred from her presence, and she cannot write to me, I am at a loss of how to win her." He leaned his head on the table, but Godwin thought that the action could be more to do with him being in his cups than as to his despair over his lady love.

"Up! Up!" admonished Percy as he dealt again.

"Who is this clerk?" Godwin asked confused by Captain Jack's explanation.

"A fool," said Samuel, "as are we all." He lifted his glass in a toast. "To all the fools who fall in love." There was a happy clinking of glasses and a moment of silence as they all drank before turning back to the cards.

Godwin's thoughts went to his lady, Miss Bellevue. What a baroness she would make! She was reserved and regal, so unlike the silly ninnies that were the staple of the *Ton*. He knew she liked the arts from her father's boasting of her talents. He thought she would be delighted to see the salons of the Louvre Palace.

He wished he could take her to Paris but was unsure what would be left there in the midst of this damned war. And first he had to win her away from his brother. Godwin was not as polished as Cedric in gaining a lady's affection and the fact that his brother had pitted himself against him was troubling. Godwin rolled his drink in his glass, until Percy interrupted his musings.

"A card, Godwin?" he asked.

"Oh, Yes" Godwin answered automatically, and scowled as his cards added to twenty-two. He threw them aside.

The captain also threw in his cards. "You do not understand," he said as the others played out the hand.

"Well then, pray explain," Godwin said as he sipped his drink.

"Pray I was never such an idiot as Hartfield," Percy said to, Samuel. "Tell me it is not so, brother."

"Oh you were worse," Samuel said laughing. "Mooning about love."

Percy punched his brother on the shoulder but it was all for fun and there was no true malice in it. Godwin wished he could be so jovial with his own brother.

"Go on man. Tell Fawkland the tale," Samuel urged Captain Hartfield. "Lud. How did you get yourself in such a pickle? Were you not the man who said you would never be caught in marriage?"

"Oh aye," the captain agreed. "I have long teased other men who are smitten by love and now here I am with the same affliction," Captain Jack lamented. "No, Samuel. I shall not relate it. You only want to have a lark at my expense."

"Yes, of course," Samuel agreed taking another card. "But you know it is a good tale."

"That it is," Captain Jack said. "But I have told too much already and there is no good advice for me." The captain downed his drink as the others laughed at his chagrin.

With much prodding, Captain Jack explained that his lady love, Miss Lavinia Grant was convinced that it was more romantic to fall in love with a poor man than a rich one.

"If only all women would feel so," lamented the lieutenant as he scowled at his losing cards.

Godwin realized that Captain Hartfield's lady love was the very same woman who was Miss Bellevue's accomplished shuttlecock partner from this afternoon. "A small blonde lady?" Godwin questioned, "I believe I know of the woman."

"A blonde angel," Captain Jack corrected.

Godwin was still baffled. "But pray tell. Who is this Mr. Hart?" Godwin asked tapping the table for a card from Lord Percival Beresford, who was still playing dealer.

"No one. He does not exist. Or rather, he is me," Captain Hartfield explained.

"How did this happen?" Godwin urged, now intrigued.

"As you all know, I am grounded," Captain Jack began. His glare kept anyone from commenting on how he lost his ship. "I had thought I would try my luck to attend the opening night's ball here in Bath and see what lovely lady I could find. Of course I was readily admitted due to my strong pedigree."

"I have hounds with a better pedigree," Samuel Beresford teased, and his brother admonished him.

"Let the man speak."

"Have another drink?" The lieutenant prompted Godwin.

Godwin shook his head. "Go on then, Jack," he said and again glanced around the room.

It had nearly cleared of patrons. Only one table besides their own was still active. It must be nearing dawn, Godwin thought. He wondered if his brother would be back in his rented rooms by now.

"You know, normally I stay far from the fashionable world and the marriage mart," Captain Jack continued. "I am a smart man and have no intention of taking a wife until I give up my commission which the way luck is treating me, may be quite some time. Anyway, I always thought there was more fire in the streets than in the parlors."

"Aye," agreed the lieutenant, saluting the captain with his drink, but Percy and Samuel exchanged glances as if they might disagree.

"But this night, this one night, I attended the opening night ball here in Bath," the captain said.

"The opening ball is a masquerade," Percy commented. "How would the woman even know your identity?"

"That is just the thing. I wore a mask, but lacking any costume of note, I donned my own uniform."

"I must be drunk," Godwin said rubbing his eyes. "If you were dressed as yourself, how did she mistake you for a clerk? Does the girl have eyes, or is she so much the ninny that she does not know a captain from a clerk?"

"She did. She does," Jack said as he threw away his cards. He continued with a sigh, "The next thing I knew, I was holding this paragon of feminine beauty in my arms. Oh, but we danced. It was like dancing with an angel on a cloud. We danced to the scandalous music of Johan Strauss, the Vienna Blood Waltz. Ah, what music! What a woman!"

"Where was her chaperone?" Godwin asked askance that any would allow a man to dance a waltz with her charge at first glance.

The captain had closed his eyes and let the memory of the night flood him with its warmth while the others had to make do with spirits. "When I looked into her eyes, I knew there would be no one else for me. I knew right then, that I loved her... but that was when she began berating me."

"What?" Godwin interrupted.

"She said that I had no costume."

"Which was the truth," Godwin agreed reasonably.

"I did not want to disappoint the lady, but because she was right; I sought to deceive her. 'Of course I have a costume,' I said. 'I am not a captain at all. I am but the captain's clerk.' I regaled her then with all the machinations I had to attempt to gain access to said costume when all I needed to do was look in my own cupboard.

Oh, her laughter. Gentlemen, it was like the clear ringing of the bells of heaven. But I shall never hear her laugh again. I lied to her and now there is no way to tell the truth, but to out myself as a liar and a cad. Furthermore, even if I did, she would not have me. She wants a poor man." Captain Hartfield sighed and took a big gulp of his drink to fortify himself.

"Did you declare your love for her?" Godwin asked.

"Of course I did. I told her at the end of our dance. 'I am in love with you Miss Lavinia Grant.' And to my surprise, she said, 'I am in love with you as well, Mr. Hart.' For that is the name I gave her: Mr. Hart. Then before I could tell her true, she spoke of the great romance of falling for a man with no position; a man she just met at a ball, and a masquerade, no less, and I saw no way to correct her."

"Then what happened?" Percy questioned. The cards

were pushed aside now, as they listened to Captain Jack's tale.

"I returned to my ship." His face became more glum as he remembered the condition of his ship. "I never should have written to her," the Captain said, "but I could think of nothing else, but her sweet face. I decided to send her a love letter. Then I thought, how should sign I it? I could not sign it Captain Jonathan Hartfield, so I signed it Mr. Hart. My lady's chaperone found said letters and learning they were from a clerk was incensed. Now I am barred from corresponding with her."

"So correspond in your own name," Godwin suggested.

"I cannot," said Captain Jack. "She fancies herself in love with Mr. Hart and will have none of it."

The table burst into laughter fueled by their acquaintance's woe and good drink. "He is the first man to be cuckolded by himself," Percy snorted into his cup.

"I am not a cuckold," Captain Jack complained.

"In time," Samuel joked. "In time."

"He will be jumping at shadows," Percy added

"She is a maid." Captain Jack roared. "I will not have her honor impinged."

"Careful, Lord Beresford," the Lieutenant added clapping Percy on the shoulder and nearly unseating him. "The Captain will be calling for a duel to assuage her honor."

"I will be his second," Samuel joked, "for all his stupidity he is my friend."

"You are unfair to me, Brother," Percy said. "You should stand with me. After all, the captain can engage

Mr. Hart as his second, or even as his first, I suppose, but who shall I have to stand for me if not you Brother?"

"Ah, but fighting a ghost can be a dire thing," Samuel said. "Look how badly it went for Hamlet."

The men continued laughing and poking fun until Captain Jack was ready to take a swing at Samuel, but Godwin, the least drunk of the group, came to his rescue diffusing the situation.

"You must write to her again," Godwin urged. "If you love her, you must never give up."

"What would I say?"

"Say that you beg her forgiveness," Godwin urged. "If she loves you, she will have you. You must win the lady's love with truth and sincerity not with guile."

"But you know the war," Captain Jack said. "I was confined to my ship. What could I do? Now, it has been weeks. I have not called upon her. I have not even written to her in my own name. She is beautiful. She has, no doubt, already moved on to other suitors. Any young woman of quality would have done. What was to hold her to my love? I gave her no token. I am a fool"

Godwin urged Captain Jack to let his lady know his love for her endured.

"Yes," agreed Percy.

Samuel got up to find pen and paper for his friend.

"What shall I write?" the captain asked.

"You have to ignite the hope in her heart," Samuel suggested as he sat the ink and paper carefully in front of the captain.

"You must be yourself," Percy urged.

"Myself," Captain Jack repeated as he attempted to get the ink bottle open.

"You have to tell her the truth," Godwin said, "but in person. Ask first to call upon her. Then, when you arrive, tell her that you were ashamed you had no costume, and that you told a tale for her amusement. When she laughed, you embellished the tale just to hear the sweet sound of her laughter, but when she said she would only love a poor man, you knew you could not be true, lest you lose her entirely."

"Right," Captain Jack said, still struggling to open the ink. "Truth."

Godwin took the ink bottle from him and opened it. "Yes. Truth," he directed. "Now, by this correspondence, tell her only you are in port and you wish to call upon her. Tell her the truth of the matter in person."

It had been Godwin's experience that good news never arrived via letter. It was better to speak in person. Had Miss Bellevue considered her engagement to him good news, he wondered. He did not think so. He would have to find some way to remedy that.

As his former shipmates aided Captain Jack with the letter writing, the door opened and Godwin's brother Cedric entered. Godwin would have confronted him immediately, but Cedric was already quite drunk and would not remember it. Godwin wanted Cedric to remember what he said to him. Cedric stumbled past without seeing him and settled at a table with some other card players.

Captain Jack, with a multitude of helpers, worked on his correspondence to Miss Grant, as Godwin thought of his own Miss Bellevue. How was he going to convince her of his sincerity? He thought of the walk home with her earlier tonight. He liked the feel of her standing beside him.

Even when she was not at her best, she was as regal as a queen. He would have very much liked to have carried her up the front stair to her home, but she was proud, and he would have her no other way. She was such a fierce thing when she had smacked his brother. The thought brought a smile to his lips and he glanced over at Cedric.

The group at the table where his brother sat was becoming quite loud. Godwin then saw that Cedric had placed a shiny bauble on the table, and the others were not willing to allow the bet. Godwin recognized the item as the silver comb from Miss Bellevue's hair, reminding him of the appalling behavior that warranted his brother a slap and more besides.

"Bloody arse," Godwin hissed as he stood and went to the opposite table where Cedric was playing. He swept the comb into his hand and said, "I will cover my brother's bets."

Godwin thought about taking his brother to task for betting the comb, but he decided against it. Cedric was deep in his cups and Godwin had been drinking too. No good would come of chastising him now. Tomorrow he probably would not remember the comb at all, and that would be for the best.

Cedric complained briefly that Godwin had taken the comb and that he could cover his own bets, but in a few minutes he was back to playing, the comb forgotten. Godwin went back to his own table for paper and ink to write a note himself and ended up penning a brief message to Miss Bellevue. He wrapped the comb in the message and sealed it. He paid a messenger to take it to her house before nine o'clock, and in a short time, the captain managed to get his own message written and sent to Miss Grant.

Godwin bid the gentlemen good night and glanced at Cedric who looked like he had no intention of going back to the hotel at all tonight. Godwin tightened his jaw. He was incensed at his brother, but words with him would have to wait. At least his brother was safely at the card table rather than with another woman.

Godwin headed out into the cool night air. It did not cool his wrath, but it would clear his head. Godwin decided he would not think of Cedric any more tonight. He would only think of Miss Bellevue. That brought a smile to his lips.

Part 3

The Baron at the Ball

11

----

*M*iss Julia Bellevue would not contemplate of the events of last night. She would not think of the incident with Cedric Gruger at the Pratt picnic nor her walk home with Lord Fawkland. She knew she had to go to the Grand Pump Room this morning. Julia hoped that the healing waters there would cure her wantonness, but nothing would stop the gossip. She knew that. She did not want to go out at all.

If she could, Julia would have crawled back into bed and stayed there, but she could not. She had to face the rumors. She had to face Mr. Gruger and Lord Fawkland. She could only hope that she would not make another misstep. She could not afford to.

It was still early when a maid came to the door of Julia's room with a small package for her.

"A messenger brought this for you, Miss," she said with a curtsey.

Julia could not imagine what it might be. She took

the package and turned it over in her hands. Who could be sending her gifts? It was too small to be anything but jewelry. Was Lord Fawkland sending her jewelry? Or Cedric? What did that mean after the picnic? Julia held the package for a long minute. Though he had not asked her, she was still Lord Fawkland's betrothed; only he could send her jewelry. It would be improper for her to accept such a gift from Cedric, but everything Cedric did yesterday was improper. Filled with apprehension, she tore open the package.

Inside was her sister Jane's comb, the one Cedric had taken from her hair at the Pratt picnic, and a brief note penned in a rolling hand.

Please accept my most humble apologies.

There was no name on the note. At least she wouldn't have to explain what happened to the comb to Jane. Should she accept Cedric's apology?

"Is there an answer, Miss?" The maid asked.

What could she say to Cedric?

"No," Julia said flatly and the maid left.

Mr. Cedric Gruger had been her friend as a child, but what was he now? If she married Lord Fawkland, he would be her brother...or was he something more now? The thought sent waves of apprehension through her. She was still betrothed to his brother. Did she want to be betrothed to his brother?

Last evening, Cedric had not asked for her hand in marriage; he had only...what? She shivered thinking of his hands on her; his lips kissing her. What exactly did Cedric want from her? Did he want to marry her in his brother's stead? She studied the note. The hand was strong and sure and she traced the letters with her finger.

"Julia?"

Julia hid the note under her pillow, just as her sister, Jane came to her door. "Are you nearly ready to go?" Jane asked. "We have a busy day ahead of us if we want to get to the Grand Pump Room and then to the ball tonight."

"Yes, of course." Julia said, holding out the hair comb. "I just didn't want to forget to give this back to you."

"Oh bother," Jane said passing the comb to her own maid who had brought her gloves and reticule. "You needn't have worried. Whatever I have is yours. You know that." She clutched Julia's hand and smiled at her. "It is going to be a wonderful day. I know it."

"Yes," Julia replied trying to smile back. She was glad her sister did not realize she had lost the comb last night, nor the circumstances of that loss. She would have the morning to collect herself and decide her feelings about the Gruger men.

"Come along," Jane said, pulling on her gloves, and Julia hurried to accompany her sister.

Lord Fawkland went by Cedric's rooms the next morning, but apparently his brother had spent the night elsewhere, or Cedric's man was lying to him when he said that his brother was not in. Still nothing could blunt his good mood. Godwin was engaged to the most fascinating woman in Bath. The thought brought a spark of excitement for the day.

No doubt wherever Cedric was, as drunk as he had been last night, he would still be abed. Godwin hoped he could dispel any rumors which had appeared this morning. He had a keen desire to protect Miss Bellevue from them.

As he walked Godwin remembered when he first taken note of the girl who was now his fiancée. Before he left for the Royal Navy he had known her only as a child, but he was only a child himself then. He remembered when he had first perceived Miss Bellevue as a young lady.

It was, after his father's death. Godwin had been distraught, not so much because he was close with his father, but because he was aware of the responsibility being thrust upon him. He was also aware of his shortcomings and his youth. He wondered how he was to become the Baron Fawkland in more than name only.

Godwin had seen Miss Bellevue again on the day he returned home from the Royal Navy. He had been engaged as a midshipman prior to becoming a lieutenant, only he never got the chance to advance. Godwin's career was cut short when his father had died. He had just turned seventeen. Only seventeen when he became the Lord Fawkland with all the responsibilities that entailed.

Miss Julia Bellevue had been the only bright spot that day, he remembered. She had inspired him to be better. Godwin had been so off balance with the weight of new responsibility but Miss Bellevue had been so poised, so strong. She was but a child of twelve or so, nearly six years his junior, yet she seemed so grown up. If she could act so, as a girl on the crest of womanhood, he could do no less.

Godwin had received the news of his father's death via a letter from his mother. He was busy when the Quartermaster had given it to him, so he stuck it in his coat to read later. That evening by the light of a lantern he read the somewhat crumpled letter. The lines on the correspondence had been so crossed and re-crossed that it took him some time to realize his mother was speaking of his father's demise. Godwin re-read the passage twice to be sure he had not misunderstood.

The man he knew as his father was always so strong, constantly busy, never a day sick in his life. It did not seem possible that the man was dead. Godwin learned from his mother's letter that his father had some sudden chest pain after breakfast, but refused to rest. He blamed it on bad eggs and went into his study. His mother had found his father dead at his desk late that afternoon when he did not come down for tea.

Godwin loved his father as much as any child would, but the elder Baron Fawkland had never been much of a family man. He would have shipped both of his sons off to the King's Service post haste if his wife had not released a flood of tears for Godwin's younger brother, Cedric. Their mother had lost both an infant son and a daughter between Godwin and Cedric and his father had fallen victim to her tears. He agreed to keep a tutor and wait until young Cedric was older to send him away.

Godwin, however, was charged to go. After all, he was the elder brother. It was worthwhile for him to learn to lead men. One day he would be a baron. The days were long gone when a baron or even a baronet held a force of arms for the King, but the tradition still held, at least in his father's mind. His father…

Godwin read the correspondence from his mother again with misgivings rather than grief. He was not sure exactly what his mother expected of him, so like a good young officer he went to his Captain with the letter. The Captain read the letter stoically and told young Godwin, "I will grant you a furlough immediately."

"Yes, Sir. Thank you, Sir." He replied stiffly.

Only his training kept him from arguing with his commanding officer. The war with Napoleon was just heating up. He had wanted to do his part for King and country. His place was here, with the men: Samuel Beresford and Jack Hartfield. He had eaten with them; fought with them; joked with them, and learned with them. He had thought to fight old Boney with them and put the little Frenchman back where he belonged. Godwin had thought to advance at least to Lieutenant and protect England. Instead he was going home. It had been a letdown. It felt like the height of cowardice, but he would follow his captain's last order.

As the newly made baron he had to give up his friends, and his career; although, truth be told, his service in the Royal Navy was never anything but a stop gap on his way to inheriting. Godwin had never expected the title to be placed on his shoulders at the dear age of seventeen, but it had been.

He had gone home to England then in quite the rush. He had sailed on the first transport, and during a brief stop in London where he spoke to his father's man, Mr.

Marks, he was disappointed to discover that his father's affairs were not in the order he had hoped.

"It was all so sudden," Mr. Marks said. "I am sure your father never meant to leave you this burden. He thought to live for a long time yet; to see you settled and hold his grandchildren on his knee."

Godwin was uncertain what to say to that. He certainly hadn't been ready for settling down or children just then. Though, he also hadn't been ready to be a baron. Instead of commenting, Godwin took his leave, but before he could get out the door, his father's man reminded him that the uniform that he still wore was no longer appropriate. He gave the young baron the name of his father's tailor.

It was in somewhat of a daze that Godwin contacted that tailor to inform him of the need for suitable garments for a gentleman in mourning. He collected the garments on his return home, but he did not put them on right away. They felt so foreign. As long as he was in uniform, he felt in control, but eventually he had to let go of the safety line. He was a Gruger, and now the Lord Fawkland.

He dressed in the black clothes and pulled on his new black gloves. He stared at himself in the glass. He did not look like himself. The stark black seemed to leach the color from his face. It was only then, that it hit him that his father was really dead. Everything now rested on his shoulders: the entire running of the estate, the welfare of his mother, his younger brother. There must be a myriad of other matters to attend to, but he was uncertain what to do first. He spoke to Mr. Marks again and attempted to make a somewhat dubious plan for the running of the estate.

One of the letters of condolence struck him. It was from Mr. Bellevue, a landowner who lived nearby. He remembered Mr. Bellevue was his father's best friend, and the words written there seemed honest. Mr. Bellevue offered his help and advice saying that he would be honored to give any aid he could to his best friend's heir. He asked to call upon the young baron, and Godwin's heart swelled with both pride and apprehension.

When he arrived home it was obvious from his mother's letter that she would be closeted in her rooms crying. He had no idea how to comfort her, so he left her to her female acquaintances. Her lady's maid periodically asked him to visit her and he did so. A man took up his obligations without protest; even at his young age, he did not complain. His brother though...Godwin had hoped that Cedric would have grown up a bit while he was at sea. No, instead of being a help, his brother was a hindrance.

Their mother was the only person that was ever able to talk any sense into Cedric and she was not at her best. After Father's death there was no one to take Cedric to hand: Certainly not the servants who feared him and not Godwin, who as Cedric frequently reminded him, was not their father. Mr. Bellevue offered some advice on directing Cedric's energies into more acceptable directions, but as Cedric got older, there was no reining him in.

All of the responsibility was on Godwin, and so he had done his best to shoulder it. He was a Gruger and he was a baron. He would do what needed doing. His uncle met with him at the country estate; on the very day Godwin's old ship was to sail for the West Indies... without him. He looked out at the gray sky and tried to let go of the part of him that wanted to be with his mates out on the open sea. He felt he would rather face Napoleon than his own younger brother. When he learned that his kind Captain had died of yellow fever in that god-forsaken land, he wept...in private of course. But no matter how he felt, that life was over now. He turned to face the new.

Godwin spoke to Mr. Marks about getting his father's affairs in order in London. His uncle stayed on at the estate for a time, but his own home was several days ride away. So in the country, it was Mr. Bellevue who became Godwin's mentor in the day to day endeavors. Godwin had a shrewd head on his shoulders and learned quickly. The Fawkland estate prospered under his hand.

He kept a townhouse on Grosvenor Square and saw to the upkeep of the country estate which boasted a manor house and acreage attached to it, along with a fair wood for hunting. Meanwhile, Cedric drank and worked his way through the village girls. Eventually, Godwin paid for his brother to have a separate apartment in London and an allowance. Perhaps that was ill chosen, but he needed peace and his brother would not allow him that. Besides, was it not the job of the matrons and chaperones to see their charges safe? They were certainly more experienced at the task than Godwin himself.

Occasionally, Godwin invited some of his bachelor friends to shoot or ride at the country estate, but he held no hunts or extravagant house parties. He preferred small bachelor gatherings which precluded him asking his mother to act as hostess. Mr. Marks suggested that he begin to search for a wife to help with the hostess duties, and his uncle suggested that as a baron he would require an heir. Godwin avoided those conversations when he could.

He had put aside his black gloves and mourning clothes and yet found he preferred the comfort of the black. He wore no ornament but his heavy gentleman's ring. Still as the Lord Falkland, Godwin cut a dashing figure in town. He was tall, blond and virile. He went to the occasional gambling hall where the play was deep and visited St. James Street often but avoided the gatherings which presented the season's debutantes.

Mr. Marks reminded him time and time again, that he should go to these balls and soirees; that it would behoove him to find a bride, but Godwin was not interested in the silly girls who frequented the marriage mart. They reminded him too much of his helpless mother. She had veritably fallen apart when his father died and was more like a child to be cared for than a woman to be a helpmate to her son. So when Godwin thought about a bride of his own, he remembered a tall girl with wild dark hair and unfathomable deep blue eyes. He thought of the girl who stood head and shoulders over his brother on the day Godwin came home from the sea. He thought of the quiet young woman with poise and substance who kept her own council, the daughter of his mentor and now good friend, Mr. Bellevue.

She was still young at the time, but Mr. Marks and his uncle were becoming troublesome about the necessity of a wife. So Godwin had proposed the arrangement to her father because he remembered Miss Bellevue's grit. She was the girl who had inspired him with a glance and Godwin felt he knew her through her father's stories.

Now that Godwin had met Miss Bellevue again, he was beginning to see her more clearly for himself. The more he learned about her the more perfect Miss Bellevue seemed. He loved that she spoke her mind, and even that she had slapped Cedric. He supposed no one had done so for many years, perhaps ever, considering how their mother coddled Cedric especially after Father's death.

Godwin would have liked to have held Miss Bellevue in his arms to comfort her, but he understood her need for independence, especially after Cedric accosted her. Once again Cedric had made a mess of things. Once again Godwin felt coerced into a situation for which he was not fully prepared; attempting to pick up the pieces, but if Mr. Bellevue's opinion of his daughter was to be believed she was a discerning woman. She would see Cedric for the man he was...and also see Godwin for the man he was. Godwin had to believe that.

He remembered her father's tales of her accomplishments with a smile as he approached the entrance of the Grand Pump Room. He had moved to help Miss Bellevue when he spotted her alone with Cedric, but she stood up to his brother on her own and truthfully, it was refreshing to find a woman that did not need a nursemaid. He had enough of that with his mother. Godwin was unaccountably proud of his betrothed. She was all her father said she was and more.

"Welcome to the Grand Pump Room, my lord," the doorman said. "May I direct you?"

"No, thank you," Godwin replied, straightening his cravat.

He just wanted to wander through the rooms and see if any gossip was being spread about his brother and his betrothed. Cedric had seen to it that Godwin was quite the expert at dispelling gossip, though some rumors were beyond even his ability to quell. He hoped that no one had seen him walking Miss Bellevue home, all disheveled, but that was probably too much to expect.

12

———

*J*ulia enjoyed the walk to the Grand Pump Room, despite her injured foot. She and her sister were there later than Jane had hoped to be; as it took longer to get ready than she had expected. Julia would have rather stayed home painting, but it had been her idea to come and take the waters. She only hoped they cured her wantonness.

"I am not confident this is the best solution for your broken foot," said Jane as they stood in front of the Pump Room. "But I do admit it seems a great bit of fun. Shall we go inside?"

Julia was bracing herself for the interior of the Grand Pump Room, which would be full of people and music and the strong smell of minerals; an overload to her senses. Hopefully all of the trouble would be worth it. The humidity of the room was wreaking havoc on Julia's curls and she could feel them beginning to wilt around her face.

"I am ready, and for the tenth time my foot is not broken, the toe is just a bit bruised," said Julia.

Julia's toe was still swollen and a shade of purple she had only seen before on her paint palette, but she could put some weight on it now, and didn't hurt as badly as expected. Still Jane insisted on helping her through the Pump Room doors. Inside enormous windows, fully two stories tall, let in the morning sunlight.

The room was large enough to accommodate twice the number of people it currently held. Several here today were elderly or wretched, but she was not the only one who appeared in good health. Women and men, dressed in party-worthy clothing, gathered around the fountain, chatting and laughing as if it were a parlor game. In one group, women were laughing and each time one of the women drank, the group cheered.

The source of the water was a fountain pouring from a stone vase, which was only slightly shorter than the man beside it. He was dressed in a servant's livery, filling glasses with the water pouring from the vase and handing them out to the people standing nearby. The air was humid. Julia could feel her hair frizzing around her face, escaping from Jacqueline's best efforts to tame it. However, Julia was grateful for the French maid's attempt and her sister's insistence on wearing their best morning dresses when she saw who else stood beside the fountain.

"We meet again Miss Bellevue!" Mr. Cedric Gruger said brightly, as he took her arm most possessively. Julia attempted to pull away, but he gripped more tightly, his fingers digging into her arm.

"I was so disappointed when you did not stay for the

rest of the picnic. You missed quite an evening." He continued, the smile on his face never wavering.

Julia wanted to crawl inside the vase and disappear down wherever the water came from. Mr. Gruger was still handsome in his dapper morning coat and breeches, but his smile made Julia's skin crawl. It no longer seemed filled with lighthearted fun. Instead, it seemed mocking and sly.

"I..." Julia began but found herself tongue tied.

Cedric went on as if she hadn't spoken at all. "I'm sure you did not mean to leave in such a rush. I do hope you are all right."

How dare he speak of why she left when he was the very reason! She raised her chin a little. "I felt unwell," she said haughtily glaring at his hand on her arm. "Then, as now." Cedric released her; she took a step back, and Jane caught her hand.

"Perhaps something you ate," he said. "My brother also left early."

"My environs more like," Julia replied quickly.

Jane missed the true meaning in their exchange and she gave Julia a quizzical look before speaking.

"Lady Pratt throws the most wonderful parties, but my sister was feeling a bit under the weather; hence, our excursion here today." Jane explained as she gestured at the vase where the water stood. She glanced around and asked, "Is your brother, Lord Fawkland, here as well?"

Cedric frowned at the mention of his brother.

Julia smoothed her hair down and looked Cedric dead in the eye. He did not flinch. If he felt any shame at all for his behavior the previous evening, there was not a hint of it on his face. In fact, he looked her up and down with a lingering gaze that made her sizzle with rage, bringing color to her face which Cedric apparently mistook as a blush. Julia took a deep breath and looked away. She supposed, she should thank him for returning her sister's comb, but Jane did not know it had been lost. Anyway, it was his fault the hair comb was lost in the first place.

Though Julia must have done something inappropriate to lead Mr. Gruger on, what it was she still did not know. How could she halt his attentions when feigned dismissal was a flirtation? How did one convey *actual* dislike? Julia was no good at these social games.

"Godwin is around here somewhere," Cedric said with a shrug. "I spied him earlier, but he did not see me. That was by design." He leaned in close again. "Will you be attending the ball at the Assembly this evening, Miss Bellevue?"

As it was their turn in line, Julia managed not to answer Cedric. She stepped away and the footman handed them each a glass of cloudy water, with the smell of acrid minerals rising from their depths. Julia tried not to breathe in as she drank. The strong mineral taste made the water seem medicinal indeed. She hoped it cured what ailed her. Cedric drank his in a single swallow, but it took Julia three. Jane took only one sip with a sight grimace before answering for her sister.

"We hope to attend, but I cannot guarantee it. Oh, here is Lord Fawkland." Jane said coolly.

Julia turned around, a shy smile on her lips, but it faded when she saw Lord Fawkland's expression. He was moving through the crowd with a thunderous look on his face. Thankfully, Julia was not the target of his ire; his glare was reserved for his brother.

"Good morning, Godwin," Cedric greeted in a bright voice, his mocking smile still firmly in place. He took a step closer to Julia, brushing her shoulder with his. She froze. She did not want Cedric that close to her. It brought back a peculiar feeling from the night before.

"Good morning, Lady Keegain, Miss Bellevue." Lord Fawkland said politely greeting them before turning on his brother. "Cedric, I require a word with you."

Cedric did not budge from his spot; although it was clear Lord Fawkland wished a private word. Cedric twirled his empty glass between his fingers.

"I am engaged at the moment, as you can see." His eyes lingered on Julia's neck making her shift uncomfortably. She felt the unwelcome warmth of a blush overtaking her cheeks.

"Cedric, I must insist that..." Lord Fawkland began.

"I suppose you have come to scold me for some incident or other. You truly must learn to relax, brother." Cedric interrupted.

Lord Fawkland's jaw tightened but he said nothing more. Julia's eyes were drawn to that jaw. She wanted to smooth away the crease between his eyebrows and make him smile again. She wondered if the brothers had spoken since last night. Was this about her? She thought horrified. Surely not!

"You have Father's temperament," Cedric went on. "Such tension will drive you to an early grave."

"I see another source of upset, Cedric," Lord Fawkland said in a low tone.

"Truly?" Cedric replied with a smile in his voice. "Pray tell, what is the reason for your poor temper then?" Cedric laid a hand on his brother's shoulder and continued solicitously. "Let us ferret out the problem and cure your ills."

Godwin looked thunderous for a moment and Cedric quickly withdrew his hand and took a step back. Julia realized that Godwin did not want to have this discussion in front of the women, and Cedric was refusing to leave. Julia felt distinctly uncomfortable. Perhaps she and Jane should excuse themselves. She did not know what to do, and of course, Jane was more confused than she was. Julia wondered if she should say anything; though she would probably only make matters worse.

Jane laid a hand on Julia's arm. "Certainly the waters of Bath are restorative," Jane said. "I'm sure you can speak with my sister at a later time, Mr. Gruger. It is clear that your brother has something urgent to discuss with you."

Godwin threw a quick glance at Julia and ran a hand over his cravat nervously.

"Well, granted, it is difficult to discuss one's shortcomings especially in front of a woman you are trying to impress," Cedric said placidly.

Lord Fawkland looked distinctly dismayed that the conversation had taken this turn.

"It is no matter," He said at last, deftly changing the subject. He schooled his expression to one of serenity and took a breath, settling himself. "We will discuss this later, Cedric. But rest assured we will discuss it. I would not trouble the ladies with such ... issues. Lady Keegain and Miss Bellevue, please excuse my rudeness. I would speak of more pleasant things."

Julia nodded and Jane hesitantly agreed. "Of course, Lord Fawkland."

Lord Fawkland turned determinedly to Julia. "Miss Bellevue, I request leave to call upon you this evening so we might renew our acquaintance."

"My sister and I will be attending the ball at the Assembly rooms this evening." Jane answered before Julia could reply.

"I shall be delighted to see you there." Cedric said. "We were only just beginning to get reacquainted last night, and since I have thought of nothing but your beautiful smile."

Cedric's words sent a chill through Julia. She wanted to take a step back again but the crowd of people behind her, still queued up at the water fountain, left her no room for escape. Jane on the other hand was beaming, having gotten the entirely wrong impression. She clearly thought there was some affection between Julia and Cedric. Lord Fawkland's face had, somehow, grown even more frightening at his brother's words. Julia shifted nervously from one foot to the other and winced as she stepped too heavily on her hurt toe.

"Where is that smile now?" Cedric cajoled. "You look so distressed. Has my brother made you cross? I know he certainly vexes me on occasion."

"Cedric," Lord Fawkland said sharply. "We should not speak of our differences to a lady. Have you no manners at all?"

A long look passed between the brothers. Julia did not know whether Cedric was frightened by Lord Fawkland's expression or if simply decided he had tormented her enough.

"Perhaps, I have taken too much of these lovely ladies time with unpleasant talk. I shall take my leave," said Cedric, bowing low to Jane and Julia, far more than necessary. He held Julia's fingers a moment too long and lazily let one finger trace a secret path on her palm as he brought his lips to the top of her hand. She pulled her hand away and Cedric turned to Lord Fawkland. "Whatever you wish to say, dear brother will have to keep, but not to worry. I'm sure you will think of some additional reprimands for me, to make the wait worthwhile. Until this evening, my dear," Cedric said silkily.

"I'm not..." Julia stuttered. I'm not your dear, she thought.

"I will count the moments," Cedric spoke over her words and then he left, pushing through the crowd with a confident swagger. Women stared after him. Julia wanted to throw her glass at the back of his head.

"Julia?" Jane said questioningly, obviously confused by the interaction between the Gruger brothers. Julia tried to smile back at her and then looked down. She hoped Jane took her expression for shyness.

They stood awkwardly after Cedric's departure. Julia did not know what to say to Lord Fawkland and he seemed at a loss as well. Cedric's final words seemed to fill the air, blocking any further discourse.

"Do you know those ladies?" Lord Fawkland asked

finally and nodded toward a group of women at the far side of the room.

They were lurking beside the windows whispering behind their fans. It was the telltale appearance of gossip. The women hid their mouths behind their fans, but their eyes kept returning to Julia. A flush spread across her skin. Julia bristled as Cedric came up to one of the women and kissed her hand.

"I do." Jane replied. "They were at the picnic yesterday. I would not have expected such behavior from Lady Stewart."

Lord Fawkland scoffed and shook his head. "You do not expect gossip and cattiness because you are so optimistic about the world, Lady Keegain."

"Is optimism a fault?" Jane asked giving Lord Fawkland a hard look.

"Quite on the contrary," Lord Falkland said kindly. "Your optimism is to be admired. It is a pity the world often cannot come up to such standards."

"I will go over there and speak to them about their rudeness." Jane said as she passed her still nearly full water glass to the footman who was collecting them.

"No. Do not bother, Jane. It is not worth the trouble." Julia laid a hand on her sister's arm.

She wanted to march over and shake the women herself, but it would only bring more attention to the gossip, and she did not want to be anywhere near Cedric. Julia had a sinking suspicion she was the subject of their talk. She frowned. How many people had Cedric told? He was only lending more suspicion to the rumors around her.

Lord Fawkland frowned as well when Cedric looked their way and toasted them with his glass. He moved away then, but Lord Fawkland looked from the whispering women to Julia. She could feel the heat of a blush fill her face. She could nearly see the dots connecting as he put two and two together. Realizing this gossip was about her.

Lord Fawkland's frown deepened. He passed the footman abruptly; ignoring the man as if he had not seen him and sat his glass in a conveniently nearby planter. Then Lord Fawkland strode purposely across the room to the gossiping women while the footman threw a confused glance at his back and then collected the glass from the planter.

Julia knew that Lord Fawkland was aware something happened between her and his brother the previous evening. She still vainly hoped he did not know what. She felt her stomach churning with anxiety as she contemplated how much he knew of her wanton behavior, and yet would it be better to have this secret known between them?

She felt a flush heat her face, deeply embarrassed. Julia was now certain the women were talking about her. When Lord Fawkland realized what the women were saying, Julia saw by the scowl that crossed his face that he was upset by their discourse. Still, if he had seen her with Cedric he knew the gossip had at least a kernel of truth to it.

He was sweet to think he could stop the talk, but how could he defend her, and should he even try? Sometimes it was best to just ignore such things. Had she not had a lifetime to learn how to deal with rumor? In her heart she could feel the warmth of Lord Fawkland's arm beneath hers as he walked her home and how tenderly he supported her to her house, but he could not support her reputation.

She watched Lord Fawkland cross the room. The women straightened when he approached, turning simpering faces his way. They fawned over him as they had Cedric but he paid it little mind while his brother basked their attention. His face was as hard as cut marble. Julia would have given anything to hear what he said to the ladies, but Jane urged her to look away. She watched covertly through veiled lashes.

Lady Stewart blushed and the honey sweet expression quickly slid off her face, but even embarrassment looked pretty on her. She lifted her eyes and glared at Julia cross the room. Then she raised her hand and caught Lord Fawkland's. She simpered and he stood uncertain holding her hand. Dear God, the woman was flirting with him, Julia thought. She felt her face near burn with anger. Julia could see the confusion on Lord Fawkland's face. Then Lady Stewart released him and flounced out with the rest of her entourage.

"If those ladies were speaking about Lord Fawkland walking you home I am afraid that his attempt to quell their talk will have only made the rumors worse." Jane sighed.

Lord Fawkland? Julia thought. She was confused for a moment. Nothing had happened between her and Lord Fawkland. When he walked her home he had been a perfect gentleman. It was Cedric who had been untoward. Then she remembered that Cedric had said it was dark.

He was right no one had seen her with him. People had only seen her with Lord Fawkland and in such a disheveled state! Or they noticed both her and Lord Fawkland had left the picnic. Her heart sunk to shoes. Her wantonness had spread further rumors about Lord Fawkland's rakishness. Rumors that she was now coming to believe were ill founded. She had dragged his name down yet further with her own. She was awful.

"He has known me for a day," Julia said, "And all I have done is worsen his reputation and make myself into...

Jane hushed her. "Oh, Julia do not take it personally. They cannot truly know anything,"

Julia did not have the courage to tell Jane how wrong she was. Someone must have seen her. It would have been easy for someone to spot her walking home with Lord Fawkland. She was so ungodly tall, no one would mistake her for another. Julia bit her lip. The chance of keeping her house in Bath was slipping farther and farther away.

Lord Fawkland returned to them, scowling. "I cannot stand gossips. I hope that will be the end of it for you. Miss Bellevue, but I am afraid that is rarely the case." Lord Fawkland looked down at Julia and she could not look away from his coal-dark eyes. There was a warmth there she had not seen before. She hoped it was not pity. She realized she did not want him to pity her.

"Thank you, Lord Fawkland," Julia said. Thinking he

was kind for defending her in spite of the detriment to himself.

"It is no trouble." Lord Fawkland said. He cleared his throat as if he wanted to say something else, but instead he bowed slightly. "I will also be at the ball tonight. I greatly look forward to seeing you there. Now if you will excuse me. I must find my brother who has disappeared again." He closed his eyes momentarily and sighed as he left them.

Julia was not the only woman to watch Lord Fawkland leave. He did not swagger, but the crowd parted for his long stride nonetheless.

"I hope I did not disappoint him," Julia said thinking that if this mess of rumors she created made Lord Fawkland leave her cold, she could hardly blame him.

"He does have a frighteningly masculine countenance does he not?" Jane replied.

Julia looked at her sister. That was not what she meant. Whatever else she felt, Julia did not fear Lord Fawkland.

13

_____

Godwin followed Cedric from the Grand Pump Room, trying to keep the man in his sights. Godwin could not allow Miss Bellevue to become an object of his brother's amusement. Gentlemanly feeling, of which his brother seemed to have none, urged him to protect the woman but it was more than that. He remembered what he had seen in her as a child and what had come to fruition in the woman. He was prepared for most anything, but not that she had grown into a beauty. Most of the time, he let his brother have his way, but not this time.

Cedric turned the corner. He appeared to be returning to his apartments here in Bath, and Godwin hurried after him, but before Godwin caught up with him, Cedric abruptly stepped from one of the narrow alleyways and surprised Godwin.

"You are following me brother. Why?" He asked crossly.

"You are quite aware of why," Godwin said. "You accosted my betrothed."

"Accosted is a very strong word," Cedric complained.

"I do not want to have this conversation on the street," Godwin said.

"I do not want to have this conversation at all," Cedric returned and started to walk away.

Godwin caught his brother's arm, yanking him around. "Maybe you should have thought of that before you kissed Miss Bellevue."

Cedric chewed on the side of his cheek for a moment as he often did when he was contemplating a lie. Perhaps that habit was why he lost so much at cards. Godwin thought idly. Every thought was on the boy's face.

He watched as Cedric let a sly smile fill his face and lifted a shoulder in a glib gesture. "Perhaps she kissed me."

"Do not!" Godwin snapped, shoving his brother further into the ally and holding him against the wall. It took all of his control to not smash his brother's head against the smooth white stone. "You accosted her. You kissed her. You took the comb from her hair. You left her upset, unkempt, and open to gossip."

"Ah, the comb," Cedric said, his hand going to his jacket pocket.

"I sent it back to her," Godwin growled. "Is it not enough that you touched her; you had to steal from her too? Do you have no honor at all?"

Cedric frowned in confusion and Godwin realized he had no recollection of the rest of the evening or betting her comb at cards. "The hair comb," Godwin said again.

"I took it when you were drunk enough to not miss its absence."

"Taking it guaranteed she would speak to me again, to get it back."

"And that is why you bet it at cards?" Godwin's eyes narrowed dangerously. "Well, she has no reason to speak to you now. None. You will leave her be."

"You have no right to tell me what to do."

Godwin ground his teeth. If the whelp said, you are not my father, like he was wont to do as a child, Godwin swore he would hit him. How could this creature be his brother?

"You have had your fun," Godwin said at last. "This is the end of it. She is my betrothed, and this ends here." Godwin turned away.

Cedric spun him back around.

"You cannot marry Julia," he said. "You cannot."

"Indeed?" Godwin raised an eyebrow at his brother. "You are on a first name basis with Miss Bellevue?"

"It's not fair," Cedric protested. "I have known Julia for years. You have not."

"Julia," Godwin repeated his voice a low growl. The boy spoke so familiarly, as if they were lovers. His eyes narrowed; a flash of rage shot through him like an explosion at the mere thought of Cedric despoiling her. Cedric had angered him before but not like this. He would not bear it. He clenched his jaw so tightly it ached.

"Miss Bellevue," Godwin corrected. "Do not address her with such familiarity," he said warningly. "She is promised to me and I will have her to wife." The thought of marrying Miss Bellevue shot a feeling of excitement through him, mixed with pride and protection. It almost overwhelmed him. He could not leave her to his brother's devices. He would not. He had never been so sure of anything in his life.

"You cannot marry her," Cedric repeated. "She was my childhood friend. I know her and she will never have you. Miss Bellevue will see you for the cold-hearted bastard you are," Cedric said bitingly.

The words hit hard. Miss Bellevue had met him with meager civility. She had barely spoken with him and there was no affection in her attitude. She had not received his suit warmly. No. She was quite cool, and that coolness settled around his heart, freezing it. He could not ever remember being so apprehensive; not since he was seventeen and facing all the challenges of his title.

"She will marry me, or she will lose her house in Bath," Godwin said.

"And that is why you are a cold-hearted bastard. You do not deserve her."

"Her father approved the match. He wanted to see her settled, and I do not think the woman shall willingly let go of the house, Cedric. Most women value security. I cannot see that she would choose to lose it."

Godwin spoke forcefully, but he did not feel so confident. Miss Bellevue did not seem open to the engagement at first but that was merely the awkwardness of the situation, Godwin reminded himself. Though he had little time to court her and was not skilled at such things. He would make her see that he was genuinely affectionate towards her. She was an intelligent woman. She would accept his suit. She would see through

Cedric's façade. She had to. "She will accept my suit," he said.

"She won't!" Cedric spat back. He was standing, fists tight and red faced. Godwin was reminded of him as boy of two ready to have a temper tantrum. He thought idly Father should have taken the strap to Cedric sooner and more often before he died.

"She prefers me," Cedric said finally.

"She did not prefer you last night when she slapped you," Godwin said.

"A token protest." Cedric returned glibly.

"Token?" Godwin said.

"They all protest, Godwin. Else, they would be labeled whores."

"Dear God, Cedric how many times have you done this?" Godwin said appalled. "She is a lady, not some low-born strumpet. This will stop. I've covered for your mistakes in the past, but no longer, and not Miss Bellevue. She is my betrothed and is not to be toyed with."

Cedric grinned slyly at him.

"I mean it. She is not another of your light skirts, Cedric. Do you understand?"

Cedric still said nothing.

"Do you understand me?" Godwin repeated darkly.

Cedric took a swing at him. Godwin, who was expecting such behavior from his hot-headed brother, caught his fist and pulled him close, so he could not engage in fisticuffs.

"You are the very devil himself," Cedric sneered and stepped back, but he turned to face his brother again, giving Godwin a hard look. "What did they do to you at sea, Godwin? You used to be fun. You used to have a heart. Now you think of nothing but duty and work. You have dried up inside."

"I used to be a child," Godwin said shoving his brother away. "Someday I suppose you will grow up too, Cedric. Eventually, even you will have to learn that the world is not here for your express amusement. A husband, a father, should generally be an adult," Godwin said. "I tell you now; I will have Miss Bellevue to wife."

"She will never agree to marry you, Godwin. She cares far too much what others think and say of her." Cedric straightened his coat and met his brother's eyes. "Always has. Always will," he said with finality.

Godwin watched Cedric stride away. He vowed that Cedric may get the last word, but he would convince Miss Bellevue to agree to marry him. No matter what it took, because losing her would break something within him; something vital.

JULIA SPENT AN HOUR AT HER EASEL THAT AFTERNOON, adding only a single puff of cloud to the unerringly blue sky on her canvas. She could not concentrate. She stepped back, dripping paint onto the floor, and looked over her work. If she did not go to the ball tonight she might be able to finish the painting, but then she might as well resign herself to being a spinster.

She tossed the wet paintbrush onto the tray of mixed paints and dropped onto the seat beneath the doublewide windows. They were thrown open to let in the cool breeze that came with the setting sun, and the curtains rose and fell like the rhythm of breathing. If Julia did not go to the ball, if she couldn't face the *Ton*, then she might as well just tell them the rumors were true straight out.

It made no difference anyway. No one would want her now. Her own betrothed, who was now proving himself to be better than what others said of him, knew that she was most certainly worse. Lord Fawkland knew she had allowed his own brother to take liberties with her. How could she face the man now? How could he still want to marry her? Why should he? Why should anyone?

Julia buried her face in one of the colorful pillows on the window seat.

"Julia? Are you awake?" Jane knocked at the door, three light taps.

"I was painting," Julia said as she stood up. She gestured at the canvas, and the drying brushes; then sat back down and looked out the window to the street below. "I just need to clean my brushes,"

"Oh posh," said Jane. "One of the servants can do it."

But Julia shook her head. She was very careful of her brushes and didn't want them drying all askew. She had already left them too long. They were sticky with paint. She would do it herself. "Must we go tonight?" Julia asked, although she already knew the answer.

"Of course we must. We must keep our heads high, and act as though nothing is amiss."

"Oh Jane, you know I am horrible at this sort of thing." Julia protested.

Jane smiled encouragingly at her. "You did very well this morning."

"I haven't messed this up entirely?" Julia asked softly, looking up at Jane from the window seat. Her sister sat beside her and enfolded Julia in her arms.

"No. I do not think so." Jane comforted her. "Rumor will die once you are married. I think as long as you choose one of the Gruger brothers..." Jane's face took on a troubled look. "You don't have your eye on anyone else do you?"

Julia thought of her promise to herself last night: to marry someone who was not a Gruger. That seemed ill begotten now. Despite all the men her sister had introduced her to in Bath she could barely remember their names. None had struck her as Lord Fawkland and Cedric had. Though she remembered she had also promised herself she would not marry a rake.

"No." Julia said reluctantly, "I didn't have my eye on else."

"Well, good then. We will take things one step at a time. Lord Fawkland maybe your betrothed but Mr. Cedric Gruger appears quite taken with you as well," Jane said.

Julia blushed. Cedric was far too taken with her. More than Julia was comfortable with. She didn't know how it had happened. How could she explain herself? Julia rose applied herself to her brushes while Jane talked. Not really hearing what her sister was saying.

"Perhaps Lord Fawkland will step aside for his brother. I cannot think a gentleman would hold you to a contract that you found distasteful. Do you think Lord Fawkland will behave as a gentleman? Julia?"

Julia thought of how he had walked her home and respected her wishes. "Yes," she said absently. "He is a gentleman."

"Then if you are finished with the brushes, you should get ready for the ball. I will send Jacqueline directly to do your hair. Come."

Julia followed her sister out of the attic studio.

"I know you do not enjoy the finding of a husband, Julia. You do not enjoy the dancing and parties, and of course, the pressure of the timeline does you no favors, and now, your sore foot is an added hindrance, but once you are married, I think you will be content," Jane said. "I truly do. You will have your own home then, and of course, children." A somewhat dreamy look came over Jane's face as she spoke. Julia was not so sure.

Julia washed in the basin and donned her dressing gown. She slipped her foot into a small foot bath a maid had brought, wincing as her sore toe hit the hot water, but in a moment, it felt better. She closed her eyes enjoying the warm water while she picked the paint from beneath her fingernails and waited for Jane and Jacqueline to come and hurry her along. Her sister would obsess over every detail of their outfits, and they would be flawless, but no amount of finery could help Julia act a proper lady.

Cedric had seen right through her attire to her true nature, a wanton woman like her mother. Though she had gone over her behavior the day of the picnic many times in her mind, she still could not pick out the moment when she had given Cedric any indication that she wished him to make such advances. Would he attempt them again? In her imagination she could feel the grip of his hand on her arm and her heart beat fast. She was not sure if it was fear or desire, but she did not like it.

She felt rather giddy when Lord Fawkland had touched her, but she did not fear him, and when she had been alone with him, he had been the perfect gentleman. He had time and place to dishonor her when he walked her home, but he had not done so. He had been kind. He had been so unlike his brother, but was that because he did not want her? Was he disgusted by her base nature? Was it not better to have a man who understood what she was...like Cedric? She shuddered as a trickle of fear crept up from her belly. She rubbed a hand over the spot on her arm where he had gripped her. There was no bruise, but the arm was tender nonetheless.

How had he gone from the boy she liked as a friend to this man? People did not change, she reminded herself, only perhaps he had done so, and for the worse. And what about herself, she wondered. Had she changed?

When at last her hands had been scrubbed free of paint, she took her foot from the basin and dried it with a flannel. She dabbed her toes dry, being extra careful of the sore big toe. Still Jane had not come to fetch her, so Julia went in search of her sister.

"Jane?" Julia called, opening the door to her sister's room and stepping inside.

To Julia's surprise Jane had not yet dressed. Her hair was done, but she was still sitting in her dressing gown.

Her eyes were closed. There were only two hours until the ball and Julia knew, in Jane's mind that was hardly adequate.

"Are you ill?" Julia said inspecting Jane's face, but her sister was neither pale nor clammy; in fact, she looked as bright and beautiful as always.

Jane laughed. "No, I am just a little tired, but I am most excited for this evening."

"If you are sure," Julia began.

"Yes," Jane assured her kissing her cheek. "It is going to be a wonderful evening. I know it." She called her maid and asked her to bring a box while Jacqueline brought an assortment of combs and brushes to do Julia's hair.

"A moment," Jane said to Jacqueline as she took the box from the other maid.

Julia's face screwed up with a question.

Jane caught Julia's hands and smiled at her. Jane did look happy and as always, Jane's good humor was infectious. "Now, close your eyes and hold out your hands. I have a present for you."

Julia closed her eyes and held her hands out flat. "What is it?"

A weight settled on Julia's palms, something so soft and silky it flowed like water, trying to slip from her hands even as she grasped it. She opened her eyes.

It was a dress far too magnificent to ever wear. It was the palest shade of butter yellow and all over the bodice was embroidery worked in gold thread, the shape of tiny flowers glistened as the light caught them. Golden leaves peeked between the flowers. The fabric was exquisite, the stitching perfection, and though Julia had no mind for clothes she knew enough to know the gown must have cost a fortune for the embroidery alone.

"This is far too much. You know I could never do it justice, Janey. Please, wear it yourself. It will look amazing on you." Julia held the dress out toward her sister, but Jane shook her head and backed away.

"No. You have never owned a dress like this and you deserve one. I had Claudette finish it for you yesterday. Now, if you cannot find a husband in that dress then perhaps you are hopeless," teased Jane.

The gown was entirely too beautiful to reject. "Fine, I will wear it," Julia relented, "but please know; from this point on that I am entirely content with your hand-me-downs. Do not get your hopes up, though; by the end of the night, you will be adding hopeless to my list of attributes."

Jane seemed to have not heard a word she said after Julia agreed to wear the gown. Jane had turned at once and begun pulling jewelry from her collection. Jacqueline lifted the fine fabric over Julia's head. It fell around her like a cloud. It truly was beautiful with a high empire waist and puffed sleeves. It was golden elegance.

14

---

*J*ulia watched out of the window of the coach as they went past the ubiquitous fountains in Bath. There were so many of them here, and they were all so beautiful. Julia took a breath and tried to relax. They had arrived at the Assembly in Jane's coach with several acquaintances of Jane's. It was well after the start of the night and the ballroom was already filled to the brim with the members of the *Ton*. Julia was still nursing her bruised foot, and Jane had required an entire extra hour to prepare.

The Assembly rooms were only a short distance away from the Grand Pump Room. From the outside, the Assembly did not seem an enormous building. It did not look like it could hold as many rooms as it boasted, but the strange horseshoe shape of it allowed for a variety of rooms dedicated to frivolous pursuits. Chandeliers hung from the ceiling and hundreds of candles and lanterns lit the area. While the white stone of the building's exterior had been dulled by weather to something of a slightly fawn color, the pillars inside were as white as an egg shell. An orchestra played as couples danced; the women's gowns a bright blur.

"Everyone is staring at me," Julia hissed as they entered the ballroom.

"I told you we would make an entrance," Jane said. "With that dress, you could rival any lady here tonight, only you must stop slouching. Chin up, back straight," said Jane, stalking farther in to the crowded room. "You are lovely."

Despite Jane's words, Julia felt ridiculous. Her hair was a massive curled confection on top of her head, making her appear even taller.

"*Juste magnifique*," Jane's French maid had said when she finished styling Julia's hair. "*Vous ressemblez à une reine.*"

"At least a princess," Jane had said nodding at Jacqueline.

"I do not think I should deign to rival royalty," Julia said dryly.

Julia's hair was strung with a net of pearls, and another strand of pearls encircled her neck, but compared to some of the other women in attendance, her outfit lacked the overly garish lace and frills. Instead, her dress was elegant and the embroidery was exquisite.

"Stand tall, Julia," Jane said. "You do look regal. You must not slump. We should put you in a position to be found by Mr. Gruger. Even if the Lord Fawkland has so upset you, I am certain Mr. Gruger will certainly request a dance with you."

It was only then that Julia realized that she still had not told Jane the truth of last night's events. She had been so upset wrapped up in her own thoughts this afternoon and Jane always seemed to know what was wrong without being told. This situation was not the fault of Lord Fawkland. This was about Cedric and her own unbecoming behavior last night. She hadn't thought to explain. How could she? Especially not now. There was no time.

She would have to tell Jane tonight. It would be alright. Jane would understand and Julia would feel better to share the whole sordid mess, but right now she just wanted to be inconspicuous.

"I do not want to dance, and even if I did my foot would not allow it." Julia wrapped her arms around herself. In the crush it was all she could do to avoid getting trod upon and she was very careful of her sore toe, making her shy even more into the corner of the room than usual.

"Jane please," Julia begged. "I just want to sit somewhere and try to be unobtrusive."

Normally, Jane would not let her get away with hiding, but with her sore foot, Jane finally took pity on her sister. "Very well," she said. "Let's find a quiet place. We will hope Mr. Gruger can find you."

"Look," Jane said nodding in the direction of Julia's friends. "There is Miss Grant. Shall we go and speak with her? Perhaps Miss Muirwood is with her or Lady Charity."

Julia did not protest and they started across the hall towards the women instead of positioning herself for the gentlemen. She realized that Lavinia was trying once again to convince Lady Charity that she loved her penniless Mr. Hart. This was good. Julia could lose her own problems in a conversation about Lavinia. Yes, it was much preferable to talk about another's woes and Lavinia would fill all the silences.

"He is my one true love," Lavinia said with a sigh.

"Are you still taken with that clerk?" Jane asked.

"I thought you had not heard from him since the weeks after the opening masquerade." Julia added.

"She received a letter this morning." Lady Charity said. "And managed to conceal it before her aunt found her out. Though after all this time, I would not answer it."

"Oh but, I must," Lavinia protested.

"Waiting so long to write is an insult to you. I would have none of him." Charity said haughtily.

"A letter to a man in the service of the Regent is one thing, as a patriotic duty, but to carry on a correspondence with someone so unsuitable..." Jane sighed. "Can you not talk sense into her?" she asked of Lady Charity.

"I have plenty of sense and sensibility," Lavinia replied. "I want to marry for love. I have told you too, Julia. Do you not think it would be romantic to be so in love that a man's position is of no consequence?"

"I have tried, speaking to her," Charity said with a shrug to Jane. "It is no use." She turned to Julia. "You know how stubborn she is when she gets a thought in her head."

Julia nodded agreeably. "So you have sent him a reply?" Julia inquired of her friend.

"I could not," Lavinia said miserably.

"Good," Jane said.

"Oh But," Lavinia said with wide liquid eyes. "I want to see him. I die to see him."

"Is he in attendance?" Julia asked looking around the room as if she could recognize the man by his manner.

"Yes. He is here. Or he will be. He said as much in his correspondence this morning."

"How exciting! So you will meet him again," Julia said, catching her friend's hands.

"Do not encourage her," Jane said.

"Yes," Lavinia's brow winkled in thought. "I think. I feel a bit faint," she said fanning herself.

"Come; do try to drink something Lavinia," Charity suggested, tugging her friend toward a man in livery who stood beside another stone fountain. A small queue had formed and they came up behind Flora Muirwood.

"Oh, I couldn't," Lavinia protested. "I shall not drink the water, but I do believe I shall have a flute of wine." She looked around for a man to fetch it for her or perhaps she was just looking for her Mr. Hart. Julia found herself also searching the room.

"Wine does sound more refreshing," Julia said thinking of how awful the water actually tasted. "I've always thought that the water has an odd and off-putting smell."

The others began talking about the water, and if the water here at the Assembly Rooms tasted better or worse than the water at the Grand Pump Room. Julia thought they were equally awful. She did not know if she was nervous because she wished to see Lord Fawkland and

Mr. Gruger or because she did not wish to. She worried her gloved hands together as she searched the room for the two brothers, knowing that both of their blond heads would be easy to spot above the smaller men in the crowd. She did not see them.

Flora Muirwood laid her hand on Julia's arm, and she startled at her touch. "What do you think, Julia?" Flora asked.

"Oh pardon," Julia replied. "I was wool-gathering. What did you say?"

"I was wondering if you would go to the musicale or the ball tomorrow night?"

"I have not decided," Julia said. "I suppose it depends upon who is going where." She smiled at Flora. "But I am not much for dancing at any rate with my sore foot."

"Oh, what happened to your foot, dear?" Flora asked.

"She hurt it playing shuttlecock, at the picnic" Jane supplied. "Will you be attending the ball tomorrow night?" Jane asked Miss Muirwood.

"The Poppy brothers are escorting me and Miss Muirwood," Charity said. "Oh come, Julia. I was hoping to have some friends along as well."

"Michael is not much of a conversationalist," Flora added.

"He is just shy," Julia said.

Charity had coaxed a gentleman into bringing them glasses of wine and they stood talking and sipping the beverage while looking for Lavinia's captain. Jane was nearby conversing with several married women. Julia felt almost normal here with her friends. She started to relax. The evening was almost pleasant.

It was just having fun, like they had enjoyed last summer without confusing kisses and husbands and everything that had happened since she found herself engaged to Lord Fawkland. Charity pointed out Lady Stewart's gaudy slippers and Neville Collington's dark gaze, and Julia commented that none of them actually knew the face of Lavinia's clerk on sight.

"Oh I do not know it either," Lavinia said worriedly. "It was a masquerade."

Julia's gaze traveled to over Neville Collington and the man with him. "Who is there with Lord Wentwell?"

Lavinia's gaze followed where Julia had been looking and her eyes widened. "There has been a coach full of rumors about Lord Wentwell this season," Lavinia warned. "Even more than your betrothed," she said fanning herself profusely.

Julia scowled thinking, why did Lavinia have to remind her of her betrothed. She had almost managed to put the whole mess out of her mind. "What about the man with Lord Wentwell?" Julia asked again. "Do you know him? Is that your Mr. Hart?"

The three women all started to turn as one, and Charity hissed. "Pray don't look!"

They were less obvious then, peering over their fans one by one.

"That man is not my Mr. Hart," Lavinia said.

"That is Lady Patience's elder brother, Lord Reginald Barton" Charity said. "You know him, Julia."

Julia frowned wondering if she had ever been introduced to him. She did remember Lady Patience though. She was one of Jane's friends.

"And Lord Barton is ginger," Lavinia looked heavenward and then gave Julia a poke. "As if I would fall for a ginger!"

"He is not *that* ginger," Julia observed. "His hair is more auburn than red. In this light you can hardly tell he is a ginger at all."

"That ginger is a future earl," Charity advised.

"How do you know your Mr. Hart is not a ginger?" Julia teased her friend. "We still do not know what he looks like. Do tell. Or do you not know on account of his mask?"

"That is right, Lavinia," Flora added. "You said it was a masquerade."

Charity chuckled. "I would laugh if your Mr. Hart turned out to be ginger."

"He's not. I would know," Lavinia said hotly. "His mask covered his face not his head. My Mr. Hart has brown hair."

"I think it is quite shallow of you to be so indifferent of a man's purse or lack thereof, but so critical of his hair color," Charity added.

"They are looking this way," Julia warned hiding behind her fan.

"How do you not know Lord Barton?" Charity asked. "I thought you came to Bath with his sister and their party."

"I don't know," Julia said miserably, wondering if they had been introduced and she was just distracted at the time, and now she looked foolish.

"Now, Lady Patience is a true ginger," Flora added peering over her fan. "At least her brother is not so bad.

He is well-built."

"His poor sister..." Lavinia commented.

"Red hair and freckles," Flora added.

"I think they are ghastly," Lavinia said fanning herself rapidly.

"I do not think freckles are so awful," Flora added. "But the red hair..."

"Hush," Charity warned. "They are coming this way."

The gentlemen in question, Lord Barton and Neville Collington, the Earl of Wentwell turned and began walking towards the small group of women. Julia blushed and wondered how they would hide the fact that they were just moments ago speaking of the men, and somewhat disparagingly.

Charity it seemed though had the matter well in hand. She beamed at Lord Wentwell. "We were just speaking of you gentlemen," she said including Lord Barton in her smile.

"It seems everyone is," Lord Wentwell said gaily making fun of the rumors that surrounded him. Julia wished she herself could be so glib.

"Miss Grant and I were discussing your sister, Lady Patience, with Miss Bellevue," Lady Charity said addressing Lord Barton. "I understand they traveled to Bath together. You were of course introduced?"

"Of course," Lord Barton said. "Lady Keegain's young sister. Charmed, Miss Bellevue."

Lord Barton bent over Julia's hand and kissed it. He conversed briefly before asking Miss Grant to dance, perhaps having mistaken her earlier scrutiny. Lavinia's eyes opened wide for just a moment, and regardless of her wish to look for her Mr. Hart, Charity pushed her towards Lord Barton.

"Were we not just speaking of Lord Barton and his sister with kind regard?" Lady Charity said with laughter in her voice.

Once Lavinia had gone Julia and Charity were left standing with Lord Wentwell. Julia turned away and would have given the man the cut, earl or no. Her reputation could not support a discourse with another known rake, but Charity chose to dance with him. Had she not just spoken of the rumors? Lady Charity knew of the man's reputation, surely, but if anyone could handle herself with such a man it would be Charity. For all her buxom form, Charity could always wiggle out of any tricky situation with ease, unlike Julia who seemed to fall into it face first and come up blushing.

As Charity and Lavinia went to dance, Julia turned around she realized that someone had also asked Miss Muirwood to dance, leaving her alone with Jane.

She would never be so discourteous to say so, but Lavinia and Charity had upset her. Her friends could say the most unflattering things and were always considered so droll. Julia was a little bit jealous that she could not be witty or coy. Whatever truth she thought was generally on her lips before she could prevent it, and no one ever thought she was witty for it.

She wanted solitude away from these social games. She thought about her painting waiting for her at home. How pleasant it would be to not have to watch her words. How pleasant it would be to recreate the stormy night sky, to hear nothing but the soft sound of a brush on canvas and perhaps the song of a nightingale outside her window.

A bout of laughter drew Julia's eyes back to her sister. Julia turned as one of their childhood friends, Mr. James Poppy approached.

Jane was fairly waylaid. Clasping his hands, Jane said, "Mr. Poppy, it has been an age. You remember my younger sister, Julia."

"Of course I do; Lovely as always." He kissed her hand and Jane's and although Julia could appreciate his clean good looks, nothing happened when he touched her. She felt no rush of heat or fluttering in her belly. Apparently he felt nothing too, because he turned almost immediately with polite interest to Jane as she spoke.

"How are your sisters?" Jane asked.

"Here," he said with a wave of his hand in the direction of Lady Patience's last sighting. "Mother is in a tizzy; like a hen trying to keep track of her chicks before some sly fox steals them away. It is a chore in this crush."

"And you are not helping her, for shame," said Jane.

James smiled at Julia showing overly large teeth in his ready grin and then turned back to Jane. "Of course I am. What sort of older brother would I be if I did not?"

The only brothers Julia had on her mind were the Grugers, mostly Cedric and their shared childhood. Perhaps she was too quick to condemn him. Perhaps he... what? It was clear he thought to kiss her and yet he had not asked permission. He had not even asked to call her by her given name. The thought of his hands on her would not leave her, and then Lord Fawkland walking her safely home. She flushed with embarrassment.

Could brothers be so different? She had only known them as boys, she reminded herself. She did not know the men.

Jane spoke with James as she took his arm. "Surely your mother is not managing all the girls alone? Is Constance not helping her chaperone?"

"My eldest sister is in the country with her newest son," Mr. Poppy said.

"Oh," Julia said, a pang striking her heart at the thought of Constance's second baby. Perhaps not everything was odious about marriage. Even if her husband was a rake, she would have her children.

Julia remembered how helpful Constance was with Jane's own coming out. She was only a year older than her sister and now Constance was twice the mother, and Julia had yet to find a man who suited her.

Perhaps she should marry Lord Fawkland if he would still have her.

An excited shiver went through her at the thought. The idea was not so terrible as it had seemed several days ago. Lord Fawkland was kind when he walked her home, but somewhere in the back of her mind was worry. She remembered the Gruger brothers from her childhood and Cedric had sworn to her that Godwin had broken one of her dolls...the beautiful one that the Poppy sisters always wanted to play with.

Cedric said he had trussed up the others for ransom. What ransom he wanted Julia never found out, because the stable master had untied the dolls from the rafters and released them to her; only the most beautiful one, the one she had named Juliet, for her mother, was broken. Her poor porcelain head smashed to bits on the path. Such a vile trick suddenly did not seem like something Godwin would do. Could she have been mistaken, all this time? Would Cedric have ever been so cruel to her? Cruel to the girls who teased her, yes. But to her? They had been friends. Still, Cedric was the trickster, she knew that. Godwin always seemed the responsible one. She could not make sense of it.

"And Gerald is quite the responsible big brother too," Mr. Poppy continued speaking of Constance elder son. He already resembles his father.

The thought of a baby just now made her heart strangely warm and a picture of a young boy with Lord Fawkland's cool gaze came into her thoughts. Jane had always insisted Julia would love her own children, but she had never been convinced until this moment. A fluttering of protective feelings rushed through her, followed immediately by a shock of fear. She could barely turn her mind around having a husband. Children were completely out of her depth. She would surely do everything all wrong.

Julia turned back to James. "All is well?" she asked "With your sister and the babe?"

"Oh Yes," he said. "But Constance is itching to go riding again. The doctor will have none of it."

"Riding! Your mother must be appalled," Jane said.

"Oh she is." He laughed. "And Mr. Nash more-so."

"Constance husband always struck me as a nervous man, but in this I must agree with him," Jane said. "I love riding to the hunt as much as the next, but being in a delicate way, a woman must take precautions." Her hand went to her own belly.

When Constance was first married to Mr. Miles Nash he was hesitant about Constance riding in the hunt, but she loved the thrill of the sport. Her dogs and her horses meant the world to her. Constance had so wanted to ride in the autumn hunt, she hid her first pregnancy for two months. Mr. Nash had been furious afterwards, but no ill tidings came of it so he was solicitous in the end.

Such a man would not do for Julia though, she thought to herself. Constance enjoyed running roughshod over her husband, and had been ever so. Julia did not want such a milksop, but she also did not want a man who would attempt rule her with an iron fist. Could there not be something in between?

Jane clucked at something Mr. Poppy had said. "And Francesca?" Jane asked "How old is she now? She has not come out yet?"

"No not yet. She is five and ten," he said. "And if Alfreda and Roberta are spoken for soon, my mother hopes to present Francesca this coming Season in London. How long will you be in Bath?" James asked.

"I hope to stay until the Michaelmas Ball at the end of September, but I may return sooner," Jane said.

Julia looked up. This was news to her. Jane had promised to stay in Bath with her for the whole summer.

"My husband will want me back home," Jane said. "If Julia is settled sooner, we may return to plan the wedding." Jane grinned at her, but Julia did not grin back.

What if she wasn't settled sooner? Jane had promised her the summer here in Bath. Even if she could count nothing else, she could always depend on Jane, but now, it seemed as if Jane wanted to leave Bath early. Why? And why had Jane not shared this news? Julia suddenly felt very rushed.

"And you Miss Bellevue?" Mr. Poppy said. "I am sure my mother would love for you to stay with us if your sister needs to return to her husband."

"Thank you," Julia said simply. She did not want to stay with the Poppys. She wanted to be in her own house in Bath with her sister. A niggling voice said the house would not be hers for long. She wanted to scream.

Jane gave Mr. Poppy a look, and he feigned puppy dog eyes at her. His eyes had a warmth that neither Cedric nor Lord Fawkland had, he was simply too brotherly. Maybe she wasn't so easily moved by a smile. Perhaps it was only the Gruger brothers that unbalanced her so.

15

*A*t that moment Julia spied Lord Fawkland. He was speaking with a small group of women just to their right. They were, as she expected, fully engaged with him. She decided not to look at him. There was another man at Lord Fawkland's side that she did not know. He had brown hair. She wondered briefly if he could be Lavinia's Mr. Hart, but somehow her eyes were pulled back to Lord Fawkland himself. He was easy to gaze upon.

He turned towards her. Oh bother. As the man looked Julia's direction, his height gave him a clear view to her. She dragged her eyes away and then hid her scrutiny beneath the guise of her fan. She peered over it stealthy. Had he seen her?

Her father had chosen this man, Julia reminded herself. The papers were all drawn up, all she had to do was accept him, and then her whole life would be in his hands. No. She could not make a decision like that on how he looked. She would not. Besides he still had not properly asked her. Lord Fawkland turned back to his companion, laughing aloud at something the man had said. It was a glorious sound. It reverberated within Julia, all the way down to her toes. She turned away, looking for someone else to take her attention.

The Poppy sisters, Alfreda and Roberta drifted over with Flora Muirwood who had just returned from her dance. Jane and Julia spent some time talking with Mr. James Poppy's sisters, and a few minutes later, Mr. Michael Poppy, James older brother also joined them.

James Poppy asked Flora to dance and Julia noticed Michael Poppy, near Jane's shoulder talking with his sister Alfreda. Alfreda was scolding him in low tones, about his sulking in corners instead of having fun in Bath.

"Have you danced with anyone at all?" she hissed. "How are you to find a wife when you will not dance and will not speak? The ladies all think you are a dullard."

"Surely not," Julia said kindly. Julia remembered Mr. Michael Poppy as the shy bookish older brother of James. They had not been well acquainted even though they had grown up near each other. Michael was four years James' senior, with Constance between them and Julia younger yet.

Michael was not unpleasing to the eye, but he was so shy, she wondered if they would manage to say more than a word or two to each other. She studied him from veiled lashes.

"Go on," Alfreda said, giving her older brother a little

shove. "Lady Keegain will dance with you, or perhaps Miss Bellevue."

Julia opened her mouth to protest that she had hurt her foot, but then Michael would think she didn't want to dance with him. She could not do that to him. She could handle one dance, as long as he didn't step on her toes. Please, she prayed, let him not ask her.

Julia hoped he would ask Jane, but instead Michael Poppy had already turned, his dark eyes arresting her. He held out his hand as he spoke, "May I have the next dance, Miss Bellevue?"

He was a sweet, shy man. She could not let him down.

"Yes, Mr. Poppy," Julia said placing her hand in his and catching her dress in the other.

He led her onto the dance floor in silence and shifted her hand to his arm as they proceeded to join the other couples. Mr. Poppy rather shyly inquired if she was introduced to Lord Percival Beresford and she replied in the affirmative. Lady Amelia Atherton was his partner for the dance. Julia made a quick glance around the dance floor for Lady Patience, but did not see her directly. She hoped that Jane stayed put with Michael's mother and his sisters. Surely they would have enough to talk about that they would not stray and she could easily find Jane again after the dance.

As the dance began Julia placed her fingers on Mr. Michael Poppy's palm. He closed his hand slowly, gently with only the slightest pressure. His hand was very warm in hers and she met his gaze. She expected that he would not be a very good dancer, and she would fear for her toe, but he surprised her with his grace.

He was not often in Bath, or even at the gatherings in London. James had said Michael preferred his own company to that of others, and yet, he danced with a quiet competence. In a moment she had traded partners to Lord Beresford. A moment later, she was back with Michael, who smiled at her, and she wondered why she had dismissed him so. Michael had a wonderful smile with the same full lips as his brother but smaller teeth. It was a pity that society saw so little of his smile. It was quite engaging.

He held her with ease, but allowed the requisite space between them. He did not crowd her or make her feel uncomfortable. The truth was, though, as pleasant company as he was, she felt nothing. There was no rush of heat that flooded her like it did when Lord Fawkland held her; no feelings of tension like when Cedric touched her. There was simply, nothing. She may as well have been dancing with her father. As the dance neared its end and Michael brought her back to Jane and his sisters, Julia realized her toe was protesting with a solid ache. She did her best not to hobble.

As they left the dance floor Julia passed Cedric Gruger and her eyes were drawn to him. Her heart beat frantically at the sight of him. He did not notice her. He was in animated conversation with a gentleman a little more than half his height, while a gaggle of women looked on. Good, let them entertain him for the evening. She did not want to be his sport. Julia's eyes slid away from him and scanned the room for Lord Fawkland. She did not see him.

"My sister said your father chose a husband for you," Michael Poppy ventured.

Julia nodded, but she was not sure what to say.

"Is that your betrothed talking to my brother?" he asked, and Julia realized that Lord Fawkland was now standing with Jane and the Poppy family. As Julia and Michael approached she heard Lord Fawkland speaking to Jane and the Poppys, asking them all to dance, one after the other. He seemed quite personable. Julia liked him with a smile upon his face.

Fawkland's voice was respectful and pleasant, but it did not only touch her ears. It reverberated down to Julia's bones. She found herself realizing just how much he affected her; much more than Michael did. Perhaps she wasn't a wanton after all; or she was only a wanton when the Gruger brothers were concerned.

Fawkland's cravat had been loosened, destroying the elaborate knot his valet had like worked to achieve, and his hand went to it, ineffectually smoothing it.

Again her eyes were drawn to him: to his hands on his cravat, and his chest and how his waistcoat fit him. She could not help but think of how he supported her when he walked her home, or how he had said he would carry her. A picture formed in her mind of her nestling against that strong chest as he held her and she remembered the scent of sandalwood. With her Amazonian size the thought of resting in his arms, the thought of him picking her up and carrying her, was certainly pleasurable. She shivered with the thought and drew her eyes away, looking up to his face only to realize his gaze was lingering upon her.

He cleared his throat and once again smoothed a hand nervously over his cravat. "Good evening, Miss Bellevue. Would you be so kind as to allow me your dance card?" She could of course, refuse him. Lord Fawkland's brow was drawn close together, his serene façade ruffled. This was the nearest thing to anxiousness she had seen in him and her heart softened.

Julia fumbled at her wrist. "I..." she began. She wanted to tell him that her foot hurt and that she didn't want to dance again but she couldn't make the words come from her mouth. Her fingers shook as she slid the ribbon over her hand and passed the ivory covered booklet to Lord Fawkland. He flipped it open and studied the list of dances.

"With your permission, Lady Keegain," he said to Jane. "I would choose the waltz."

Jane glanced pointedly at Julia, her look clearing asking Julia's preference. It was an intimate dance. It was Jane's choice as her chaperone, not hers. Jane could forbid it. But didn't Jane say to act normal to foil the gossips? What was normal? Fawkland was, according to her father, her fiancé. He would be expected to dance with her.

If she failed to dance, would that fuel the fires of conjecture? If she danced a waltz with anyone else it would certainly be scandalous, but did she want to dance at all? What if Cedric asked? Her heart leapt into her throat. That would be disastrous. She looked at Lord Fawkland again, and paused. He was so handsome, and his face so hopeful. The thought of being in his arms...She found herself giving Jane the faintest of nods and Jane approved him rather reluctantly.

"Of course. You are her fiancé," Jane said with a tight smile.

Lord Fawkland fairly radiated gladness. Then he scrawled his name on her dance card in a bold hand. Twice.

Rather than give the booklet back, he held out his hand for hers and slid the loop of ribbon delicately back upon her wrist. His touch did not linger there, but left a blaze of heat in its wake as his finger dragged slowly over her fingers and wrist. She found herself staring into his eyes again, at the spark of heat in them like a glowing ember in their charcoal depths.

She noted his rumpled tie, his starched white waistcoat and his perfectly fitted formal dress coat. It was cut away at his trim waist sweeping down into the tails meeting the line of his dark trousers and accentuating his great height. It was with an effort that Julia brought her eyes back to his face. Lord Fawkland's jaw was set and he did not look quite so kind as he had when he escorted her home.

"I will see you shortly," he announced. Then he unsuccessfully attempted to straighten his cravat once again, and with a brief bow, Lord Fawkland turned to Alfreda Poppy and escorted her onto the dance floor.

Julia watched Lord Fawkland's departing back until she realized she was staring. As he danced with the other young woman, Julia looked down at his signature on her dance card. It overtook the boundaries allotted on the card for the dance and she was reminded of the bold strokes of the brush she made on canvas when she was sure of her intent. There was no hesitancy there. No uncertainty. A person who wanted to dance before or after him would have to squeeze their name around his. She smiled at the thought.

Fawkland he had written. Not Lord Fawkland, nor the Baron Fawkland. Nothing so grand as that, and nothing so forward as Godwin, just Fawkland. The F was tall, as was the k and l and d, each touching the top and bottom lines in perfect looping symmetry. There was a familiarity to his style of writing.

She turned to watch him again, but Jane brought her back into the conversation with the remaining Poppys. She still allowed her eyes to follow Lord Fawkland, but only when she could do so without being obvious. He had been ever the gentleman, but she had felt the heat in his eyes. Was it possible that he still wanted to marry her, even after the events with his brother? Did he not blame her for the incident with Cedric? Did he think she had knowingly encouraged Cedric's advances, or did he think that she did not realize what she had done at all? She could not have her husband think she had invited the attentions of another man. She was not like that. At least she did not want to be. She could see Cedric had designs upon her, but Lord Fawkland was harder to fathom.

As if summoned by her thoughts, she caught sight of Cedric at the edge of the room lurking by a window. He glanced up, spying her eyes upon him. Cedric broke off his conversation, leaving a wake of disappointed women as he moved across the room. She did not want to speak with Cedric. She certainly didn't want to dance with him, and yet, she feared he would persuade her.

Perhaps Julia could beg off dancing with her sore foot. Yes, that would do. It was actually quite painful. The dance with Michael had stressed it and she wanted to sit down.

"Good evening, Miss Bellevue. You are a vision of loveliness tonight." Cedric said when he reached the ladies. Julia thanked him softly, wishing she were anywhere but here.

He turned to greet Jane as well, inviting them to walk with him. "If this is your first visit to the Upper Rooms, you must allow me to take you both on a tour of all the rooms. I have been in every one and know some of their history."

Julia thought uncharitably that no doubt he had been in every room, propositioning other young women he had separated from their chaperones, though you would never know it just looking at him. Cedric's voice was smooth like poisoned honey and his face was the very picture of innocence. Cedric's face was softer than Lord Fawkland's Julia realized almost cherubic; lacking his brother's strong jaw. It was not right for a man to appear so angelic. An angel's face hid a devil's heart was the saying, but Julia could not believe fully it. Cedric had once been her friend. Was that person not still within?

People did not change, she reminded herself. She found herself caught up in his smile, as in their youth right before he proposed some dangerous trek...but she usually had fun. She shook off the lethargy with the thought to refuse him his offer of a tour. She was no longer a child, and such treks were dangerous now.

But Jane spoke before Julia could refuse his offer. "Although it is not our first time here; perhaps you have some new insights. My sister is quite taken with the history of Bath."

Julia worried her lip as they turned to follow Cedric from the ballroom. Jane nudged Julia up to walk beside him, though she would have preferred to make for the nearest exit, or find a bench on which to sit. She wished Jane would stop helping her. This was only digging her in deeper. Cedric held out his arm for her and she had no choice but to lay her hand upon it.

"Miss Bellevue." Cedric said as he took her hand and held it.

She was reminded of how he had gripped her arm, but his voice was passionate and private, as if he were speaking only to her. Shivers ran down her spine. Was it only yesterday that she had accepted his advances? Had a simple stolen kiss driven all feelings of affection from her and replaced them with animosity? Had she given him some signal? She could not imagine what she had done to let him think his advances were expected...wanted even, but she must have done something.

He put his other hand on hers possessively and she felt as if she couldn't escape.

After the ballroom, the Tea Room was a respite. Though smaller, it held only a few groups of people swaying to the distant refrains of music from the ballroom as they talked in small groups. Banquet tables were laid out with trays of wine. Cedric commandeered three goblets from the nearest as they passed, and handed them out to Julia and Jane. Julia sipped the wine, more for an excuse to hold the cup with both hands and edge away from Cedric than out of any desire for the wine.

"Every time I see you, you are more beautiful than the last," Cedric said. "If you continue on this way, I will not be able to speak at all the next time we meet. I shall be struck dumb."

She certainly hoped that was true. "What luck that would be," she blurted caustically.

Cedric opened his mouth to reply and then closed it. A smirk came over his face as he whispered. "I'm sure we would find something to do to pass the time."

She glowered at him, all semblance of romance gone. In the next instant he smiled again, and she was suddenly struck by the thought that his smile was only a mask. A perfect mask in his angelic face that had every one of the *Ton* fooled.

Jane frowned at Julia and Julia stared back. Jane was above such petty games of the *Ton*. Could her sister truly not see what a conceited cad Cedric was? No. Jane still thought Lord Fawkland was the one who upset her. Julia had told Jane that Lord Fawkland walked her home so Jane thought it was Lord Fawkland who took liberties. If only she could tell Jane the truth of the matter now without actually speaking. There was no privacy and no way to convey to her sister her feelings.

"Now, the rooms in the Assembly," Cedric said importantly, "were first used by the commanders in the

Roman legions. This was all built thousands of years ago for the Roman army." He gestured grandly.

That was not exactly true, Julia thought. The temple was built around 70 AD, but most of the actual bathing areas grew up around the temple over the next three hundred years. The army used the baths, but it was not built for the army specifically. But she did not contradict Cedric.

"It was called *Sulis* for their pagan god."

Aquae Sulis, Julia thought. Did he think he knew all the history of Bath? Julia was quite sure she was just as knowledgeable, probably more so. As she opened her mouth to say so, her sister interrupted.

"I am sure you are much more versed than either of us." It was a blatant lie and Jane knew it, but Jane was good at smoothing over gauche remarks. She had had lots of practice with Julia as a sister.

"Did you know about the curse?" Julia asked.

He frowned. "What curse is that?"

"Oh," she said blithely. "There is a curse that the ancient gods are said to perpetuate on anyone who steals an article of clothing from another in Bath."

Jane laughed.

"You are making a jest," Cedric said.

"No. It is true." She paused thinking what she knew of the Romans. They would definitely curse someone who stole their clothing while they bathed. "I believe the curse is doubled for anyone stealing jewelry," she added. Now that part was made up, but she smiled when she thought Cedric went just a little pale.

He sputtered for an answer, but just then Lord

Fawkland appeared at her shoulder. "I believe our dance is about to begin," he said, taking Julia's hand. Lord Fawkland's timing could not have been better, but Cedric stepped forward and there was a moment while the two men glared at one another. They squared off in a silent battle of wills. Julia could feel the building tension and even Jane shuffled nervously on her feet.

Cedric was fuming. Still smiling of course, but the tendons in his neck stood out and she could see his gloved hands had tightened at his sides.

"Godwin, you are interrupting our conversation," Cedric said.

"I have the honor of escorting Miss Bellevue for the next set, and I refuse to give up the privilege, even for you brother...especially for you."

"It is our dance," Julia said breaking the tension.

"If you will excuse us," Lord Fawkland said addressing Jane.

16

———

Julia, still flustered, let Lord Fawkland lead her back toward the dance floor. Surely he remembered her hurt foot. What little grace she had for dancing would be curtailed by her limp.

Lord Fawkland paused, noticing. "Does your foot still pain you? Would you rather sit than dance?" he asked, but the music was starting and they were already on the floor. It would look unnatural to leave the dance floor now, but he cared nothing for that. He was only concerned with her welfare. She remembered that the dance he had chosen was the waltz, a new and particularly intimate dance.

Julia blushed and shook her head, unable to speak.

It should have been awkward, dancing so, but it was not. He took careful steps to the rhythm of the music and lifted her with ease into the air to spin her around, dress twirling. Julia knew people were staring but she could hardly bring herself to care.

He was so very close. For just a moment she caught her breath. She could smell the cherry scent of his pipe tobacco clinging to his clothes, his sandalwood soap and beneath it all, the faint scent of him. He was so very warm. The way she had felt with Cedric was nothing like what she felt with Lord Fawkland.

Julia wanted to close her eyes and lay her head against the firmness of his chest, but she resisted. She finally managed to speak.

"Thank you for your kindness, Lord Fawkland. I... your brother...you do always seem to arrive at just the right moment."

"My brother is too forward with you." Lord Fawkland was showing no signs of exertion despite the dancing. His statement almost made her fall in shock, but his arm tightened around her waist and his opposite hand kept her steady as he caught her, never missing a step.

Her eyes opened wide. "I don't know what happened," she said babbling, and trying to get her feet under her. "I am sorry."

"Are you alright," he asked, holding her scandalously close.

"Yes. Yes fine."

"And your foot? Should we stop?"

"No," she said thinking if she left the dance floor in the middle of the dance, the rumors would never stop. "I am fine," she repeated. "Your brother...Mr. Gruger and I seemed to get along so well as children," she said trying to re-ignite the conversation.

"I remember," Lord Fawkland said. He hardened his jaw and Julia thought that he was on the verge of saying something that pained him, but he just sighed, and held her close to him to keep her steady. Far too close, and yet she did not feel so ill-at-ease as she did with his brother. She did not want to flee. She wanted to lay her head on his chest and feel his heartbeat. She sucked in her breath with the thought.

"He is not who you think he is," Lord Fawkland said finally. "He is not even the boy you once cared for. He no longer steals baubles from our mother's jewelry box. He has moved on to..." He stopped then cutting off his own words as if he had said too much and instead led her into a turn. She twirled around and a moment later was back, close in his arms.

"I know Cedric," he said. "He will go to any lengths to ensure he gets anything I have ever desired. He simply takes what he wants with no regard for anyone else."

"Surely not," Julia began to protest, defending Cedric, but even as she spoke, she knew Lord Fawkland's words were true. Julia thought about the kiss last evening. Lord Fawkland was right. Cedric did not ask to kiss her. He had simply taken.

"Your loyalty does you credit," Lord Fawkland said. "I know you were Cedric's friend," he said. "But I do not think he was ever yours. Despite his charm, he is not the man he seems."

Lord Fawkland's closeness was making her giddy. She did not want to step away. If they only talked, he could not hold her in his arms and she wanted to be in his arms. Wanton, she told herself, but she could not bring herself to care. They were close enough for her to admire the intricate carvings on his buttons, the wrinkles in his cravat where it had been retied, the faint shadow of stubble on his cheeks and the hardness of his jaw.

Julia did not want to spoil the moment with her questions, but she had to know.

"And are you the man you seem, Lord Fawkland?" she said trying to get it all out in a rush, stumbling over her words. "I would have the truth. Might I have your word that we may start out with a clean canvas, so to speak? Whatever the rumors, I would have the truth from your lips." It was a long speech for Julia and she looked up hopefully at him. She had expected many reactions, but none was the sadness that entered his eyes. He took a moment to compose himself before replying. There was an edge to his voice. "This is very irregular," he said

"Truth is irregular?" she asked.

"In the *Ton*? Yes. But perhaps not with you."

"Whatever do you mean?"

"Miss Bellevue, you are the most forthright woman I have ever met. There is no precedent for the situation in which we find ourselves. Perhaps truth is the only way to proceed and you shall hear it from me. But not here," he said and she nodded, resolved to just enjoy his closeness and the silence. The music filled her with joy as she let herself be romanced. Lord Fawkland twirled her and held her and looked into her eyes as the dance ended and she saw kindness there.

She had not noticed her sore foot at all until the dance ended and suddenly it pained her again. She knew she should sit, although she did not want to leave Lord Fawkland's arms. In his arms she felt content and whole. She felt cherished. For this feeling, she realized she would have given up the house in Bath and more besides. Perhaps Lavinia was right about being in love.

Was she in love with Lord Fawkland? Julia did not know. She only knew her foot would not handle another dance. It was aching something fierce and she hobbled off of the dance floor with Lord Fawkland holding her as he had done last evening, letting her grip his arm for support, while his other arm supported around her back.

"I would carry you," he said. "To keep you from any discomfort, but the gossips would never stop."

She nodded. "I can walk," she said.

The second dance began. Couples moved around the dance floor and for a while, Julia and Lord Fawkland sat in the alcove where Lord Fawkland had led her and watched them in silence.

Julia did not feel the need to talk about the weather, or the *Ton* or to tell him anything about her archery lessons or Cedric or the recent dance. She just sat in compatible silence and let all they spoke of sink in. He was near enough that she could still smell the sandalwood soap.

He turned to her with a sudden thought. "Did you get your comb alright?"

Julia was momentarily confused. Lord Fawkland had returned the hair comb, not Cedric! How could he have gotten the comb? Did he go back and find it on the grass? Had he confronted his brother about it?

That was why his written name on her dance card looked so familiar. It was the same handwriting as the note she received with the comb this morning. She did not recognize it earlier for the letter he had written her weeks ago was penned so much more formally. Oh but this meant that he had seen everything that transpired with his brother.

"Yes," she said simply. "The comb is my sister's," she added. "I am glad I did not have to explain its absence."

"I am also glad," he said. "And..."

She watched confused while he reached in his jacket pocket. He brought out a small collection of pins tied with a red ribbon.

"My hair pins," she said wondering if he had returned to the Pratt's gardens and crawled around on the ground himself to find them. They were somewhat of a precious commodity, but she had thought them all lost. Now she stood looking at the pins in his hand. She had no reticule. "I have nowhere to put them," she said.

"Here." He untied the ribbon and began placing the pins in her hair, one at a time. His fingers were light as a butterfly, but nonetheless, she could feel each touch.

"I am sorry my brother treated you so." His voice was soft, gentle and yet had a sincerity that she had not often heard. The next song finished and Julia thought she should find her sister, but she did not want this moment to end. It was a quiet contented kind of silence, the kind of silence she enjoyed in the morning when she painted and the sun came warm in through the window.

"We should go back," she said at last.

"Yes, of course," he answered. He stood and tucked her hand under his elbow and she felt secure.

They stood in silence and walked slowly back towards Jane while the dance ended and Julia's pulse settled.

◦◦◦◦◦◦◦

BY THE TIME LORD FAWKLAND RETURNED JULIA TO HER sister Jane had danced several times herself and was looking a bit pale.

"Jane, are you alright?" Julia asked her.

"Just fine," Jane said. "Though I believe I need to sit." Julia could not agree more so the three of them went in search of some chairs. They found several in a corner of the ballroom, near some of the older chaperones. The Poppy sisters had gravitated back over to where their mother was seated. "Finally," Jane sighed, sinking down into one of the unoccupied seats. Julia was only too glad to sit with her.

It was there that Percival, Lord Beresford found Lord Fawkland. He greeted the women politely, if somewhat hastily, before addressing Lord Fawkland.

"I require your assistance, Fawkland" he said simply.

"What is it?" Lord Fawkland asked somewhat annoyed that his time with Miss Bellevue was once again being interrupted.

"A friend in need," Lord Beresford said enigmatically.

"Who?"

"Captain Hartfield needs you to speak to his lady."

"He should speak to her, himself," Lord Fawkland protested.

"He needs someone to explain that his feelings are true regardless of the deception played earlier." Lord Beresford explained. "You must tell his lady love that he truly is a captain. She does not believe him and he cannot convince her. She is sure this is another ruse, and that he is a cad. You must speak to his character. You know the man, Fawkland."

"You know Hartfield as well, Lord Beresford," Fawkland argued.

"Not half so well as you do."

"Samuel then," Lord Fawkland said. "Commander Beresford served longer with Hartfield, than I and, at the moment, I am otherwise engaged." He gave Julia a longing look.

"You would have my brother speak delicately to a lady's chaperone?" Lord Beresford asked slowly. Julia did not remember much of the particulars of the members of the *Ton* but even she knew that Commander Samuel Beresford was known to be a rather outspoken man.

"You said the maid. You said nothing of the chaperone," Godwin protested.

Julia frowned, realizing just whom they were talking about.

"Are you speaking of Lavinia's Mr. Hart," she asked. "The clerk is truly a captain?"

"One and the same," Lord Beresford agreed.

Julia clapped her hands excitedly. "Oh how wonderful."

"You see, Miss Bellevue understands," Lord Fawkland stated. "Miss Grant will as well. The matter is not so hard to explain."

"I am afraid your friend Miss Grant, has some rather strange notions of romance," Lord Beresford said to Julia.

Julia started to rise to help if she could, she would speak to Lavinia, but sitting seemed to have worsened her pain. She winced the moment as she put weight on her foot. Lord Fawkland steadied her and helped her to sit back down.

"Do not over tax yourself Julia. Let the gentlemen handle this," Jane urged.

"Yes, do not worry Miss Bellevue, Lord Beresford and I will sort this out." Lord Fawkland promised. "We shall return with the couple directly." With that Lord Fawkland and Lord Beresford strode across the ballroom and out of sight presumably in the direction of Lavinia and Captain Hartfield.

"Let the gentlemen handle it," Mrs. Poppy sniffed dryly when the men had gone. She was comfortably seated next to Jane and had witnessed the whole exchange. "It has been my experience that men of that age can barely wipe their own noses. When they reach the age of forty, they can sometimes be trusted to carry a message," she said.

Jane laughed. "In that case, I shall look forward to when my husband turns forty."

Julia could not deny the warm contented feeling taking hold of her, but the feeling did not last.

Whispers followed Lord Fawkland as he traversed the floor. Several women looked back over their fans towards Julia. It was clear who they were talking about.

"One would expect such a man as Lord Fawkland to dance with her."

A woman's voice from somewhere behind Julia cut through the din. The sound was shrill, and seemed pitched for her to hear.

"The Baron of Bastards."

Julia gritted her teeth, her face burning.

"A shame but not a surprise, given her breeding."

The woman drew out the last word, as if relishing it. Julia had heard it all before, the slander and the slurs.

"Harpies," Jane hissed. She did not keep her voice low. Like the other woman, her sister's words were pitched to carry and the biting, cold laughter from the woman stopped as Jane caught Julia's hand. Jane was after all, a countess, and no one really wanted her disapproval.

A hush ran through the nearby crowd. Julia stared at the floorboards, studying the swirls in the wood and the dull marks of footprints across the waxed surface. She wanted to run, but her foot precluded such movement. In a moment, her head would stop swimming. She would not prove them right with an outburst. If Lord Fawkland could handle the talk with poise, so could she. There was no retort from the other woman, and in a moment the chatter rose to its previous levels. Julia let out her breath.

"Are you alright?" Jane asked squeezing Julia's arm in reassurance.

There was a sour pit in her stomach, but she no longer felt the desire to thrash the snarky woman. Julia nodded. She wished Lord Fawkland would hurry back. She searched over the tops of people's heads for his tall countenance. She didn't see him. Instead, her eyes caught Cedric's form. She looked quickly away, but was too late. He had already noticed her gaze.

17

She had not yet recovered from the gossips when Cedric appeared by her side. Fury filled her. How dare he even speak to her? What he did at the picnic was the reason the ladies were gossiping. They wouldn't be talking about her tonight if he had not kissed her and mussed her hair. She stood, a little wobbly on her sore foot. She grasped the chair to steady herself. When he would have greeted her, she glared at him.

Cedric frowned at her. "What has happened to your foot?" he asked.

"I injured it," she said.

He seemed a bit taken back by her cold attitude, but pressed on. "You did not mention your foot this morning at The Pump Room," he said.

Julia didn't answer.

Jane answered for her. "My sister had a mishap playing shuttlecock yesterday. Her foot pained her later in the evening."

Cedric turned back to Julia, the ever-present smile even brighter than usual. Obviously he knew that Jane was making up an excuse for her, but he said nothing as Jane continued.

"I fear the dancing was a bit overtaxing for her."

Julia thought how this was all Cedric's fault. She wanted to kick him. Lord Fawkland had told Julia to kick nothing more firm than a shrub, but perhaps an exception could be made of Cedric's shin. Maybe she should use the other foot. What a ninny she was. And then she would be entirely the cripple.

Cedric faltered a bit. "Then you are not dancing?" Cedric asked. "I had hoped we would be able to speak."

"I think not," Julia said.

"You danced with my brother," he accused.

"I did," Julia said.

The thoughts were festering in her head. She could barely think at all. She had been turning her actions at the picnic over and over in her mind. All day her thoughts had churned around and around. She had not done anything at all to tell Cedric his advances were wanted. She had told him he was being inappropriate. This was all Cedric's fault. He had led her away from Jane. He had taken liberties. It was Cedric's fault that she left the picnic early. It was his fault that she hurt her foot. It was his fault that the gossips would not stop, and now he was here. Right in front of her. Making things worse. How could he? If she was not surrounded by the *Ton*, she would slap him again.

Cedric's smile faded for just a moment as he caught

her eye, but he recovered quickly. "Will you walk with me?" he asked.

Jane glanced at Julia, a frown forming on her brow.

"No, I will not." Julia said simply.

No doubt Jane would be reluctant to leave her alone with any man after last night, but she took Julia's refusal to heart. "I do not think that is wise after recent events," Jane said.

Cedric looked at Jane as though for the first time, and then threw a questioning look a Julia. He tried again false sweetness dripping from his words. "I must beg your pardon, Miss Bellevue" he said. "I know. I have been unaccountably forward."

She looked at him. Did he expect her to forgive him? She didn't answer.

"I had hoped to do this with far more tack and elegance, but my brother has forced my hand. He always manages to meddle at the worst times," said Cedric, drawing himself up to face Julia and Jane. "And it would be entirely improper for you to spend so much time and attention on my brother." Cedric grabbed for Julia's hand, clutching it tightly.

He closed his eyes for a moment and then continued. "I have loved you since we played together as children. I suppose I forgot for a moment that we are now grown, and such familiarity can be misconstrued. I did not wish to offend you."

He had forgotten nothing.

He sank to one knee in front of her, and Julia stared at him. This could not be happening. She was engaged to

Lord Fawkland, his own brother. The room turned as one, tittering at the display Cedric was making.

The Poppy sisters beside her all gasped as one. Julia looked desperately towards Jane and Jane looked at her. Julia thought the panic must be evident in her eyes.

"Wait," Julia hissed looking for some way to escape, but Cedric did not stop.

"I have loved you forever. I want to spend my life with you," Cedric continued earnestly. "I do not know what I should do without you, Julia. I think I should probably go mad." He had grasped her hand now, pulling it to his lips, and she did not know how to escape.

The room felt like it was closing in. There was not enough air. She could only think of Lord Fawkland's words. *He is not what he seems. He simply takes... He will go to any lengths to ensure he gets anything I have ever desired.*

"If you have any kindness within you, my dear Miss Bellevue, you will say yes. You will say you will be my wife."

"Your w-wife?" Julia felt the room tilt.

Yesterday he had treated her like a light skirt in a tavern and now he was asking her to marry him? She wanted to flat out refuse him. She wanted to run. She wanted...the world to stop moving. This could not be real. This was a dream that had turned into a nightmare. Perhaps she had fallen asleep before the ball. Perhaps in the coach and she was not even in Bath yet. Perhaps she was still in the carriage on her way to Bath and none of this was real. Perhaps Father would still be alive, and nothing would have changed.

The room felt strangely fuzzy and distant. Suddenly

Jane was there at her side clutching Julia and pulling her aside. Julia near stumbled and stepped down hard on her sore toe. It had the effect of snapping her out of the fuzziness with the sudden pain. Reality came back with a jolt, but Cedric was still kneeling before her.

She felt the stillness and realized the music was still playing but most of the dancers had stopped. Everyone was looking at her. She felt the heat of a blush fill her face and could not speak at all. What could she say? She opened her mouth and closed it again, like a dim-witted baby bird. If she had two good feet she would have run, but as it was she could do nothing but stare at him.

Jane came to her rescue. "My sister is clearly over-whelmed by the sentiment and the unusual setting for a proposal. Please give us...give her...some time to consider."

Julia did not need time, but she did not contradict her sister. She was so grateful to Jane.

Cedric did not look pleased, but he nodded. "Very well."

Julia's feet were leaden as Jane stood and dragged her away still dazed. When they were out of the ballroom and in the ladies' retiring room, Jane gave Julia a little shake.

"Did you know...expect this..."

Julia opened her mouth to speak, and emotion suddenly overwhelmed her. She burst into tears, ugly sobbing tears that would not stop. Julia was not a woman easily moved to tears. She could not remember the last time she had cried. Yes. She could. Father's funeral.

"Is this not what you wanted?" Jane asked in confusion, realizing Julia's tears were not happy ones. "A husband before summer's end? And one I thought you may actually have felt some affection for?"

Julia could not get control of her tears. She just sobbed harder.

"What is wrong? You told me you preferred Mr. Gruger and since he is Lord Fawkland's brother the solicitors think they may even be able to allow the house here in Bath to pass to him rather than cousin Rupert."

"Wha—no." Julia made an effort to speak coherently. Jane did not know it was Cedric who had accosted her. Jane thought it was Lord Fawkland. Had Jane written to the solicitor? Oh this was even worse than Julia expected. She just cried harder. "I should..." said Julia.

"Should what?" Jane said.

"I should...but...but...but."

"But what?" Jane demanded wiping Julia's face with a dampened handkerchief. A few curious ladies had moved in close, but Mrs. Poppy managed to shoo them out.

At last, Julia got Jane to understand that it had been Cedric, not Lord Fawkland who had so upset her the night before. Lord Fawkland had only seen her safely home.

Jane was shocked, but only for a moment. "Are you alright for a moment?" she asked. "I will call the carriage."

"I will call it for you," Mrs. Poppy said.

Jane continued to wipe her face. "Come now," she said at last, pulling Julia limping towards a door. "Please little sister, you must stop crying. Your face will be all a-blotch," Jane said as they hurried out a side door to the carriage.

"Oh, what shall I do?" Julia asked taking a breath.

"Well, we shall not lose our heads," Jane said after they had entered the carriage. "It will be alright. We will sort this out."

"I just want to go home," Julia said.

"I know, dear. I know," Jane said smoothing her sister's hair.

GODWIN WAS GOING TO KILL HIM. CEDRIC LIKED TO STIR UP trouble. He liked to cause mischief for his own amusement, but this time he had gone well past mischief and deep into mayhem and Godwin was going to kill him. Godwin had learned of what happened from the Poppys when he returned to find Julia missing and everyone gushing over Cedric.

"What have you done?" Godwin asked eyes narrowed and fists clenched.

"Do not make a scene, brother," Cedric said.

"We are leaving," Godwin growled.

"Are you not going to offer me your congratulations?" Cedric asked.

Godwin grasped his brother's coat and moved in close. "Let us go. I've called for the carriage."

"Perhaps I am not ready to go," Cedric replied.

"You are." Godwin laid a hand on his brother's shoulder and steered him towards the door. "I have given our apologies," Godwin said tightly. "We are leaving."

The doorman opened the door. Godwin stepped through putting Cedric in front of him. The warm night air did nothing to cool the tension between the two brothers.

Cedric pulled away. "Unhand me."

"No Cedric. I am finally taking you in hand. You have done enough to tarnish our good name. These games stop now."

"This is no game, Godwin."

"No. This is bad form. The lady is a member of the *Ton*, not some village wench. Have you not caused enough trouble?"

Cedric jerked his arm away from his brother. "Go to hell," he hissed turning back towards the ballroom.

Godwin put his hand on the door, blocking his brother's entrance.

By now, the footman had stepped forward. "Please gentlemen," he practically begged. He would not lay hands on a gentleman, but he certainly wanted them to remember their manners.

"We are leaving," Godwin said again. "And you are going to refrain from contacting Miss Bellevue."

"I shall not. I have asked Julia to marry me," Cedric said.

Godwin grabbed his brother by the coat and pulled him close. "By her father's will she is my betrothed," Godwin hissed. "You had no right."

"I had every right," Cedric growled at his brother. "You may be the eldest, but you are not the best of our father's sons."

Godwin never saw Cedric's right hook until it connected with his face. He rocked back against the door and Cedric was on him one moment, hitting him again, and then as suddenly as he had come on Cedric was thrown back; the fight stopped.

A man in a naval uniform had come between them and another had pulled Cedric off. Godwin recognized Commander Samuel Beresford. "Pray, do not quarrel," the large man said, stepping between the two combatants. Lord Percival Beresford stepped forward a moment later to help his own younger brother, should Samuel need assistance, and Captain Jack Hartfield made the third, holding Cedric by the scruff of the neck like a spitting stray cat.

As quickly as it had begun, the fight was averted.

The doorman stood wringing his hand and muttering. "Sirs, please. Sirs."

Cedric straightened his jacket and glared at his brother as he pulled free of Samuel Beresford and Captain Jack's hold.

"This is not over," Cedric said to his brother. He turned on his heel and stepped into the carriage that was waiting. The very confused driver urged the horses on and the carriage sped away.

Godwin stood rubbing his cheek, looking from one to the other of the gentlemen who had stopped the fight. He assumed that his friends had followed him outside when he left with Cedric. He was glad they were there. Otherwise, he and his brother may have made a scene with their fisticuffs. He hoped it was stopped quickly enough to avoid more talk. He looked quickly over the men's heads and saw no one else. Perhaps they would be safe from rumor, but that was probably a vain wish.

"I'm sorry to have disturbed you," he said to his friends.

"Not at all," Lord Percival Beresford said dismissively.

"He looks to have darkened your daylights," Samuel said gesturing. "You may have a black eye in the morning."

Well, that would add to the talk, Godwin thought.

"You should put a steak on it," Percival suggested.

Godwin touched his cheekbone gingerly and licked his lip. It felt cut too, the faint coppery taste of blood on his lip. How could his brother have done so much damage to his face so quickly? If he had been expecting the attack, he supposed he would have been quicker to defend himself, or would he have, he wondered? Cedric was after all, his little brother. Even after everything would he have hit him? Godwin sighed. "I am most grateful for your help," Godwin said looking a little shame-faced. "I truly am sorry."

"It was no trouble," said Samuel relighting his cigar from one of the lanterns. "I've broken up more than one fight on board ship."

"Tossing the combatants into the drink generally cools them off," said Captain Jack with a chuckle. "We should leave though."

"What of Miss Grant?" Godwin asked.

"I've been given leave to call upon her and I think it best not to push my luck tonight."

"I seem to have lost my carriage," Godwin replied as he realized Cedric had taken the carriage he called. Godwin brushed off his coat and straightened his sleeves thinking to go back in and call for another if he did not look too bedraggled. Perhaps he should send the footman inside.

"Do not concern yourself," Percival Beresford said.

"We were considering going to the club. You can ride with us. You look to need a good snifter of brandy anyway." Samuel continued.

"Perhaps," Godwin said. "But what of your ladies? Lady Patience and Lady Amelia?"

"Barton escorted his sister and Lady Amelia home," Samuel explained.

"I think Lady Amelia was overrun with rumors about her father, the Late Duke of Ely," Percival explained.

"Ah. Rumor," said Godwin angrily. "Yes. I think a drink would do me fine."

Part 4

The Baron's Bride

18

Julia Bellevue and her sister Jane had not lingered at the Assembly Ball after Cedric's proposal. As they hurried out the side door to the waiting carriage, it was impossible not to notice that everyone was abuzz. Julia could feel their eyes on her as she and Jane hurried away.

The inside of their carriage held no respite for Julia. Although it was dark and the accusing voices of the *Ton* were shut out by the distance, Julia could not shut out her own thoughts. She had no idea how to stop the rumors now. Everyone had seen Cedric Gruger kneel and propose to her, despite the fact she was already his brother's betrothed! The news of Cedric's humiliating proposal would only fuel the earlier rumors of her being seen with Lord Fawkland, but those too could be laid at Cedric's feet. It was Cedric who had tried to take liberties with her; Lord Fawkland only saw her safely home.

How had she gotten herself into this predicament?

She had tried to ignore the rumors earlier in the evening. She thought she was doing well. Both she and Jane had thought that the talk would die down, but instead, Cedric had brought all the rumors to a peak with his gauche and very public proposal. She supposed she was at fault for the spectacle. She could have chosen to walk with him in private. Jane could have accompanied them; she would have been safe enough. But how was she to know what he was planning? She was never good at this sort of thing; these social games. Now, Julia could not bear to show her face. Even Jane did not know how to combat the looks and innuendo.

The thought of Cedric himself, made Julia near shake with fury. He knew there were rumors. He knew her situation was tenuous and he chose to cause havoc. Cedric could have waited. He could have apologized to her alone and made his intentions known before he made so public a demand. If he cared for her at all, if he sought to protect her reputation; he would have done so but he chose instead to make a scene. He chose to disgrace her, not once, but twice. He had once been her friend, but now, he seemed intent upon this cruel manipulation. How could she even consider his proposal? How could she consider Cedric at all when the thought foremost in her mind was how this must appear to Lord Fawkland? He was an upright man. She remembered his vexed countenance, but he had only looked so when Cedric had done something untoward. Lord Fawkland was not an angry man. Even she was angry at Cedric; she still wanted to kick him in the shins.

Oh, she was not ladylike. What would Lord Fawkland think of her?

This thought brought a new flood of anxiety. She wanted to cry again. She wanted to run home and throw herself on her bed and sob because although Lord Fawkland was her betrothed, he would never have her now. Not after this deluge of aspersion. Not after he had seen her with his brother. Not after Cedric proposed! She tried to see the events from Lord Fawkland's eyes. There was no reason for Cedric to propose so publicly, so quickly, unless there was more to their acquaintance than a walk in a garden, even with the kiss. Fawkland had only just come to Bath, and she was cool to him; he must believe she rebuffed his suit because there was more than friendship between her and Cedric, and Cedric had manipulated that assumption. This was even more dreadful than she had first thought.

The truth was, Lord Fawkland had not in all actuality asked Julia to marry him. Certainly, there was the matter of her Father's will, but that was only a legal document, not a proposal of marriage. Since she had arrived in Bath, Julia had been making Lord Fawkland's life more difficult. She was the cause of the rift between him and his brother. In the short time she had known him already Julia had caused Lord Fawkland more trouble than happiness. Why should he want to marry her? Perhaps he was too polite to rescind their supposed betrothal outright, no matter how much he wanted to. And that was why he had not asked her to wed. The thought made her breath catch and she held back another sob. Even without her mother's curse, with her own low breeding

Julia brought nothing but misfortune to those she cared about.

"Julia, we are home," Jane said softly.

Julia looked out of the coach and realized it was true. They were in front of the townhouse in Bath, the house that had in some way been the start of this whole fiasco. If she had just let the house fall to Cousin Rupert, she could have spared herself some of this pain. She did not need a husband. She did not need one, but she wanted one, and strangely, she realized the husband she wanted was the one her father had chosen for her. Lord Fawkland. Godwin. Why had she not just bent to her father's will in the first place? Her father knew her. So much turmoil would have been avoided if she had consented at the first. Would accepting Lord Fawkland have been such a hardship? Would she even have the option of accepting him now, or had he decided that he was glad to be rid of her? The thought filled her with a near physical pain that settled into melancholy. Is that why his brother pressed his suit, she wondered, because Lord Fawkland did not want her? Of course he did not want her.

Thoughts of dancing with Lord Fawkland rushed through her mind with a singular heat. She remembered him almost touching her as they talked on the archery field. She remembered his hands on hers as he helped her home, and the scent of him; his gentle touch as he put her pins back in her hair; his hand on her waist as he lead her though the waltz. Indeed the soft brushes of his fingers against her hair or the cloth of her dress were more titillating than all of Cedric's kisses. This was not a man of anger. This was not a man with violent sensibilities. This was a kind man. She sighed. He would not want to lay eyes upon her again. She had caused so much trouble.

"Julia?" Jane said again, and Julia at last roused herself to leave the carriage.

The footman helped her down and they entered the house. She was soon settled on the sofa in the parlor. Jane asked if she wanted a basin of warm water for her hurt foot, but Julia hardly noticed her sore toe. It was overshadowed by her sore heart, she supposed. Julia shook her head. "I have made such a mess of everything," she said. "Jane, what shall I do?"

"Perhaps you should explain," Her sister said as she sat beside her on the sofa. "I do not understand this flood of tears. You once told me that you preferred the younger brother. I thought that you would welcome his suit. Am I to understand from your tears, that you now prefer the elder?" Jane asked gently.

"I know. I thought Mr. Gruger was my friend, but I have in recent days revised that opinion," Julia said, her voice trembling. "It was not Lord Fawkland who made advances towards me; it was Cedric. Lord Fawkland was only ever kind. He walked me home. He was ever the gentleman, and I have ruined everything."

"So all the rumors are wrong," Jane clarified. "It was Mr. Gruger who was forward with you? Who upset you so?"

Julia nodded. "I do not know what I did to encourage such action, Jane," Julia whispered. "I have tried to find some error I made in judgement. I have tried to see where

I gave Mr. Gruger some indication that his advances were wanted, but I cannot see it. You know I am not well versed in these things. But it was ...Cedric was so overwhelming...He frightened me."

Jane stood to light some additional candles and after a moment turned back to Julia. "Perhaps you should tell me what exactly happened," she said as she sat back on the sofa. "Explain it to me."

Julia felt a hot blush filling her face. "I cannot." Julia put her face in her hands. After a moment, she realized that her reluctance to share the incident with her sister was making it sound even worse than it had been, so she tried to rally her thoughts.

"Mr. Gruger kissed me," Julia said finally. "Is that not enough? I would have been ruined. Though I suppose I already am now." She sighed. "He kissed me, and then he pulled the comb from my hair... He...He..." Julia stood and began to pace.

Jane waited, giving her time to think and to organize her thoughts. Julia's pacing turned into a limp.

"Julia, please sit," Jane urged. "I can see your foot is paining you."

"I cannot," Julia protested. "He said; it was dark. No one would know; and that... I could keep a secret." Her voice had dropped to a whisper. "He pulled me against him and kissed my neck. And then, my mouth. I slapped him and I ran. That's when...well, I hurt my toe." Julia finished sheepishly. "Lord Fawkland found me then and walked me home," she said.

Jane bit her lip and sighed. "You are young," Jane began. "A kiss is certainly dangerous, but when a gentleman particularly likes a lady...He might sometimes become a bit ...overly ardent," Jane said. "Are you sure you did not misunderstand his intentions?"

"What?" Julia said confused. "What are you saying, Jane?"

Jane was silent for a long moment while Julia tried to puzzle out what Jane meant. At last she spoke again. "I am not saying you did anything to encourage his advances, but you did know each other as children...even as forward as he was...perhaps he thought..."

"What? That I expected such behavior? That I wanted such advances?" Julia interrupted angrily. "Do you think that he should be able to take liberties simply because we were childhood friends?" Julia's voice rose in pitch.

"No. Of course not," Jane said. She sighed again and rubbed between her eyebrows as if she were getting a headache.

It was a night for headaches, Julia thought.

"I must be blunt, Julia. As it stands, the perception of the *Ton* is that one or both of the brothers took liberties with you."

Julia opened her mouth to voice her objections, but Jane stopped her. "I hate to voice it, but with Lord Fawkland's reputation as a rake, some may think he has despoiled you, and his brother was making a grand gesture to save you."

Julia's heart sank. How could she be so completely ruined?

Jane was still speaking. "Despite all of this unpleasantness, a betrothed may be forgiven. The sooner married; the sooner forgiven. If you marry one of the

Grugers, either of the Grugers, the rumors will die. It will take a while, but marriage will calm the talk. Many a rake has calmed after marrying. Either way, we cannot hope for another offer, at least not this season, and perhaps not the next. Marrying Mr. Gruger would solve this, but if you will not have him, then what of Lord Fawkland?"

Julia did not answer right away, and Jane patted the seat beside her. "Come, sit," she said.

Julia limped over to the sofa and sank down feeling dazed. What of Lord Fawkland? Julia thought. She sighed. Lord Fawkland had always been gracious and upright. When they were at the archery field and when he walked her home, he did not make any advances. He offered to carry her, but that was only because of her sore toe. When they danced, she thought...Oh, when we danced! His arms were so strong around her, and she could almost smell the faint scent of sandalwood and cherry pipe tobacco as she thought of him. He was the perfect gentleman. Her face fell. She was suddenly fearful. Not once did he hold her hand too long or take any liberties. Even at the archery field when he was coaching her shooting, and it would have been so easy to touch her, he did not...never once. She wrung her hands. He was not...ardent. Not that she would want him to be like Cedric, but she did not know his feelings. What if Father thought of this whole betrothal and Lord Fawkland never wanted it at all? Never wanted me?

"I do not know," Julia said softly. "He hasn't asked me, Jane. He hasn't truly asked me to marry him." She felt her lip tremble as she spoke. She turned to Jane with a worried frown.

"But Mr. Gruger has." Jane replied. "And very publicly. He will need an answer. He offered a proposal of marriage, Julia." Jane hesitated a moment. "That does not forgive his actions, but as forward as he was, he was once your friend. Could he not be forgiven?" Jane asked at last. "Although he was overly zealous, and made a mistake, Mr. Gruger sought to correct it; to let you know his intensions were genuine."

"But do you not see, Jane? He has done just the opposite. I said no, but he wouldn't even hear me. I cannot marry a man who does not even hear the words I speak! It was as if I said nothing at all; as if my words were just so much noise. I fear he does not know me at all, and moreover, does not wish to know me, or even hear me. I pushed him away, and then I...I slapped him and I ran. I can think of no clearer way to show my displeasure with his actions. I do not know why he would think I would accept a proposal of marriage except that he has left me with little recourse. He has trapped me, Jane. This is exactly what Cedric planned. I cannot give in to him. If I accept him, he will have trapped me forever." She turned earnestly to Jane. "I cannot marry Mr. Gruger. I will not."

"Then, you must tell him so," Jane said. "And the sooner, the better. We need to lay the rumors to rest as best we can if we want any hope of getting past this, even next season."

Julia groaned. The thought of going through all of this again next year was just too much to contemplate. Her sister was kind to say so, but Julia was not so naïve.

There was no getting past this. Even she knew that; this kind of scandal would not easily die.

Jane rang for her maid. "Bring us paper and ink," Jane said. "We have a letter to compose."

"Please Jane, I would rather do it in the morning."

"It will be no easier in the morning. It is best to get it over with so you might rest easier."

"I am sure you know best," Julia agreed. Now that she had decided, Julia did wish to simply have the thing done with.

Composing the letter was agonizing, more than once Julia wanted to dissolve into tears. Even as she thought of what to say to Cedric, her mind kept going back to Lord Fawkland and what he must think of her. The thought pained her. What he thought mattered more to her than the whole of the *Ton*. She remembered him holding her as they danced, and with a pang realized that he would never hold her so again. He must hate her. Her lip trembled and she had trouble keeping her mind on the task at hand.

"Julia," Jane said. "Read it back to me."

Julia picked up the letter, still wet with ink. It was a mess of contradictions and crossed out sections. She and Jane kept taking out the things they could not say, until the letter was a series of short declarations. Even the greeting was in question.

"*Mr. Gruger*," Julia read.

Jane had suggested starting with Dear Mr. Gruger, as dear was a common appellation in a letter, but Julia had refused. The name alone looked stark on the page. Julia began again and continued to read:

MR. GRUGER,

In light of past events, I must refuse your proposal of marriage from last evening. As you know there is a previous contract between Lord Fawkland and myself. This arrangement was decided upon by my father, and as a young lady I will abide by my father's wishes so much as I am able. I am sorry if you construed the kindness meant to be shown to a brother as something more. That was never my intention.

Sincerely,

Miss Bellevue

THEY DITHERED FOR A WHILE OVER THE SIGNATURE, BUT Julia finally decided upon sincerely. She did *sincerely* wish to refuse Cedric. She also did not want to put her given name on the paper at all. She did not feel she should apologize for anything. She did not do anything wrong, but Jane insisted the letter needed a little softness. 'You are a lady,' she had said. 'You must allow the man a way out with grace.' She did not see why she should do so. He had not allowed her to leave the Pratt's picnic with grace.

"I suppose it will do," Jane said. "It does what we wish it to."

"You do not think it is too presumptuous to mention my betrothal to Lord Fawkland?" Julia asked. "I do not even know if he still wants to marry me, or in fact, if he ever did."

"The letter is not being sent to Lord Fawkland," Jane

reminded her. "It is the most expedient way to explain your reluctance."

"I could say my reluctance was because I was offended by Mr. Gruger's advances," Julia said.

"No. You could not."

"It just does not seem like quite the truth," Julia said.

"The truth is sometimes a hard thing, Julia. Now, rewrite the letter in your own hand. The sooner it is sent, the better you will feel."

Julia carefully copied the letter and managed to do so without blotching the page. After the letter was written and signed and laid to be sent to Cedric with the morning post, Julia thought she could relax. That was not the case. She was a long time in falling asleep, her thoughts turned around Lord Fawkland and her tears soaked into her pillow.

19

The Baron Fawkland did not spend long at the club with his friends. He had a single drink to settle himself, and nursed it for a good hour. The liquor burned his cut lip, and Percival fretted over his blackening eye like a mother hen. Godwin supposed he could not stay in Bath with a blackened eye. It would just add to the already rampant rumors. Godwin kept reliving the moments at the ball when he had realized that Miss Bellevue was missing; the moment when he realized what had happened and the ground had seemed to crumble under his feet. He tried to think what he could have done differently, to avoid the rumors; to avoid the fight, and most of all, to keep Miss Bellevue free of his brother's machinations.

Godwin had known something was amiss as he crossed the dance floor to return to Miss Bellevue. He could guarantee the problem had Cedric's orchestrating at the center of it. Worried, Godwin lengthened his stride, leaving Captain Jack Hartfield and Miss Lavinia Grant behind as he returned to the place where he had left his betrothed safely amidst the Poppy sisters, her own sister and her friends. The group was all in a frenzy.

It took Godwin several moments to realize the tittering was because Miss Bellevue, his betrothed, had received a very public proposal of marriage from his brother, Cedric. How Godwin had missed the advent of this event, he was unsure. Apparently he was still engaged in the tea room, matchmaking, and telling Miss Grant that Captain Jack was not entirely the liar. He could not leave Cedric nor Miss Bellevue unattended for a moment.

Now, Julia was nowhere in sight and neither was Cedric which sent Godwin's heart racing in fear. Fury pulsed through him on the heels of that fear. Once again Cedric had managed to throw his world into turmoil, and this time it was too much. "I'm going to kill him," Godwin had said in a low growl. "I am going to call him out, and kill him."

The tittering group grew a bit anxious at his words, and Captain Jack laid a hand on his shoulder. "Fawkland," he said softly.

Miss Poppy addressed him directly. "Surely not, Sir. You would not raise your hand against him. You are brothers." She fanned herself anxiously, and Godwin suddenly had no patience for such silly women.

"So were Cain and Abel, Miss" Godwin snapped, which had the effect of immediately silencing the little group's whispers.

That was ill said.

Godwin was aware that his words, said in anger, would accelerate the gossip. Fear returned in equal portion to the anger as he realized Miss Bellevue would not have him. His suit had been tenuous at best. This would be the last straw. Perhaps she already had decided for his brother. Had Cedric not warned him that Miss Bellevue hated gossip, and would go to any means to keep herself from being the brunt of it? And now he had just added fuel to the fire with his anger. He had been so careful. He had wanted to show her his best side.

Godwin had caught a whisper of the earlier rumor, which he had thought dispelled. *Lord Fawkland had walked her home, in quite a state of disarray*. He turned, but he could not make out who spoke. It did not matter. The fire was already a conflagration. There would be no stopping it now. It seemed to be a roaring in his ears. In the space of a heartbeat, everything had fallen out of control, and he had no idea how to fix it, short of fratricide. He knew he could not let Miss Bellevue marry Cedric. He could not. Cedric did not love her. He was playing with her heart to hurt Godwin. His brother would do naught but make her miserable. Surely his brother had done a fine job of making him miserable in the past years.

Godwin took a sip of his drink remembering the only bright spot in the conversation. Miss Bellevue's friend, Miss Grant gave him a slight glimmer of hope. Captain Jack's lady, Miss Lavinia Grant had the fragile appearance of a china doll, but she had stepped unafraid into this fray.

"And the lady?" Miss Grant had asked addressing Miss Poppy. "She is my friend. What did Miss Bellevue say to Mr. Gruger's proposal? Did she accept him or nay?"

Godwin had a moment of panic then thinking that if Miss Bellevue said yes to his brother there would be nothing he could do. It was after all Miss Bellevue's decision. He only wished he could have had time to woo her properly, but now he had no time at all. He was not sure he would have had the courage to ask such a question outright, but he needed to hear the answer.

"Nothing," Alfreda Poppy had said shaking her head. "Mr. Gruger was so charming, and his proposal so beautiful, but Miss Bellevue gave him no answer at all; only burst into tears."

"Tears?" Miss Grant said surprised. "Julia! Cried? Miss Bellevue?" She looked around concerned. "Where is she? Please, where has she gone?"

Mrs. Poppy strode into the little group then, calming her daughters with her no nonsense attitude. "Girls, stop whispering at once. Miss Bellevue has gone home," she answered Miss Grant, succinctly. "I have just called the carriage for Miss Bellevue and her sister. And all of you, if you have any love for the girl, you will stop your whispering this instant. Michael, dance with your sister. You, Captain, if I can impose upon you to dance with my other daughter? And Miss Grant..." Mrs. Poppy gestured, and Godwin, started towards the door, thinking to escape her orders, but the vivacious Miss Grant had put her hand on his arm.

"A moment, please Sir," was all she said. Godwin looked at the slight girl, and realized that in spite of his wanting to bolt for the door, either to find his brother or Miss Bellevue, his leaving was not going to change anything. Miss Bellevue would probably not receive him at this late hour, and it would be best not to meet his brother just now. He might indeed kill him. Normalcy was the only choice to stem the gossip, if it could be stemmed at all.

"I feel this is my fault," Miss Grant said, her delicate face creased into a frown of dismay.

"It is not," Godwin replied. "My brother has been attempting to cause trouble since he first learned of my betrothal to Miss Bellevue."

"But if you had not been so good as to come to my Mr. Hart's aid...I mean Captain Hartfield," she corrected. "This would not have happened."

Godwin shook his head. "Not now, perhaps," Godwin agreed. "But my brother would have found a way to thwart my efforts to convince Miss Bellevue to accept my suit." He looked at the Poppy girls now lining up for the very ordinary pastime of dancing. He wanted to rush after Miss Bellevue.

"I have not seen Julia cry on many occasions," Miss Grant admitted without provocation. "I do not think they were tears of joy."

He looked at the woman then, and saw intelligence in her eyes. "Do you think...?" He paused. It would not be right to ask her friend if Miss Bellevue favored his suit. "It distresses me that she is upset," he said instead.

Miss Grant smiled at him. "You care for her," Miss Grant said, and he agreed.

"I do." He excused himself and went looking for his

brother, he had to do something. The night had just gone further downhill from there. The argument with Cedric. The fisticuffs. Miss Bellevue gone and him with a blackened eye and split lip.

Godwin rubbed his sore cheekbone and accepted another drink from Jack. It was late. He thought about writing Miss Bellevue a correspondence, but decided he would call upon her on the morrow. That was the better choice. No good news ever came in a letter. He hoped his face did not look too awful, or would not look awful on the morrow. Perhaps he should wait a few days; deal with his brother before visiting Miss Bellevue....

"I am so sorry, I took you from your betrothed," Captain Jack said as he pushed the fresh drink towards Godwin.

"It is not your fault, Jack. My brother is a thorn in my side. Father should have shipped him off to the King's Service long ago. He is a spoiled child who has never learned to be a man." He leaned his head against his hand. "There is no salvaging this wreck," he said.

"Oh, never say never," Jack replied. "Or underestimate the tenacity of a woman. Wrecks can be salvaged. As a matter of fact, I am going to have little enough time to court, Miss Grant. Apparently our esteemed British shipbuilders have managed to make my ship seaworthy, and new orders will be forthcoming."

"Well, that is good news," Godwin muttered, but he could not think about Jack right now. His thoughts were all for Miss Bellevue.

The dawn was breaking when Fawkland finally turned in for a few hours of sleep. He tossed and turned as thoughts of Miss Bellevue churned in his mind. He rolled over and looked at the ceiling. Perhaps he should go to call upon her. Perhaps he should discuss this entire affair with her. It was such an awful mess; he did not wish to speak of it. He was embarrassed for his brother, and hurt for himself. He did not want to go to her from a place of weakness. He wanted to be able to tell her that he had taken care of his brother, but what if she wanted his brother and not him? Would she not have accepted his brother last night if that was so? He finally gave up on sleep. In his mind, he rehearsed what he should say to her. Only what could he possibly say to her that she did not already know? What could he say that had not been said? Miss Bellevue would either believe him or not. She would accept Cedric's proposal or she would not. The decision, as it always had been, was hers.

THE MORNING SUN SHONE BRIGHTLY ON THE CALLING CARD on the silver plate. Julia stared at it. The angled script of Mr. Cedric Gruger graced the card and she felt her stomach clench in anxiety. So this was his response to her letter? To call upon her? The summer sun was streaming into Jane's sitting room where the two of them were conversing over tea. After their late night discussion and letter writing, the sisters were late in rising, but it was still early for visitors. They had not gone downstairs. They were still in their dressing gowns leisurely completing their morning toilet.

"Shall I tell Mr. Gruger you are not receiving visitors?"

Harrington asked.

"The letter was clear," Jane added. "You do not have to see him, Julia."

"I think I do," Julia said with a sigh. She reached out a hand to clasp her sister's for a moment. Jane had been right about sending the letter last night. Julia's mind had settled, and she felt she had shed enough tears over the actions of Mr. Cedric Gruger. She would tell him she had refused him and the matter was ended.

"Where shall I meet him?" Julia asked her sister.

"It is obvious from the hour that he expected to catch you at the concluding stages of your toilet and be admitted to your dressing room," Jane deduced.

"He shall have to wait then," Julia said with a shrug. "Gentlemen are accustomed to waiting for ladies; though he is no gentleman." Jane smiled at Julia's flippancy.

"The morning room, I think," said Jane. "It is bright, and not too formal, nor private."

The butler frowned. "Do you wish to serve, my lady?"

"No," Julia said. "Not even tea. That is the point, you see."

The butler nodded. "Very good. I will show him in when you are ready, Miss Bellevue."

"Tell him if he wishes to wait, he may, but inform him that he will find no difference in speaking in person than he did in the correspondence," Jane said.

"Yes, Countess." Harrington did not crack a smile, but his eyes lighted. "Shall I have him wait in the foyer? Say that Miss Bellevue has not yet decided where she shall receive him, but he is welcome to await your pleasure?"

It was rude to leave him cooling his heels so, but Julia

agreed. She quite liked Harrington at that moment for suggesting it.

Still, once Harrington left, the reality of the situation hit her, and Julia was flustered. They were not yet dressed for visitors. "It will take an age," Julia said.

"Does it bother you that Mr. Gruger has to wait?" Jane asked.

"No. No it does not."

OUTSIDE THE MORNING ROOM, JULIA WAS PACING ON HER sore foot. She could not be still.

"I can stay with you," Jane said.

"No. I think I need to do this myself," Julia said. "Mr. Gruger thinks I can be manipulated. He thinks I am still a gullible child. I am not."

Harrington had left Cedric standing in the foyer for a good forty minutes before showing him into the morning room and Julia could put this meeting off no longer.

"I shall be right here, if you need me," Jane told her. Jane had seated herself at the window, just outside the door of the morning room. Any closer and she could listen at the keyhole, Julia thought with a smile.

The summer sun beamed in the windows. The breakfast area would be bright and cheery, but Julia was feeling anything but cheery. She nodded at Harrington. "I am ready," she said with determination.

"Yes, Miss," Harrington said as he opened the door for her.

Cedric wasted no time in touching her. As he greeted

her, he caught both of her hands in his and kissed them. "I am afraid I did not make myself clear," he said.

"You were perfectly clear, Mr. Gruger" Julia said pulling her hands from his grasp, "as was my letter of reply."

"Let us sit and talk," Cedric said, leading her to a seat in the breakfast nook. "Have you eaten?" he asked.

Was he attempting to invite himself to breakfast? How had she not seen how impertinent he was! Julia had no intention of this conversation taking longer than needed, and that most certainly did not include breakfast. "I am not hungry," she said, still standing which required Mr. Gruger to remain standing as well. Instead of sitting, she walked across the room to the window, positioning the table between them. "Say your piece and be gone, Mr. Gruger. I have nothing further to say to you."

"You jest!" Cedric said. "You are but playing a piece,"

She stiffened. "I do not."

"Surely you can see we belong together. We have been friends since childhood."

"I am no longer sure that is true, Mr. Gruger. I do not know that you were ever my friend." She worried her hands together.

"You are listening too much to my brother."

She stilled and looked at him. "Am I, Mr. Gruger?"

"Cedric," he said gently. "You remember when you used to call me, Cedric?"

"We were children. We are children no longer, Mr. Gruger."

"Nonetheless, we were friends. Can we not be friends again, Julia?"

She ignored the familiarity. She folded her hands together in front of her and looked at him with resolve. "Friends do not manipulate one another," she said.

He scoffed, but she continued.

"Friends do not hurt one another. A friend does not take a friend's property, nor ruin a friend's property, or her reputation. They do not leave one another open to ridicule and gossip." She turned and fixed him with a stare. "Do you have nothing to say for yourself, Mr. Gruger?"

"You always did care too much what others said of you," he snapped, and Julia took a step back, surprised by the sudden venom when she expected an apology.

"And you cared too little," she replied.

"So you wish to be a baroness," he said. "That I understand. That's what all women want, isn't it? Money. A title."

She was struck dumb. How could he say that to her? "I never desired a title," she said.

He tsked. "No? Come now, Julia. It is only the title that makes you prefer my brother to me."

Now he was being too brash. She sputtered, trying to think of a retort. Julia knew she should not have mentioned her prior betrothal to Lord Fawkland in her letter of refusal.

"You think he will have you, but he shan't. My dear Julia, you are grasping," Cedric said as he moved closer to her. "You see, my brother cares about what others say as well. I caution you. Do not make a hasty decision. I may change my mind, and no one would blame me. After all, I am a respected member of the *Ton*. I do not have to offer for you in my brother's stead, nor take a wife with a sullied reputation."

"Sullied?" she repeated, her voice strangled. "I am not. Your brother did not..."Julia began, but Cedric with even more poor manners interrupted.

"Oh Julia," he said with feigned pity. "When will you realize it is not what you are; it is what people believe you are?"

"What have you done?" Julia asked horrified by the thoughts running through her mind.

"The *Ton* is awfully easy to convince of sin, Julia." Cedric tsked and smiled and spoke in that honeyed tone that had fooled so many women of the *Ton*. You know what they will say. He brought his handkerchief to his nose in an affectation, before shaking his head, and whispering conspiratorially: "the poor deluded woman, in love with a rake like my brother. You must be aware my brother is known to be the father of one bastard." He smiled his sickening smile at her. "Oh Julia it will be so easy for them to believe the worst of you considering your parentage. You have no one but me."

She squeezed her hands together to keep from picking up one of the brass candlesticks and bashing him in the head with it. She could not believe this was happening. Did he think so little of her? That she would be so desperate to accept such a proposal? That she would tie her life to his despite the disregard he had shown her? She had been right to refuse him. He had been manipulating her from the start. Did he think to convince her to marry him; by saying she was not good enough for anyone else? She could not quite believe her ears.

"I...I shall have myself," Julia stuttered. "I have my own self-respect, and I think it is high time you took your leave, Mr. Gruger."

"Julia, be reasonable. Pride is cold comfort. Do you not see that my proposal is your salvation? After all that has happened, no other will offer for you. It is just like it always was when we were children. Nothing has changed. The women have not changed from the spiteful little girls they were. They will not accept you, and having a title will not help you any more than having the nicest porcelain doll would help you...or the best shoes or the latest fashions. They don't like you, Julia. You do not belong, and you never will. You just don't know how to play the game, and you do not even have the wit to see that. "

Julia felt like she couldn't breathe. It was him. It was Cedric who had broken her dolls as a child. It seemed he also had not changed and now, his cruelty nearly broke her heart... How could he be so awful? How could she have been so blind for so long? Lord Fawkland had warned her. He had told Julia that his brother was not who she thought he was, and she thought the baron was being arrogant. He was not. He was only being truthful.

Cedric held out his hand to her. "But I have always protected you, Julia," he said. "Let me protect you from this scandal now. Just say the word and as my wife, you will be under my protection."

Julia's face blossomed red with anger and embarrassment.

"Under your thumb, you mean," she blurted. "No! I would not have you if you were the last man on earth."

"I might as well be," he said.

Julia gasped. "Leave now, Mr. Gruger," Julia said loudly. She rang for Harrington who must have been waiting on the other side of the door with Jane, he appeared so quickly. The butler moved forward between them. Jane had also entered the room. Harrington was stocky enough to escort Mr. Gruger out himself if things got ugly, but Julia noticed two more footmen had come to the door behind Harrington.

Julia realized that all these years Cedric was as much a part of making the scandal as he had been in protecting her from it. How could she have been so blind? Perhaps he was right. No one would want her after this, but that was no matter. She could not marry Cedric. He was nothing like the man she once thought he was. He was a monster.

"Shall I show the gentleman out?" Harrington asked, with just a bit of a lilt on the word gentleman. Harrington was addressing Jane but his glance shifted between the two ladies.

Julia answered him. "Mr. Gruger was just on his way out."

"Yes, Harrington," Jane added "Please show him the door."

Harrington came forward and put a hand on Cedric's

arm. "The Lady Keegain has requested that you leave, Sir," he said in a tight voice.

"You shall not find another husband," Cedric threw as a parting shot.

"Then, I shall get a cat," Julia said. "And if you ever show your face here again, I shall teach it to scratch your eyes out!"

Cedric took a single step towards her.

The other two footmen stepped up.

"I am going," Cedric spat, straightening his coat, and stalking out the door.

Julia was shaking so badly, she could not quiet herself. Once Mr. Gruger was gone, Jane reached for her sister and enfolded Julia in a hug. Julia did not cry. She had used up all her tears. She stared wide-eyed out of the morning room window at the bright sunshine. She was still shaking, and could not tell if it was anger or frustration.

She had lost everything now. Cedric was right in one respect. If Lord Fawkland did not want her, no one would have her. But it was the right decision. She knew she had been right to refuse Cedric. What the *Ton* said did not matter. She could never have married him.

"I shall get a cat," she said again, and Jane squeezed her tighter. They stood together for a long moment.

"I think we should leave Bath," Jane said at last. "I would rather like to be home."

Julia nodded mutely. "The house will go to Cousin Rupert," Julia said softly.

"Shhh," Jane eased her. "Do not fret over it."

"I should pack my paints...and the easel."

"I will have the servants do it," Jane said, still holding her sister. "They have the rest of the house to pack as well, by the end of summer. Let us leave before the rumors Mr. Gruger has planted take root."

Julia nodded. "Yes. Let us go home, Jane."

20

By the time morning came, Lord Fawkland had formulated a plan. He had already told Captain Jack. Now he had to find his brother. He decided to check Cedric's rooms first, but Miss Bellevue was never far from his mind. Cedric was not in his rooms, so Godwin simply paid the bill and let the owner of the hotel know that Cedric would be leaving soon.

Lord Fawkland checked every gaming hall and bawdy house. As he went through his brother's haunts, he gave each of them notice that he would no longer honor his brother's debts.

Lord Fawkland stopped his carriage on the front street, at the edge of the rough side of town. He mentally catalogued the pubs he knew Cedric frequented. He was prepared to go through the entire list when he caught sight of the man in question, Cedric. He looked to be in a towering rage. A little rage might do him good, Godwin thought.

Lord Fawkland turned his carriage and followed his brother. Godwin thought that Cedric did not look like a man who had just been happily affianced, which calmed Godwin somewhat. He no longer wanted to kill him on sight. Godwin still wanted to call him out, but the urge was somewhat mitigated. In any case it would not solve the immediate problem. It would not quell the rumors or make his lady rest easier. When at last Cedric entered a pub, Godwin followed after him.

Cedric had just ordered a drink, when Godwin walked into the pub.

"This deuced maggot pie, does not need a drink," Godwin said grabbing Cedric by the back of his neck.

Cedric would have taken a swing at him, but the angle was wrong, and the footman took offense to the gentlemen brawling inside the establishment.

"If you have some grudge," the waiter added. "Take it outside."

"Oh, indeed we will," Godwin agreed, giving Cedric a shove towards the door. "By the look of you, brother, the lady has more sense than to agree to your terms." Godwin was surprised by how happy that fact made him.

"She hasn't agreed to yours either," Cedric said sullenly, and Godwin's heart soared. He hadn't realized how much the uncertainty had worn on him. He knew Miss Bellevue was a woman of sense.

"I'm going to tell you how it is and you are going to listen." Godwin gave Cedric another shove. "You have ended my patience, Cedric. You are brought to a point non plus and this is how it will be."

"How it will be?" Cedric scoffed. "You haven't the

bollocks to do anything to me. Shall I blacken your other eye?"

"It is not what I am going to do; it is what you are going to do, Cedric. You are going to offer your services to His Majesty's Navy... or Army if you prefer. I will even buy you a commission. I do not much give a damn as long as you are far from me and Miss Bellevue, but that is the last farthing I shall spend on you. You are, as of this moment, penniless. You shall have no funds for your rented rooms or your tarts. You have no allowance and no apartments in London. The sooner you sign up, the sooner you may have your military stipend. Do it now, and keep some measure of dignity."

Cedric straightened his coat. "I am the son of a baron."

"As you so readily remind me, our father is dead. You are the brother of a baron. The younger brother, which means that I hold the purse strings. And as of right now, you haven't a sixpence to scratch with. I have sent messages to all of your establishments informing them that I will no longer honor your debts. If you want a glass of wine or a pint of ale you will have to have cash on the line. Mark me. No one will take your vowels. I have bled very freely for you, but no longer, Cedric. This last trick of yours has finished my patience. You have embarrassed me and embarrassed my fiancée. It ends here."

"The *Ton* will shun you if you treat me in this way."

"If I have to, I shall truss you up and put you on a ship myself."

"You and what army?"

"What Navy," Godwin corrected. "I am giving you the

honor of walking there on your own two feet. If you are still in town tomorrow, I will have you conscripted. In case you were not aware, England is at war." Godwin paused. "I will leave you the courtesy of the carriage, until tomorrow. Use your time well."

❧

GODWIN MET UP WITH HIS CAPTAIN JACK HARTFIELD about an hour later at one of the clubs in town. "Did you do it?" Captain Jack asked.

"I did. He is my brother, but I can take no more." Godwin sat at the table with his friend.

"And if he does not sign up?"

"He will be on your ship or another by dawn," Godwin said. "He is too piss proud to let anyone know that he has no money."

"Good then," Captain Jack said. "I will send the shore patrol around at dawn to save you the trouble." Jack waved the waiter over.

"I think I shall like to see him carted off," Godwin said as he ordered a drink. "I will feel much better once he is safely away from Bath."

"And what of your lady?" Captain Jack asked. "How goes it?"

"I know not. I doubt she would wish to see me at all after this mess. I have embarrassed her beyond measure. The rumors are rife. I not only walked her home, but I have, according to the gossips, invited her alone into my carriage. An incident that apparently occurred the week before either of us even arrived in Bath," Godwin said.

"The gossips of the *Ton* are idiots," Jack agreed, "but fighting rumor is worse than fighting ghosts."

"Still the other rumors are bad enough. We have also apparently have kissed under every tree in every garden in Bath."

"Oh," Captain Jack said, rolling his drink in his glass. "I have heard all those, but the latest is worse."

"What is worse?" Godwin asked concerned.

"The whole line of rumors from several years ago, about your mistress by the sea has resurfaced."

Godwin groaned. "She's not my mistress. She never was."

"And the latest is that Miss Bellevue carries your child, but your brother was kind enough to offer for her when you would not."

"What!"

"They are only rumors," Captain Jack said.

"Lud," Godwin said, feeling rather sick. How had his brother managed this? Despite his efforts Cedric had still found a way to best him.

"It is not your doing," Captain Jack said. "As you stated, half of these events appear to have occurred in Bath when neither of you were yet here. Anyone with any sense knows they are lies." Captain Jack sipped his drink.

"As you have just said, the *Ton* has no sense." Godwin groaned. "My fault or not, I cannot fix this," Godwin said hopelessly. "He has won. I can do nothing to stop the rumors. My good name and worse, hers, is in tatters."

Godwin's face fell, as Captain Jack lifted a glass. Jack hesitated. He sat the glass down again and studied Godwin. "You love her," he said.

"It does not matter."

"Of course it matters."

"I cannot remedy this, Jack. It has gone too far. I do not see how I can marry her. She has not accepted me."

"Ah, so you have asked her and she is leaving you off just like your brother?"

"Well, no. Not exactly."

Jack frowned at him. "I do not understand. You just said you loved the girl."

"Yes. I believe I do."

"And have you confessed your love?" Jack asked. "How has she answered your suit?"

Godwin lifted a shoulder. "It never seemed the proper time, Jack. I wanted her to get to know me, and I never felt sure...and now..." He shrugged again.

"You have not asked her, then?" Captain Jack surmised. He finished his drink and waved the waiter over for another.

"I have not spoken directly," Godwin agreed. "But it was a most awkward situation. We were already betrothed by her father's writ, and..."

"A letter!" Captain Jack interrupted. "And from the solicitors! My good man, were you not the one who told me nothing good ever comes in letters? You must speak plainly and honestly."

"Why would she hear me?" Lord Fawkland asked, looking into his glass as if for wisdom.

Captain Jack reached over and took Godwin's untouched drink from in front of him.

"What are you doing?" Godwin asked him as Jack took Godwin's drink and downed it. "Hey!"

"I am saving you from going to your lady love with the smell of brandy all around you. You need your wits about you, not spirits. Now you must at least give the lady the option to dismiss you. A wise man told me, you must in all honesty confess your love, and lay your pride on her tender mercies. Follow your own advice, Fawkland. Go. Talk to her."

"I'm afraid it is too late. Nothing will quell the gossip. A speedy marriage will only give credence to the rumors."

"Blast the rumors," Jack said. "If you love her, marry her. You do love her, do you not?"

"Yes," Godwin said miserably. "God help me, I do."

"Not a speedy marriage then. A long engagement," Jack suggested. "I know most of the *Ton* are simpletons, but they can count, at least to ten with their gloves on. The rumors end in nine months and you shall have your lady love."

"Why would she have me, Jack? I've been such a fool."

"If my Miss Grant could forgive my foolishness, your lady can forgive you. The letter I sent her was nigh unreadable; I was so in my cups, but she still welcomed me." He shuddered as he thought of it and shook his head. "What were we thinking? Writing to a lady in such a state?" he asked Godwin, with a wry smile, but then continued without waiting for an answer to his question. "As my Lavinia says, love can bear many wrongs."

"Lavinia?" Godwin said. "You are very familiar."

The color rose in Captain Jack's face, but he would not be persuaded. "Go!" he commanded in the voice that ordered men. "Your lady awaits. You can do nothing until you speak with her. Every moment is a moment in time lost."

Godwin stood and smoothed his cravat. "Wish me luck," he said as he worried the cut in his lip with his tongue.

"I wish you love," Jack said and with an inflection that sounded strangely like his lady. He lifted his glass in a toast. Godwin laughed, but he left the establishment, intent to see if Miss Bellevue would have him.

Captain Jack was right. He was being foolish. He had to talk to her. Godwin straightened his cravat again and made himself as presentable as he could be with a blackened eye and headed determinedly toward her townhouse. When he reached the house, however the butler told him that Lady Keegain and Miss Bellevue had already left Bath.

"Where did they go?" he blurted.

"I am sure, it is not my place to say, Lord Fawkland," Harrington replied.

"I understand," Godwin said. "But I need to speak with Miss Bellevue."

Harrington still said nothing.

"You know me, Harrington. I've been here with Mr. Bellevue, God rest him. Her father was once my friend and I am not my brother."

Harrington cleared his throat. "I do believe the lady wished to avoid contact with your brother," Harrington said.

"I concur," Godwin said. "And I have seen to Cedric. Now did they go to London or to Lord Keegain's country manor?"

Still Harrington was closed mouthed.

"Pray, do not make me ride in both directions," Godwin said with an exasperated sigh. "I know my betrothed was upset. I want to make this situation better for her, if I am able, not worse."

Harrington gave him an appraising stare. "I hear that London is rather uncomfortable in the heat of summer," Harrington said at last.

Godwin grinned. "Thank you, Harrington. If she will have me, remind me to raise your salary."

"I shall, my lord," Harrington said gravely, and Godwin laughed, his spirits lifting somewhat for the first time all day.

"I do not relish the thought of working for Cousin Rupert," Harrington added stiffly. "He should answer the door himself."

As Godwin left off speaking with Harrington, he thought about what he should do. The sensible thing to do was to wait until the morrow, see his brother safely away, and then travel himself the first thing in the morning. That was the sensible thing to do. He looked at the sky. The sun was barely past its zenith. Keegain's country manor was not so far as London. There was much of this day left, and he did not feel sensible.

21

---

ane and Julia's carriage and the other conveyance bringing all matter of items from Bath pulled up in front of the Keegain county house. It was only a small amount of what was actually in the townhouse in Bath. The servants had packed the essentials for the journey and Jane left the rest of the house for them to close, as the sisters had left in quite the hurry. Julia imagined the outrider sent ahead to tell the earl of their arrival was only an hour or so ahead of them, but at last they had arrived home. Finally, they would be out of the carriage. The footman helped them down, and Julia watched Jane's shoulders relax with a feeling of liberation as she exited the carriage. This was Jane's home. She immediately directed the servants and then turned away allowing them to do their jobs unencumbered. They unpacked the carriages with practiced ease and without Jane's active intervention.

Julia breathed in the fresh country air. She had always

loved Bath. Bath was her home, but now this would be her new home. She would no longer have Bath.

"Shall we go sit in the garden after dinner?" Jane asked her sister. She took her arm and it was a comfort.

"Do you think the roses are blooming?" Julia asked.

"They were not when I left," Jane said. "But they should be by now." Jane turned to one of the servants. "Have water brought so that we might refresh ourselves," she said.

The maid curtseyed. "Yes, milady."

Julia could see that her sister was glad to be home. Everything about her attitude shouted joy to Julia. Jane led the way up the steps to the front landing, her eagerness and excitement causing Julia to smile in spite of herself.

Jane's husband Randolph Keening, the Earl of Keegain came out to meet them at just that moment. "We were not expecting you quite so soon," he said. "White hoped to have lemon cakes for tea."

"That sounds marvelous." Jane hurried to her husband on the steps and Julia was sure if she had not been there, Lord Keegain would have kissed her. Instead, Jane squeezed her husband's arm gently. "I am glad to be home," she said beaming up at him.

"Likewise," he said smiling down at Jane as if he wanted to touch her more intimately. Instead, he looked over at Julia with a smile.

Julia did not think the earl was a handsome man. He was fit but considerably older than his wife and shorter than Julia: not even half a head taller than Jane herself. His hair had prominent spots of grey at the temples and a bit of scalp showed through the sparse hair at the crown of his head. He made up for this lack with a full beard which he kept immaculately trimmed. Even though he was not attractive in Julia's opinion, his eyes were kind and his face lit up at the sight of Jane and that was enough.

Keegain looked directly at Jane then. A moment passed before he spoke. "And am I paying the solicitors to find a loophole and rewrite the will?" The Earl of Keegain asked. There was no censure in his voice, but Julia felt embarrassed anyway. She blushed and looked away.

"This does not appear to be a happy homecoming," he said.

"No," Jane agreed simply. "I am afraid Bath was quite ghastly. I am unaccountably happy to be home." She squeezed his arm again.

He frowned a little and looked at Jane as if for an explanation, but something in Julia's face must have warned her sister to not dig up the whole mess just now, and the earl saw as much with only a look at his wife, and he shrugged off the whole matter quickly.

Lord Keegain smiled at her and Julia felt self-conscious. "Well, do not worry little sister. I am sure my Janey has the matter well in hand. Together, we shall find the best way forward for you."

They went into the house and considered their next action. Julia desperately wanted a cup of tea. Everything was better with tea, she thought, but it was obvious that Jane and her husband were itching to be alone, and her sister married almost two years. It was almost outrageous, but then it was also sweet and she wanted that for herself. The gentleman who came to her mind was Lord Fawkland. There was no inkling of another, and then quick on the heels of that thought were the nagging remembrances of the rumors which came up in her mind like little demons, his and hers. She had a hard time pushing them away. This was how it would be from now on, she thought. She had to resign herself to that fact.

The maid came back and curtseyed. "Your water is ready," she said to Jane, and Julia assumed she meant the basins Jane had asked for to wash the dust of the road from their skin. Tea would wait, Julia reminded herself. She did not want to inconvenience her sister. She was not in her own home.

"I am a bit weary," Julia said to Jane. "And I'm sure you will want to rest before dinner as well. It has been a trying couple of days."

Jane's eyes lit up and Julia was certain her sister was glad for a bit of privacy with her husband.

"I'm sure you can do with a bit of rest and refreshment," Keegain said. "Travel is so draining."

Julia noted he had moved Jane's hand from his arm, and now stood with one arm around her waist. Julia remembered Lord Fawkland's arm on her waist in just that way as he helped her up the stairs with her hurt foot...as he danced with her. His hand was so warm, there in the small of her back. There was no comfort in these thoughts. They would only make her maudlin. She brushed them away from her mind, and smiled at Jane and Lord Keegain.

"I will have a late tea sent up to you, Julia," Jane said.

"When is dinner?" Jane asked turning back to look at her husband. Her sister's face was already sunny.

"Dinner will be at eight," the earl said, "but it is just the family here this evening if you would like to adjust the hour?" he looked at Jane.

"Dinner at eight," she repeated. "I see no need to change." She turned back to Julia. "I will send Jacqueline up to help you dress for dinner and fix your hair, if you want to rest now," Jane said.

"That would be wonderful," Julia replied with a tight smile.

The maid showed her to her room as if she did not know which guest room Jane would put her in. It would not really be a guest room any longer; it would be her room and it would always be a guest room, Julia thought. She wondered if the awkwardness she felt with Jane and her husband would ever go away. She felt a third wheel on a cart. She was never so aware that without her they could be a couple. They could speak freely. Even though, Jane had said she was her sister and she would always be welcome, Julia thought, she would also always be the odd one, the extra spinster aunt.

She had sworn that this would not happen and at the same time she had dreaded it. Julia knew she was inept in pleasant conversation. She knew of her deficiency, and still she had tried to dance and flit about society as if she were one of those social creatures. Why had she been so foolish? That was not her. It was no wonder she managed to make a mess of things. She now thought she should have just married Lord Fawkland as quickly as she was able, before he changed his mind; even if he had been an ogre. She sighed. But he was not an ogre. He was tall and handsome and virile and kind. She realized suddenly that he was everything she had once hoped for, and she had been so cold to him. Why did she not believe her father had her best interests at heart? Her father knew her. She should have trusted him a little more. She squeezed her eyes shut tightly. She would not cry. She was done with crying.

One of Jane's ubiquitous maids tapped on the half open door.

"Come," Julia said and the maid came in with a brief curtsey. "I saw your door was open, Miss Bellevue. May I unpack your things?" the maid asked and Julia nodded. Yes, she thought. Unpack my things. This is my room. This is my home. "I would very much like a cup of tea," she said.

"Right away, Miss," the maid said. She left, but returned shortly and a second maid followed, who brought the tea set. Julia took a blessed sip of the hot liquid and it seemed to fortify her.

The first maid also helped her to strip out of her traveling clothes. She had brought a basin and pitcher for washing. Julia was much more comfortable after a brief wash to rinse away the grime that always seemed to accumulate on days of travel.

"Shall I press a dress for you for dinner?" the maid asked.

Julia nodded. She chose a dress for dinner, the first one she grabbed, a medium blue frock without frills. It looked a little matronly. It had puffed sleeves and a round neckline which was a bit dated, but it was cool and simple, perfectly fitting for the spinster aunt, Julia thought. The maid took the dress to press it, leaving Julia alone with her thoughts. They were not good company.

She kept running over all the mistakes she had made and the greeting that Jane gave Lord Keegain made her realize just what she had done wrong. When she had first met Lord Fawkland she had been so cool towards him, telling him he should deed her the house in Bath. She had not tried to get to know him. She had not even looked him in the eye. How many times had she looked at her shoes? How could he tell anything about her when she did not open up to him? He had tried. She remembered the conversation in the carriage on the way to the Pratt picnic when he has asked about her paintings. He had asked if she liked to go for walks. Would he have escorted her on a walk if she had said so? Would he have talked about birds or cats? Would he have shared his own interests? She would never know. She had closed him out, and now, what did she have?

Cedric was right. She had nothing. No one wanted her. No, she thought. That was not what troubled her. It was only that Lord Fawkland did not want her. Julia realized what she had tried so hard to deny. She loved Lord Fawkland. Somehow she had fallen in love with him, but he did not love her. If he loved her, he would have offered marriage. He would have proposed. But how could he love her, she warred with herself? They had barely begun to get reacquainted.

Julia wasn't tired and she could not still her thoughts. She wished she had her paints, but they were not yet unpacked. She remembered the misty grey of Lord

Fawkland's eyes; they were like a storm cloud and she wanted to paint them. She wanted to capture that color before she lost it in her mind's eye. Perhaps she should try a portrait; to capture Lord Fawkland's likeness. She had always been much better at landscapes, but perhaps she only needed the proper subject.

She sighed. Lord Fawkland was not here and neither were her paints; she had to content herself with a book. It appeared her sister had left her a text of Lyrical Ballads by Coleridge and Wordsworth, and another book of poetry by Robert Burns, both on the night stand. No, perhaps not her sister, Julia thought. Jane didn't read romantic poetry. If she read, Jane would rather have had a novel. This was more Lavinia's fare; poetry that sang of the power of love. Julia opened the book and was filled with melancholy. No one would recite poetry for her; of course, she was not really the poetry type. Although if Lord Fawkland were the one to read the verse perhaps an exception could be made.

Jane had never been much for poetry either unless she had been changed upon her marriage to the earl. Julia wondered if Keegain recited poetry for Jane. She hoped he did. She hoped Jane had all the romance she did not. Still, the earl seemed more of an enlightened type. Surely he would have something of substance in his library, Julia thought. What sort of books were in Lord Fawkland's library, she wondered suddenly. She put the poetry book aside. She considered briefly if she should try to find the library, but the journey had fatigued her and she thought instead she would just close her eyes for a moment.

A moment became an hour and soon, Jacqueline was knocking on her door asking if she was ready to have her hair done for dinner.

"Dinner this evening is only a family affair," Julia reminded Jacqueline. "Do not fuss overly much. Something simple."

"*Oui Mademoiselle*," Jacqueline agreed, "*simple*." But it seemed the woman was incapable of just pulling her hair back in a knot.

"Some of the Greek and Roman styles are simple." Jacqueline suggested. "I shall do this, yes?"

"Yes," Julia agreed. "That will be fine." She didn't want to think about anything at all, but Lord Fawkland kept sneaking into her thoughts. She closed her eyes and Jacqueline brushed her hair and arranged it with her fingers separating the curls. She was gentle and it was soothing and Julia was reminded of Lord Fawkland meticulously replacing all of her pins in her hair. She sighed and opened her eyes to Jacqueline. Instead of pulling all of her hair up, the woman gathered it to one side with a ribbon plaited through the hair, and wrapped the braid around to hold the rest. The style required only a few pins. It took Jacqueline almost no time at all.

"Your hair is *magnifiques*," Jacqueline said.

"Thank you," Julia replied. She did not think her hair was beautiful. She thought it was a nuisance; generally a rat's nest of tangles unless she braided it.

"*Tant de boucles*," Jacqueline said.

"Pardon?" Julia said with a frown. Perhaps she would use her free time to better her understanding of French.

"*De boucles*," Jacqueline said again. She paused to

think a moment. "The curls," she repeated. "Many curls." When she was finished, Julia was surprised to see Jacqueline had let the mass of her natural curls drape, her dark locks streaming round her neck and shoulders. It looked very pretty, but there was no one to see her. The thought depressed her. She pulled herself together and went down to dinner.

22

The earl seated Julia beside Jane for dinner. Lord Keegain was a congenial host, smiling almost without ceasing at his wife, but dinner was a simple affair with only Julia, Jane, and Jane's husband. Julia had never felt so ill at ease with her sister by her side.

With only the three of them at the table, the conversation stilled. At first, Julia kept quiet thinking that Lord Keegain may enjoy a more formal dinner. It was certainly appropriate to speak to one another. Even at formal dinners one spoke to the person on either side of oneself although it was considered vulgar to speak across the table. Julia thought of how Cedric had tricked Lord Fawkland out of his seat beside her at the Pratt picnic. She should have known then what a manipulative man Cedric was. Jane and her husband were looking at each other like an engaged couple, only Julia thought, no one would ever look at her like that.

"If I had known you both were coming home so soon," Lord Keegain said. "I could have invited some of the local ladies and gentlemen."

Oh praise heaven he did not, Julia thought.

"We will celebrate my return soon enough," Jane said. "I have not yet informed anyone that we have returned to the country. It was so sudden," Jane said. "We barely had time to pack the necessities. I asked Harrington to oversee the closure of the Bath townhouse."

"I am sure he will do a fine job," the earl agreed. "But are you sure it is necessary?"

The footman stood at Lord Keegain's shoulder until acknowledged. "May I bring in the first course?" the footman asked the earl.

"Yes," he said. "I am sure my wife and her sister are hungry after their journey."

"Very good. I will inform White," Gagnon replied and with a bow, he retired to the kitchen and returned almost immediately with a tureen of soup. Once the white soup with mushrooms was served, the other items of beef, venison and pigeon were set on the table.

Julia found she was hungry and the soup was delicious, but the stillness bothered her and little more than half way through the soup she paused, her stomach rolling. She never would have thought it so. She normally liked silence, but now, it allowed too many thoughts to crowd in. She supposed that dinner conversations about distressing topics were bad for digestion, but she found the quiet just as wearing. The distressing topic was still present in the silence.

A complement could not be adverse. She turned to her sister, Jane.

"What a lovely table," Julia said breaking the silence.

"Yes," Jane repeated. "Everything is lovely, Gagnon."

The footman appeared pleased with the compliments. "Thank you, Countess," he said with a brief bow.

It sounded strange to have her sister addressed so formally and Julia once again felt uncomfortable.

"Did you attend the Pratt's picnic in Bath," Lord Keegain asked. "You were so looking forward to it."

"Yes," Jane replied and regaled her husband with a description of the shuttlecock game, while Julia thought of the other events of the picnic that were not so pleasant...excepting perhaps her walk home with Lord Fawkland.

"I wish I had been there to cheer for you," Lord Keegain said to Jane, bringing Julia's attention back to her sister and the earl.

Julia hoped she would feel better after having eaten. She applied herself to her pigeon in white sauce with sautéed mushrooms. It was nicely paired with fresh asparagus in breadcrumbs and Jane's cook had added a variety of sauces which could be added to the other meats available. Everything was delicious and she found she was quite hungry after the long ride. Julia decided that food would do her good. She could not feel much worse, she thought.

After dinner, the time when most men would have retired for a smoke and brandy, came and went, while Lord Keegain sat, looking to remain at table with the women. At last he suggested that the three retire together to the parlor. The earl poured sherry for the women and a brandy for himself. Julia took a seat in the corner and to her chagrin, Lord Keegain sat in the chair opposite her. Julia had thought that she would have some time alone with Jane.

"Do you not smoke?" Julia asked.

"Not usually. I have a cigar now and then with company," he said, "but I have never really liked the habit, and today, I have two beautiful women in my company, why would I leave them?" He beamed at Jane and toasted her with his glass. Then he turned to Julia with purpose.

"Now, as you might have guessed, your sister related much of the events that transpired in Bath, but there are some small details that escape me. I hope, little sister, that you will enlighten me." He smiled brightly at her.

"I shall of course, do my best," Julia said her face heating with her nervousness. She threw a glance at Jane who nodded slightly and sipped her sherry.

Julia sat her sherry on the side table and worried her hands in her lap.

"Do not be shy," Keegain said. "We are family, are we not?" He patted her hand in an almost paternal gesture.

"We are," she agreed, but she had never had an older brother, and the conversation was strange to her.

"As I understand it," he continued, "Mr. Gruger was inappropriate at the Pratt's picnic, and Lord Fawkland walked you home unchaperoned afterwards. Is that correct?"

"Yes," Julia agreed. "But Lord Fawkland was the

perfect gentleman," she added, attempting to excuse him from any blame. If Lord Keegain asked her anything about what had transpired between her and Cedric, she was going to sink into the floor boards, or perhaps into the chair pillows. She would surely die of embarrassment. She slouched a little with the thought. Surely he would not. She threw a glance at Jane feeling somewhat betrayed. She had told Jane of Cedric in confidence.

Jane raised an eyebrow at her sister, but said nothing.

The earl caught the look. "My wife and I share most things," he said calmly deducing Julia's upset from Jane's look. "Do not be alarmed. We both think that honesty is a strengthening factor in a marriage and in a family in general. Pray, be honest with me now. We are trying to help you."

Julia nodded miserably. "That sounds reasonable," she said. She had once said as much to Lord Fawkland at the ball. She had asked for honesty in marriage. Reasonable or not she would never have the chance to know for herself now.

"Jane shared your secrets only to help you," Keegain added. "You know she loves you."

"I know," Julia said. It did not make this conversation any less embarrassing.

Lord Keegain took a breath and looked at her. He was calm and kind, but also resolute. "Jane is under the impression that Lord Fawkland was aware of his brother's activities with you at the Pratt picnic. Is that correct?"

"Yes," Julia said, her face hot with embarrassment, but she went on. "Lord Fawkland even warned me that his brother was not who he seemed. He said the boy I knew was not the same...Oh bother," Julia muttered as she tangled up her words. "Yes, he knew," she finished. She looked at her shoes.

"Did he know about his brother's proclivities only generally, or specifically; I mean to say...did he know of the actual incident at the Pratt picnic? Did he know his brother kissed you?"

Julia's face flamed, but she persevered. "He knew," Julia insisted. "But I do not see how this matters now. What matters is the proposal, and the rumors."

The earl shook his head. "No, what matters is that if Lord Fawkland wished to end your betrothal he would have done so after he learned his brother kissed you, but he did not. He walked you home. And Jane said he even asked for a dance at the Assembly Ball afterwards, a waltz. That does not sound like the actions of a man who wanted to break his engagement."

"Yes," Julia said with a sigh as she thought of the waltz with Lord Fawkland. It was so wonderful to be in his arms.

"Are you absolutely sure he knew of the kiss? Could you be mistaken? Think carefully." Lord Keegain pressed.

"Yes," Julia said firmly. "Lord Fawkland knew. I did not think so at first but he gave the comb back to me and my pins," she said, and then she stumbled to a halt. She glanced at Jane. She had not told her sister the comb was lost. She supposed now was the time to be entirely truthful. "When I ran from Mr. Gruger," she admitted, "he still had your comb, Jane. The one you loaned to me. I worried how I would get it back, but Lord Fawkland sent the comb back to me and the next day he even returned the pins from my hair."

Lord Keegain leaned back in his chair, a smug look on his face. "Do you see?" he asked Jane.

"I see," Jane said and Julia realized they had discussed her in detail this afternoon. Julia picked up the sherry and took an overly large sip to cover her embarrassment. She did not see at all. What did they mean?

"But you are a man," Jane said. "I would expect you to think as a man would think, but still, the rumors will be much worse now, since Mr. Gruger's proposal. Even if Lord Fawkland was of a mind to marry Julia earlier in the week, things have changed. How can you know if he still wishes to marry Julia now, Keegain? As much as it pains me to say, we have left quite the scandal."

"Well, have you spoken with the man since? Inquired as to his feelings for the girl?" Keegain asked. He looked from Jane to Julia, and Julia felt she had to speak for herself. She was not a girl. She was a young lady, and she had not been a child for a very long time.

"My lord brother, if our trip to Bath has taught me anything at all," she said. "It is that I am quite unskilled in all social matters but I do know that it is not my place to speak of marriage. It is the man's purview to ask if we should wed and he has not done so."

"Quite," Keegain said with a huff. "You have not received any word at all? Not even a note?" He glanced at Jane for an answer.

"No," Jane said.

"No," Julia repeated.

"Well, a man of four and twenty should be able to at least send a message," the earl groused.

"Missus Poppy said a man of forty could barely be trusted to send a message," Julia blurted, and the earl sputtered a moment and then laughed heartily as if Julia had made some great joke. She smiled in spite of herself.

"We did leave Bath in quite the rush," Jane added. "The rumors grew ugly, very fast. Perhaps a letter will follow us."

"We shall send our own letter," the earl said decisively. "Or rather our sister shall send a letter."

"Surely not," Julia said. "I would not know what to write."

"Can you not write from your heart?" he asked. "Does not such emotional language come easily for young ladies?"

"I couldn't," Julia whispered a blush rising again. "He is so..." She broke off, with a sigh, a dozen adjectives flooding her mind. She could not choose from them. He was so handsome. Virile. Compassionate...

Keegain exchanged another glance with Jane.

Jane looked closely at her sister. "Julia, have you fallen in love with Lord Fawkland?" she asked.

Julia could not answer, but after a moment she nodded. It was a wonderful, terrible feeling and she was quite sure he did not return the sentiment. If he did, he would have asked her to marry him.

"It must be a carefully worded letter, then" Keegain said nonplussed. "We cannot ask outright what his intensions are; well, I suppose I could, but I think a letter from you would be better received. But you also should not appear to be begging. You are a Bellevue."

Julia glanced at Jane, who nodded at her. Julia wanted to believe she was truly a Bellevue. She could give no more credence to the talk of the *Ton*. All they ever said were lies, but she did not know how to go about writing this letter. She was quite sure it would sound like she was fraught with anxiety. She felt truly desperate. How could she appear not to be begging, when that was exactly what she wanted to do? When had this happened? When had Lord Fawkland become so important to her? When had she fallen so in love with him?

"We must send for Fawkland," the earl continued. "And settle this matter post haste. Julia, perhaps you will better be able to put your sentiment into words with a little time to consider. You will be able to better organize your thoughts on paper so as to say what you truly mean."

Julia nodded. She wasn't sure she was truly up for the task, but she would try. She half expected to be handed a parchment on the spot. Jane certainly would have done so, but Lord Keegain suggested a walk in the garden.

"The out of doors always helps me to think," he said kindly. "Perhaps it will have the same effect on you little sister."

He helped Jane to her feet just as the butler entered with a card on a silver platter.

"My lord, A gentleman has just arrived. He says he is the Baron Fawkland, and he is quite insistent that he be allowed to see Miss Bellevue regardless of the late hour."

"Oh!" Julia said. She had gone suddenly pale and her stomach engaged in acrobatics.

"He is here? Now?" Jane said voicing Julia's thoughts exactly.

Julia could not quite wrap her mind around the fact that he would arrive so late. It was already dark and as safe as the journey usually was, no one brought a carriage out at night unless it was an emergency. There was the danger of highwaymen, but even a rut in the road caught in the dark could be a disaster along a country road at night.

"Show him in," the earl said. "See to his horse and carriage, and have White find something for his manservant."

"Begging your pardon, my lord," the butler said. "I was unclear. He did not bring a manservant, nor a carriage. He arrived on horseback."

Well, that explained his late arrival, Julia thought but it did not explain why Lord Fawkland was here at all. Was it possible that Lord Keegain was right? Did he not hate her for all the trouble she caused?

She had no time to puzzle this through before Lord Fawkland strode through the door. His riding boots had lost their shine. She had never seen him so rumpled. His breeches were stained with spots of road grime and his cravat looked like it had been re-tied in the dark. He had never looked so wonderful. He greeted Lord Keegain and Jane, hastily, but his eyes were only for Julia. She felt the intensity of his gaze like a physical touch. His face split into a smile, and Julia stilled her feet. She wanted to run to him. Instead, she gave a slight curtsey.

"Lord Fawkland," she said.

He strode forward and took her hand to kiss it. He smelled of sandalwood, and more strongly of leather and the outdoors scent from his ride, but mostly just of him. She closed her eyes as he kissed her gloved knuckles, and for the first time he held her hand a bit too long, as if he did not want to let her go. His fingers tightened on hers momentarily and then he released her.

"I do apologize for coming before you in such a state Miss Bellevue, but I felt I must speak with you in all haste, and you had already left Bath."

"Yes," she said. She looked more carefully at his face then. Even in the candlelight she could see the dark smudge beneath his eye, and that his lip was slightly swollen. "So it is true that you did not simply have words with your brother," she said.

"Sadly yes. I am afraid that only the intervention of some gentlemen who stood outside the ballroom kept the altercation from turning truly ugly."

"Do sit," Jane invited, ever the hostess. She rang for a maid, and instructed her to bring tea and sandwiches although they had just eaten.

Fawkland thanked her and seated himself on the edge of a wing chair. He brushed his hand over his thoroughly wrinkled cravat.

"I hate to speak with so little tact, Lord Fawkland," Keegain said. "But this has been a rather unusual few days and it is obvious as I venture a closer look at your face, that you were obligated to leave Bath, much as my wife and sister were, so I hope you will forgive my forthrightness. After the scene last night and your brother's forward courtship of our sister, I think it would be best for you to propose in all haste or remove yourself quite out of sight until the rumors die down, for both yourself and Miss Bellevue." Keegain's tone was the same no-nonsense one that their father had used when he expected things to go the way he wanted them to.

"Lord Keegain, please," Julia said aghast. She did not want Lord Fawkland to be coerced into marrying her. In fact, she was not sure this was the best course of action. Keegain had his reasons for being so forward; heaven knew Julia could not afford another mark against her reputation, but this was not how she had imagined the evening progressing.

"I agree," Fawkland said to Lord Keegain. "And that is in fact what I came here to do. Though you have quite spoiled the moment," Lord Fawkland said. He rose from his seat and came around the side table to stand beside Julia's chair. She found she was trembling, unable to look at him.

He waited a moment. Then when it became clear she would not even lift her eyes from the ground, he knelt down. Julia had no choice but to look at him now. She gasped. The movement brought back the moment when Cedric had knelt so at the ball, and she could not stand it. She stood and pulled away. "No!" she said.

At the stricken look that immediately filled his grey eyes, she knew she had made a mistake. He looked like he had been struck. Her hasty words were ever the bane of her existence. She had never meant to hurt him. Was it possible that he truly had feelings for her? She took a breath. She had to fix this, and speaking was the only way she could do so.

"A moment...," she said more softly. "I know... I know that I should accept your kind proposal without hesitation." She paused a moment collecting her thoughts. She did not want a proposal out of pity for her situation or because he felt responsible for his brother. She did not want a marriage of entrapment. Julia wanted more than that. She had always wanted more...a man who was kind as well as strong...a man she loved. She had to explain.

"I should accept," she said again, hating that she could not make the words come out of her mouth and her hesitation was bringing him pain. "That is what I should do," she continued, "but if I am to make a decision that affects my entire life here after, I would ask for a moment to speak with Lord Fawkland." She glanced at Jane and then at Lord Keegain. Her voice was soft but determined. "He has ridden through the dark to speak with me, and he is right. We do need to talk." She looked at Jane. "Please, may we have a moment of privacy?"

"A walk in the garden perhaps," Jane said.

"An inspired idea, I would love a walk amongst your roses," Lord Keegain said as he stood and took his wife's hand. He gave Lord Fawkland a hard look. "We will grant you privacy in your speech, but I expect you to keep our little sister in sight. She has been hurt enough."

"I do not plan on harming her in any way," Lord Fawkland said.

"Most men never do," Keegain replied.

They stood to leave the parlor, when they met the

maid bringing in the tea set. "I'm sorry," Jane said. "We will have tea shortly, and the sandwiches."

"Yes, milady," the maid said glancing at the countess and then the young couple who had proceeded into the garden.

23

The smell of the roses was sweet as Julia and Lord Fawkland walked a bit into the garden. Only a few torches were set. Jane and the earl stopped near the garden entrance and sat on the closest bench.

Julia found her voice as she and Fawkland walked a little further and then paused by a second bench, just inside the torchlight. "I feel I must apologize, Lord Fawkland, for the trouble I have caused you," she began.

"Apologize?" he said with a frown. She realized he still misunderstood. The look of pain was still on his face and she wanted to wipe it away. She caught his hand in hers. It was very forward, but some of the pain left his face and in its place, a look of uncertainty.

"We left Bath so quickly," Julia said. "I only thought of escaping rumor." He tightened his grip on her hand just a little and it gave her strength.

She took a breath and continued. She had to explain. She had to explain it all. "I did not expect Mr. Gruger to propose. You must believe me, until he knelt before me in the ballroom, I had no idea his thoughts were turned that way."

Fawkland grimaced but did not interrupt.

"I meant to write to you. I did. I was planning the letter this evening. I was thinking of what I would say... I just..." She stopped and took a breath.

He waited for her to collect her thoughts, his hand on hers, a comfort. He was so patient; so kind. She looked up at him in the moonlight and completely lost her train of thought. He was so handsome. His lip was a little swollen and she wanted to touch it; to ask if it hurt. The thought of lips went immediately to the thought of kissing. She wanted him to kiss her and she felt her own lips part, just a little. The tension fair crackled between them, but they both knew they were in sight of Jane and the earl.

Lord Fawkland cleared his throat.

"I didn't," she began again. "I didn't mean to cause further damage to your reputation," she said.

"My reputation?" he replied. "You were thinking of my reputation when Cedric left yours in such tatters."

Now Julia grimaced. "I know mine is now also soiled..." she began.

"No, you shall not take the blame for him." Lord Fawkland spat. "My brother is a bloody arse." He took a quick breath through his nose. "I beg your pardon, Miss Bellevue." He said, immediately apologizing for his foul language, but Julia was glad to know she was not the only one who occasionally blurted things without thought. Her lips curved into a smile.

"I should not have said that. Cedric brings out the

worst in me I'm afraid. But you are not to blame for his faults. Nor our quarrel. In truth the fault resides with me," Lord Fawkland said running hand over his cravat, pulling the knot askew.

Julia realized it was something he did when he was nervous.

"Our father died when Cedric was still only a child and I fear, I myself, was still too young to teach him discipline in spite of my attempts at severity."

Julia nodded. "I remember. You were the new Baron," she said. "Just back from the Royal Navy. I told your brother how handsome you were in your uniform. I had a..." She bit her lip as he looked at her now, his eyes appraising her.

"An attachment," she admitted softly.

"Did you?" He said. He looked surprised, but his eyes twinkled with joy. "You could not have been more than eleven. You were a tiny thing."

"Twelve." She never remembered herself as tiny. She had been even taller than Cedric at the time. But perhaps from the viewpoint of grown man...of seventeen, she counted the years in her head. He had seemed so grown up and ridiculously handsome in his blues, and then the black.

"I was seventeen," Lord Fawkland said. "I was so frightened. I did not know how to be the baron, but I knew how to keep my little brother in line, or so I thought." Lord Fawkland gave a small shrug.

She remembered Lord Fawkland being so firm with Cedric. Her admiration for Lord Fawkland had only soured when she thought him unkind. She knew now it was Cedric who was unkind. Lord Fawkland had never been anything but the perfect gentleman.

She remembered how he looked at seventeen...that day. A little uncertain, but determined, much as he looked now, she thought. Perhaps she was right. People did not change.

"I thought you were so grown up," she said.

"I thought you were brave," he answered. "Lying for my brother. Defending him. I wanted to inspire such loyalty in him, in my command... I remember you standing in the kitchen one evening confessing to hiding the kitchen knives when I, and all the kitchen staff, knew full well that it was Cedric who had taken them," he said. "But you took the blame."

She didn't know he knew that. That was earlier. She must have been nine...no...ten at the time. She thought that the older brother had taken no notice of her, but somehow he had.

"I wasn't lying," Julia said. "I did help him bury the knives in the garden," she said. "I thought it was a lark." She paused wondering where this conversation was going. "What did he do with them?" She asked somewhat nervously. She hated that her mind went to darker things.

"Cedric was angry because he could not go riding, so he decided no one would ride. He cut through the leathers of a number of girths and stirrups. A job you would not have had the strength or wherewithal to do at the time even if you had stolen the kitchen knives."

"Was anyone hurt?" she asked thinking that riding with a cut girth was a dangerous thing.

"No. The stable master found the damage before there was an accident."

The silence stretched for a moment. The same stable master who had taken her dolls down from the rafters where Cedric had hung them. For she now was certain it was Cedric not Godwin that could be so cruel.

"He was angry that you curtailed his fun," Julia said. "Just as he was angry with me when I would take my dolls and play with the Poppy sisters rather than him. He blamed you then, but it was Cedric who broke my favorite doll. He said he would be my friend...anyway... even though no one else would." Julia bit her lip.

Lord Fawkland's face clouded with anger.

"It is no matter," she said laying a hand on his. "It was a childhood slight. It is nothing."

"It hurt you."

"You have your own hurts," she said, slowly an idea forming in her mind. "Your own rumors." The *Ton* called Lord Fawkland a rake, it was said he had a bastard child. She could not believe such behavior of Lord Fawkland, but she felt she may have found the kernel of truth within the lies.

"My doll was not the last time your brother has let someone else take the blame for him, is it Lord Fawkland?"

He did not answer at first, and she feared her hunch was wrong. Dare she say it? "I defended Mr. Gruger," she continued. "I lied for him, but he was my friend. Friends do not betray one another, nor I should think, do brothers, not if they have any kindness in them."

Godwin shook his head.

"I do believe now, Lord Fawkland that the stories of you and your brother are entirely reversed, but the tales of the *Ton* lie between us and if I am to marry you, I need to know the truth, from your own lips. Let there be nothing false between us. You promised me that."

He nodded sadly. "The tales have grown so tall. It started with a single child, but I suppose that was not enough of a scandal. As with any bit of gossip, it grows like a wild thing."

Her heart sank believing the worst. Could she forgive him a bastard child?

She didn't know, but she had to give him and herself the chance. "People make mistakes," she said softly. She wasn't sure she was talking about herself or Cedric or Godwin. She only knew that the woman, whomever she was, and her child would have happened before their marriage vows. If he would only be truthful, she would try to forgive him. She didn't know if she would succeed, but the possibility of a future with Godwin seemed worth the effort.

"The child is not mine," he said.

Julia released the breath she found she had been holding in a sigh of relief. She believed him. "Good," she said. "Then I shan't have to try to forgive you."

"You would have forgiven me?" Lord Fawkland's face was aghast.

"I would have tried. I do not think I would have succeeded." She admitted sheepishly.

Lord Fawkland laughed and the sound of it was like music reverberating inside of her. She wanted it to go on and on, but he folded his hands steadying himself. "You are an intelligent woman, Miss Bellevue. It is as you surmised. It was Cedric who fathered the child. He was still young and I, being the foolish older brother, wanted to protect him from the scandal. I have always protected Cedric."

"You are kind," Julia said with a wry smile.

"Too kind. I provided Cedric with his own apartments in London. The girl I sent away to a cottage by the coast, and provide her with a monthly allowance. I thought that was best." Lord Fawkland frowned. "I foolishly stopped by when I had a trip to Brighton. That is when all the rumors began. I didn't mean for it to happen. I just did not think." There was a spark of anger in his voice as he told the story and she could not understand why he continued to go along with the ruse rather than repudiating the rumors.

"But why do you protect Cedric after all of this?"

Lord Fawkland's answer was simple. "He is my little brother. Some misguided sense of loyalty, I suppose. I have always envied the camaraderie of the Beresford brothers or even the companionship you share with your own sister. I wanted such a feeling between us. Cedric and I have never had much of a brotherly bond."

Even though she had once thought that she and Jane were not truly sisters, she had always loved her like one. Perhaps that was enough. Perhaps love was all that was needed. It was certainly more than what Cedric and Lord Fawkland shared. She put her hand on his in solidarity. Perhaps it was forward on her, but she didn't care. He closed his own hand over hers and they just sat together, hand in hand.

Lord Fawkland was silent for a time.

Finally he cleared his throat, hesitantly and looked at her. "I want you to know that when I approached your father, years ago, and asked him when the time came, might I be permitted to court you, it was not on a whim. I know his will has moved the matter more to the forefront. I did not want to press you, but I do want you to one day be my wife."

She supposed he was waiting for some response from her, but she wasn't sure what to say. Her pulse was racing and thoughts fluttered about her head and would not settle so she could choose one to say. He had asked her father about her? This proposal wasn't about the house in Bath or out of pity to somehow makeup for what Cedric had done. He had noticed her before. Before everything. Her eyes were wide. "You asked my father to court me? And you want me still? After all that has happened?"

"I will not pretend that Cedric's character does not force me to speak," Lord Fawkland said at last. "Though he is certainly not the only reason. I was older than you, but that did not mean I did not notice you. You were so strong, so poised, even as a child. As I grew older the other women of the *Ton* seemed silly little girls when compared with you. You stood apart from their petty games; head and shoulders above them in all areas."

Julia was surprised. Everything she thought wrong; everything she thought to change about herself was the very reason he cared for her. He did not think she was too large and not feminine, or too blunt, or awkward.

"Miss Bellevue, the more I saw of you, in Bath, the more you enthralled me. I did not wish to pressure you and in my delay I feared I would lose you to my brother. I was quite elated to learn that you had refused him, and that I may be granted another chance to prove my sincerity. You would not have been happy with my brother because he is selfish and cruel and because he would not find joy in your spirt as I do. I know it is hasty, and that we barely know one another," he said.

"It is hardly the proposal I would have wished, but it is not without reason. I wish to marry you Miss Bellevue, not to save your reputation or mine," said Lord Fawkland. "But because every minute I have spent with you has caused me to resent the minutes we have spent apart. I have fallen in love with you, Miss Bellevue. My life is brighter with you in it, and I have become irrevocably addicted to your smile. I intend to see to it that it never leaves your face. If we should follow your father's will and marry; if you will accept me, I shall endeavor to make you the happiest woman on God's earth."

He was so eloquent; she did not trust herself to speak, though it was not his words that lead her to know his sentiment was true; the truth was so clear in the anguish on his face when he had thought she might rebuff him. It did not lift until she could make her mouth move at last.

"Yes," she said with her usual articulateness. "Yes," she repeated as he brought both of her hands to his lips and kissed them. "I believe I have fallen in love with you as well, Lord Fawkland and no amount of reason could compel me to refuse you. I trust that my father knew me better than I knew myself."

Lord Fawkland pressed her gloved hand to his cheek. She brushed her fingers along the rough stubble there, tracing the strong line of his jaw. Let people think what they would. If she was a wanton woman, it was only for this man.

He reached up and touched the loose curls that fell over her shoulder.

"I see you have made your decision," Jane said, proving that she and Keegain were still there and noticed how close together she and Lord Fawkland had become, but there was no censure in Jane's voice.

Julia had nearly forgotten about them.

Nonetheless, Lord Fawkland dropped his hand.

"So little sister, have you found yourself a husband?" Keegain asked as he and Jane approached, proving they had heard at least some of what was said.

"Yes, I believe I have," Julia said with wonder.

"So be it then. I had wondered what folly overtook you that you would turn down a baron."

"Do not tease, Keegain," Jane began but Julia answered his jest.

"Because a marriage without love is no marriage at all," she said thinking of Lavinia.

Keegain's smile broadened as he gave his wife his arm. "A smart girl, no doubt, just like her sister."

"Oh Keegain, this is just what she needed." Jane said gaily. "Look how bright her face is! It pleases my heart to see my little sister happy. I am overjoyed for you," Jane pulled Julia into a tight hug.

Julia squealed. "You will crease our dresses," she said.

"You would fret over creasing that dress?" Jane asked and for the first time Julia realized that she had worn one of her oldest and most comfortable dresses instead of a beautiful one on this evening, the most happy evening of her life. Oh, she was engaged!

"Oh, I do not care a wit about dresses today," Jane said. "My little sister is in love!"

Julia giggled. Heady with excitement, Julia looked at Lord Fawkland and marveled that he wanted to wed her.

"Let me be the first to extend our congratulations," Keegain said holding out a hand to Fawkland, who took it gingerly. Fawkland shook hands with Lord Keegain.

"Come," Keegain said. "Let us go back into the parlor and break out some wine, or brandy. I am afraid this deuced war has made champagne hard to come by." At the doorway, Keegain paused, thinking. "You would have left Bath just after breakfast?" he asked.

"Actually, Sir, it was near midday, but I was too nervous to eat before I left."

Julia realized he had ridden most of the day without food. She immediately rang for the maid.

Jane went into action, asking for the earlier requested tea and sandwiches to be brought to the parlor, but Keegain rejected that thought. "No. We will go back into the dining room," he said. "Bring out the cold pigeon and beef. Some cheese and bread too."

"The tea sandwiches are fine," Lord Fawkland said humbly.

"We cannot have you wasting away before the wedding. Look at the size of you. Skin and Bones." Keegain said, looking up at Lord Fawkland with a grin.

"Thank you," Lord Fawkland said, and Keegain patted him on the back.

"I shall be gaining another brother," he said. "For my fourth little sister."

After they had a bit of snack, supper for Lord Fawkland, Keegain sat back in his chair and laced his fingers over his midriff. "There are matters to discuss in regard to this marriage," he said to Fawkland.

Julia felt like she was buzzing. It was impossible to sit still. Only Keegain could return to business when everything was entirely too exciting for that.

"Though the conditions in the will said Julia must be married by summer's end, according to my solicitors, I am also certain a formal engagement will do, to allow you both time to get to know one another, due to the fact that Julia is indeed following her father's will and not marrying another."

"That is perfectly acceptable," Lord Fawkland said. "Preferable even."

"Now you will be her husband and the property in Bath will therefore be yours," Keegain continued.

"I will gift it to her," Lord Fawkland cut in. "That is clearly how her father wished it. The house in Bath is hers, to do with as she pleases." He looked at her. "Does that suit you, Miss Bellevue?"

"Yes," Julia said, still somewhat dazed. "That will suit me fine."

"Then I shall send word to the servants still in Bath and tell them they can stop packing," Keegain said.

"Oh," Julia said. She had completely forgotten about the house in Bath and the servants packing it.

"I hinted my hopes to Harrington," Fawkland said. "But a message would not go amiss."

"Now, what of your brother?" Keegain asked. "I do not wish to inject turmoil into the happy occasion of your engagement, but I would have the matter of Cedric settled."

Julia looked at Godwin. Yes, what of Cedric? If he was so angered as to engage in fisticuffs at the ball, what would he do when her engagement to Lord Fawkland was formally announced? What would he do after they were wed? She knew Cedric. She knew his deviance. She had even participated in it as a child. Now she put herself on the other side. She would be married to his brother. Cedric would now be her brother as well. If she were truly a lady, she should love Cedric as a brother. She was not sure she could do that. She found she wanted him out of their lives. She struggled with the feeling.

"You needn't worry about Cedric," Godwin said. "I have closed his accounts and have seen to it that he will be enlisted with Captain Hartfield into His Majesty's Service."

"You do not think he will feel you are sending him away?" Julia asked.

"I no longer care what he will think, but I hope he will embrace it. Cedric always loved adventure. I gave him a choice of the Army or the Navy. He chose the Navy. He has charisma, and will do well leading men, and perhaps service to his country will teach him some responsibility. What could be better than that?" He looked at Julia imploringly. He truly seemed to want her approval.

Julia laid a hand on his arm. She nodded. "I think it is a good strategy," she said. They would be free of Cedric's influence and she hoped that Cedric himself would be happy.

Lord Fawkland nodded his eyes soft upon her.

"I think he will do well," Lord Fawkland said decidedly. "Cedric wanted to join the Navy after I came home, but Mother discouraged him. With the war, she wanted to keep him close."

"I think she just wanted to keep him safe," Jane said. "It is a mother's prerogative."

"Oh pish posh, Jane," Keegain said. "For all his faults, he is a man, not a child. You cannot keep him caged."

Lord Fawkland nodded. "You are right; it is time I stopped protecting him and let him learn to be his own man, with something he can be proud of and something he can call his own."

Julia had realized as Lord Fawkland was speaking, as much as she loved the townhouse in Bath, she already had something to call her own and it was far more precious to her than any house. Home could be a person too, she thought. She felt the contentment filter down to her bones as Lord Fawkland put his hand on hers.

24

————

*J*ulia was up early the next morning, in spite of the lateness of her retiring last night. Keegain had, of course, invited Lord Fawkland to stay. They had spent the evening talking and simply enjoying each other's company. It was a pleasant night filled with quiet comfort.

When Julia went down to breakfast, she was informed by the staff that Lady Keegain had chosen to lie in and take breakfast in her rooms. Julia remembered yesterday, Jane had been slow to rise then too. That was unusual. Her sister loved breakfast and was often awake before Julia herself. Julia wondered, was she ill?

Concerned, she went to Jane's room and knocked on the door. When Jane bid her enter, she hesitated. Keegain was in her dressing room as well, and Julia did not want to intrude, but Jane waved her in. "Come," she said. "Sit with us."

"I could take breakfast in my room if you would

prefer privacy," she said aware that they had ceased their conversation because of her. They seemed very cozy.

"Nonsense," Jane said. "Sit. Would you like to share our news?" she asked her husband with a smile.

"No," he said cupping her hand with his. The clink of crystal continued as tea was served.

"Yes. That's fine," Jane told the server. "That will be all, Lucy."

"Yes, milady." When the maid had left, Keegain said, "I think it is fitting that you tell your sister first."

Julia's heart leapt in her chest. She knew suddenly what Jane was going to say. She remembered her sister had looked wan in the mornings and she was easily fatigued when Jane had always been a font of energy. She never got tired of balls and to-dos. She was the last one to leave any affair, and yet, the past week in Bath, Jane had been anxious to be home and to put her feet up.

"Jane?" Julia said looking at her sister. She did have a certain glow, but she wondered about the earl present in the room. She could not speak of pregnancy in front of a man, albeit that he was the father of said child.

Jane smiled at her, and spoke. "I had thought to wait to tell you. You, being so unhappy upon our return from Bath, but that was before Lord Fawkland's arrival. And now that you have your own glad tidings, I feel I can share mine. I told Keegain yesterday and you are the second to know. I believe I am with child," she said.

"Oh!" Julia got to her feet to hug her sister. "How wonderful! That is why you were so interested in Connie's baby. And why you told Mr. Poppy that you may be leaving Bath before Michaelmas."

"Yes," Jane agreed. "I invited Constance and her husband to visit here later in the summer when her youngest is able to travel." Jane was smiling ear to ear.

"Oh." Julia inwardly groaned thinking of the house being full of the boisterous Poppy family and Constance's husband, Mr. Nash. Although having an infant and a three-year-old in the house in addition did not seem so terrible. She smiled.

"When is the happy event to be?" Julia asked trying not to think of the dangers of childbirth.

"Near Christmas, I think," Jane said.

"Will you return to London for the Season?"

"I may return home for the holidays with a midwife in attendance. I wished to speak to Constance about hers."

"A physician," Keegain corrected. "You will have a physician. Only the best for my wife."

Jane grew quiet.

Julia thought she would prefer a woman at such a time. It would be very uncomfortable to have a man who was not even her husband in attendance while she was in such a state.

From the look on Jane's face, her sister seemed to agree. Lord Keegain must have sensed his wife's reticence as well.

"It will all go according to plan," he said. "You will see."

Jane glanced at Julia. She nodded and picked up her tea cup again, but Julia had the feeling that her sister was not silenced on the subject. Though this was certainly not the sort of discussion she should be in the middle of.

Jane deftly changed the topic. "First, we must have a dinner party to announce Julia's formal engagement to Lord Fawkland."

"I truly would rather not have a big announcement," Julia argued but Jane insisted.

"Nonsense. Your fiancé is a baron. You cannot hide away here in the country."

"Very well, then. Just a small party," Julia agreed.

"A small party," Jane said, "with those who are truly our friends."

EPILOGUE

The announcement event was meant to be only a few close friends, but it had spiraled out of control. Married to an earl, Jane moved in a higher circle than her sister. Julia felt out of her depth as a young marquess came her way and congratulated her. She did not remember him, but they must have been introduced. Otherwise he would not have spoken to her. There were two dukes and a number of earls in attendance. Although Julia had to admit the guest list had been chosen with an eye toward friendship rather than society. It seemed the only individuals of Julia's acquaintance who were not at the party were Cedric, and Lavinia's love, Captain Jack Hartfield. The two had sailed out on the same ship just the week before. Captain Hartfield promised to keep a special eye on Julia's soon to be brother-in-law.

Julia gravitated to a corner where the music and conversation were not too loud. Lavinia and Charity came to fetch her. "You cannot hide away in a corner," said Lavinia.

"Especially since it is your engagement we are celebrating," Charity added.

Julia voiced her reluctance to mingle and Charity's solution was to place another glass of wine in her hand. Julia let the drink and the presence of her close friends fill her with their warmth. Social flowers like Lavinia and Charity might not understand but Julia was celebrating. She was content to observe the gaiety of the party guests, happily plied with food and wine rather than join with them. She carried her own joy in her heart.

"I am truly happy for you, Julia" Charity said, sipping her drink. "When there was all the trouble in Bath and you refused Mr. Gruger, I thought it was the height of foolishness. Now I see that I was wrong."

"Of course," Lavinia replied. "Julia and Lord Fawkland are in love. Anyone with eyes can see it and love is never foolishness."

Julia blushed, embarrassed to have her feelings so known even here amongst her close friends. Although when it came to matters of the heart, Julia supposed Lavinia had the right of it all along.

"Isn't it wonderful, Julia," Lavinia continued. "Your baron is in love with you and my captain is truly in love with me. We are both engaged!" Lavinia caught Julia's hand and fairly bounced with glee.

Lavinia had remained in near constant correspondence with Captain Hartfield, since his departure. They were to be married as soon as he might manage to return to her, perhaps at Christmas time.

Julia had to smile. "Yes. It is wonderful," she replied, glad her friend was as happy as she was. "Now we just need to find a husband for Charity," Julia said with a sly smile at her other friend.

"You should see to your guests," Charity deflected.

"Yes, Charity," Lavinia agreed. "We must share our good fortune."

"I cannot believe she would be the last of us to be married," Julia continued, grinning at Lavinia.

"Guests," Charity said again. "You must remember you are a hostess, Julia."

"I just do not enjoy the company of a crowd," Julia said.

"I would enjoy your company," said a deep voice that warmed Julia to her toes. She turned to find Lord Fawkland, her betrothed, at her shoulder. "I too find social events taxing," he said and offered her his arm. "Shall we walk together?"

Charity and Lavinia gave the two of them knowing smiles as they moved across the room.

Together the engaged couple spoke with several of their well-wishers. After a few moments Julia and Lord Fawkland found themselves standing in front of the doors that opened out onto the lit gardens, the aroma of the torches mingling with the scent of Jane's roses and the cool evening's fresh air. Julia looked at Godwin, who looked back at her. She felt calmer now. She felt she could handle most anything if she had Lord Fawkland at her side.

He nodded at the doors. "Shall we get a bit of fresh air?"

Julia nodded shyly and allowed the young man to lead her out onto the wide balcony that overlooked the gardens. The pair moved beyond the torch light and stood at the far edge of the balcony where they could better see the stars overhead. The scent of roses was everywhere as the garden was in full bloom. Julia allowed Godwin to lead her right up to the balcony rail, cast in shadow, where the torchlight did not reach. Together they stood arm in arm and surveyed the gardens before them. They watched couples wander along the paths and heard light laughter, and bits of conversation wafting up to where they stood.

"It is a beautiful night, is it not?" Julia asked in a low tone.

"Indeed; made more beautiful for my companion in it."

Julia blushed at Lord Fawkland's complement. She had always thought herself too large a woman to be considered beautiful, but she could hear no falsehood in his words. She smiled shyly at him and whispered. "Thank you for bringing me out here. I did not realize how stifling it was inside. I needed a bit of peace."

"Peace is what you bring to me, Miss Bellevue," he said, sincerely, taking her hands in his own. "Although it is such an unaccustomed feeling, I shall scarcely know what to do with myself."

He smiled then as if struck by a sudden inspiration. "Perhaps you would teach me how to paint?"

Julia startled and Lord Fawkland's grin widened. He had known all along then? He had known about her oil paintings? He had known that the paintings in the house in Bath were her own work. She flushed scarlet.

"You knew the paintings were mine?" she asked. "You knew? When you inquired after the artist?"

He shook his head. "Not for certain, though I surmised as much. Your father mentioned that you loved to paint. He called it your passion."

Julia felt the heat of a blush fill her face, and looked down, but he caught her chin and tipped her face up just a bit so she was looking at him. "I wanted to hear you speak of your passions," he said. "I still do." The moment caught and held. His eyes were stormy grey, just like they were on that first night when she wished she could capture the color on canvas. She should have known then. He was her passion.

"I do love to paint," she said. "Capturing something precious on canvas is like nothing else in the world; a moment caught in time."

"I shall fill the walls of the manor with your paintings as well as the house in Bath," he said. "There are some lovely views at The Fawkland Barony, if you should like to capture them."

Julia's heart caught on his words. *The Fawkland Barony.* The excitement of the engagement and the presence of the man himself had driven all thought of Lord Fawkland's title quite out of her mind.

"The barony," she whispered.

"Yes?" Lord Fawkland replied confused by her sudden upset

"Then when we marry...I will be..."

"The Baroness Fawkland," he said and she gasped.

"Oh Lord Fawkland. I cannot be a baroness. I will simply do everything all wrong."

He smiled at her, and brushed his fingers against her cheek. "I felt much the same once; you gave me courage. You are stronger than you know, Miss Bellevue."

"I would be the most uncharacteristic baroness."

"I do not see that," Lord Fawkland disagreed. "You shall be the perfect baroness. You have a regal countenance, Miss Bellevue. You are kind and compassionate and loyal to those you believe in. I can think of no baroness more noble, and if that is uncharacteristic of a baroness, I care not. I would have no other woman as my lady wife."

He caught her hands in his. "Besides, we shall have a most uncharacteristic marriage I should think. We shall be the talk of the *Ton*."

"Oh," she said. She looked down at her hands in his. They felt perfect, like a perfect pair of fitted gloves. His hands were warm and strong and yet gentle. Let them say what they would. While Lord Fawkland was holding her hands, she did not care. "I do not care what they think," she said. "It only matters what we know of each other."

"Truly?" he asked. "You do not care to know what they will say of us? Oh, but it is a good tale, especially since most married couples are notoriously boring." There was a jest in his voice and Julia could not help smiling.

"I do not think we shall ever be boring," Julia objected.

"Never. Not the Baron of Bastards and his wanton wife..."

Julia laughed lightly at Lord Fawkland's jest, but he continued.

"In time I believe they shall say that: the Baroness Fawkland was a lady of such beauty and charm that she drove a pair of brothers to fisticuffs for her hand, possibly even a duel."

Julia blushed and found herself staring into Lord Fawkland's soft grey eyes.

"And of course, as long as they are talking about us," he went on, "they are leaving some other poor soul in peace." He let one of the curls at her chin wrap itself around his finger.

"My father used to say that," Julia replied.

"Where do you think I heard it?" he asked, his fingers still playing gently with her curls.

She looked at his face. His blackened eye was nearly healed, as was his lip. She liked that she was almost eye to eye with him. She adored his eyes, his fingers on her skin, and the smell of his cherry pipe tobacco and under it all the sharp manly smell of him. She reached her gloved hand up to touch his face and smooth the wrinkled knot of his cravat. She thought she should probably learn to tie the thing herself, and a shot of excitement went through her at the thought. The world had stilled and seemed far away, as Lord Fawkland spoke in his deep baritone.

"Whatever might have been said of me in the past, the only thing that matters now, is the scandalous news that I am deeply in love with the woman whom I have asked to be my wife."

She had a sudden impulse to cling to him. She did not ever want to leave the comfort of his arms.

"There is just one more question I have to ask you Miss Bellevue," he said. The soft rumbling of his voice rolled over her like music, but she sought to compose herself. She frowned. What other question could he have?

"Of course," she said, puzzled.

His hand moved from her hair, back to her chin, and tilted her face up to his, he asked, "May I kiss you?"

For once she did not struggle for words. "Yes," she whispered.

His lips fell over hers and she melted into his embrace. His arms tightened around her and Julia's heart soared. Let the *Ton* say what they would. Their words would never touch her again, for here in the arms of her future husband, Julia was home.

CONTINUE READING FOR A SNEAK PEEK OF...

The Deceptive Earl ~ Lady Charity Abernathy
by Isabella Thorne

1

---

*L*ady Charity could not see the man's appeal; refused to see it, in fact. Of course, Neville Collington was in possession of a dangerous array of features. The Earl of Wentwell was altogether too handsome, and he knew it. Every fiber of his being shouted the knowledge as did his artful grin and his glinting eye.

Patience was already on to a new topic, recounting their shopping excursion to Lord Wentwell while they enjoyed their slight repast.

In no time at all, Patience expressed her desire to continue shopping, and she led the way, guiding the foursome toward a neighboring shop, where various novelties were sold.

Lady Charity found herself flanked by the two gentlemen and she did her best to devote her undivided attention to Lord Barton and ignore Lord Wentwell entirely. Despite her determined focus, she could not cease to be aware of the pair of devilish green eyes that burned her from behind.

Whether she had intended to or not, she had somehow piqued Lord Wentwell's interest. Charity refused to be another challenge for the gentleman to best. She did not doubt that he notched his bedpost with his conquests. She would have none of it. She would not allow herself be so used.

"Reginald," Patience called to her brother as she browsed an outdoor booth that was bursting with bolts of fabric. "You must help me find something similar to Mother's evening shawl. I am certain that this style is just the thing for her."

Charity strolled after the siblings wishing that she had never agreed to this excursion. At this moment, she would rather be sitting at home or upon her bench with simple Jean than partnering Lord Wentwell through the streets of Bath.

"My dear Lady Charity," Lord Wentwell spoke her name as if merely capturing her attention were enough to make her swoon. Charity had to admit his voice was deep and smooth as butter. She turned away from him, determined not to hear or let the man affect her.

"Are you often in Bath?" he continued, this time close enough that she might not continue her pretense without offense. She could smell the scent of him, a pleasant sandalwood smell. Only a scoundrel would overstep personal boundaries so. Still, she had to answer or be proclaimed rude.

"Only in the summer," she replied shortly. Her response was honest, but not forthcoming. She picked through a box of trinkets, weighing each in her hand and holding one up for inspection.

"Do you not prefer Brighton and the sea?" he tried again.

"My father prefers Bath."

"Then you do prefer the sea." He smiled as if he had gleaned some great insight into her character with the assumption.

"I have not been often enough to make a determination," she admitted with a simple lift of her shoulder. She turned back to her examination of the trinkets with aplomb. She would not give him a moment's regard.

"You should try the sea," Lord Wentwell leaned against the table of baubles and Lady Charity tried not to notice how the artful cut of his clothing clung to his fit frame. He looked a bit rumpled this morning as if he slept in his clothes, and yet somehow his disheveled appearance made him all the more appealing. Charity turned abruptly away, a blush coloring her face.

Lord Wentwell began to regale her with tales of the waves and the salt spray. At one point he lay his hand, warm on her elbow and she nearly dropped the bauble she held.

"Here in Bath, the heat of summer air is heavy with moisture and the scent of the mineral waters. I find it to be somewhat cloying and I do not enjoy the taste. The sea, on the other hand, ah, the sea sends quite a different message to the senses. It is freeing and quite overwhelming."

She turned to him startled at his passion.

"I should like to take you to the sea," he said fervently.

To speak so ardently was not seemly, but he continued, almost as if he were not speaking for her ears, but for himself alone. "The sound of the waves as they crash against the shore is intoxicating. It fills one up, pulls one in and rolls over the skin, like an ever present heartbeat." His voice was soft and sensual, and Charity felt a moment of unease with the conversation, though she could not quite put her finger on the reason. Goosebumps appeared on her skin although the weather was uncommonly hot.

"The clean salt of the air is quite unlike any other taste one can imagine," Wentwell said. "It lingers over the lips and leaves an altogether delightful languidness trailing in its wake." He looked at her then, his green eyes altogether darker in color than she had imagined earlier.

Charity pulled away from his touch, anger rising like a bright flame. She gasped thinking of the telling way that he described the coastal town. Their conversation of lips and waves and heartbeats was not inappropriate in any overt way; however his words sent strange feelings through her. He affected her sensibility in ways which made her insides twist.

Charity did not miss the earl's subtle context, nor his hand pressing on her elbow. She looked up and met his startlingly green eyes. They were a vivid shade of dark emerald, and he was looking at her with an interest that seemed to burn across her skin. Still Charity attempted to not take it to heart.

Instead, Charity cultivated a feeling of annoyance, for herself, and indeed for all of the young ladies who would soon begin their first season and in their innocence fall prey to Lord Wentwell's honeyed tongue. She reminded herself that Lord Wentwell was a dangerous man. He was a flirt through and through: a rogue and a scoundrel. He used his wit and smooth speech, much like one would tread a garden path. He took the path without thought of his walking. His speech, like the traveling of said limb was altogether immaterial. He used speech without effort, without thought and without sincerity so intent was he upon the destination.

It was as if his flirtation were a reflex, a muscle that must be exercised but that took no effort or care on his part to maintain. The habit was so ingrained that Charity wondered if the gentleman could make untoward statements in his sleep and dishonor a woman with the same nonchalance.

"Lord Wentwell," she began. "You need not play your games with me. I assure you, I have neither the time nor the inclination to participate. Walk alongside me, if you must, but you need not waste your breath on convincing me of the benefits of... of the sea."

Lord Wentwell laughed. He threw his head back and let forth an honest bout of laughter that caught Charity off guard.

Lady Charity did not understand Neville Collington, and although she told herself she should pay him no mind, the puzzle that was Lord Wentwell had engaged her interest and despite her best judgment she found herself wanting to know more.

CONTINUE READING....

The Deceptive Earl ~ Lady Charity Abernathy

For more Regency Romance,
Follow Isabella Thorne on Amazon

W<small>ANT</small> E<small>VEN</small> M<small>ORE</small> R<small>EGENCY</small> R<small>OMANCE</small>...

Follow Isabella Thorne on BookBub

https://www.bookbub.com/profile/isabella-thorne

Sign up for my VIP Reader List!

at

https://isabellathorne.com/

Receive weekly updates from Isabella and an
E<small>XCLUSIVE</small> F<small>REE</small> S<small>TORY</small>

Like Isabella Thorne on Facebook

https://www.facebook.com/isabellathorneauthor/

Made in United States
North Haven, CT
06 May 2022

18961668R00203